The
Sunshine
Club

BOOKS BY DEE MACDONALD

The Runaway Wife
The Getaway Girls
The Silver Ladies of Penny Lane
The Golden Oldies Guesthouse

KATE PALMER MYSTERY SERIES
A Body in the Village Hall
A Body in Seaview Grange
A Body at the Tea Rooms
A Body at the Altar
A Body on the Beach
A Body at Lavender Cottage
A Body at in a Cornish Village

The Sunshine Club

Dee MacDonald

Bookouture

Published by Bookouture in 2023

An imprint of Storyfire Ltd.
Carmelite House
50 Victoria Embankment
London EC4Y 0DZ

www.bookouture.com

ISBN: 978-1-83790-683-3
eBook ISBN: 978-1-83790-682-6

To the enduring friendship of women

PROLOGUE
2015

The small group stood huddled together around the grave. Shivering, their heads were bowed as the words of the committal were intoned and the coffin slowly lowered. The two elderly women stood, collars up against the bitter wind, arm in arm, to one side.

The vicar seemed oblivious to the fact that he had a lengthening drip dangling from his nose, but it was obvious to the two women, who nudged each other and tried not to giggle.

'She'd have a fit if she thought that was going to fall on top of her!'

'Indeed she would! She'll probably come back and haunt him!'

'Have you got the roses in there somewhere?' the taller of the two whispered, causing her companion to make a surreptitious search into the depths of her large shoulder bag. She patted her expensive hairdo in despair, aware that the weather had totally wrecked it.

'Don't tell me I've *lost* them!' Some frantic searching was going on.

'God only knows what else you'll find in there,' said the

taller woman, and both suppressed further nervous giggles. 'She'd probably have lectured you for being so disorganised!'

'She damn well would! Ah, wait a minute – here they are!' The shorter woman produced two bedraggled red roses and handed one to her companion as they both inched forward to toss them on top of the oak coffin. Some further burrowing in the bag produced a bundle of crumpled tissues. 'Here, you better have one of these.'

The priest cast a disparaging look at the two women as the drip from his nose fell silently on top of the oak coffin and increased the volume of his speech by several decibels, making everyone jump. Then, to indicate that the service was over, he snapped his Bible shut.

The tears which the women had been trying to hold back now began to flow. They dabbed their eyes as they walked slowly away from the graveside, their arms linked once more.

Tony, of Tony's Taxis, who, until then, had been gazing lustfully at the beautiful red Porsche parked under the yew tree, reluctantly redirected his gaze to the two women. Poor old girls! They certainly looked like they had need of a taxi.

'Can I give you two ladies a lift somewhere?' he asked as he opened the door of his well-polished Ford Mondeo.

'Thank you, but no.' The taller lady dabbed her eyes. 'We have our own car, you see.'

With that, she opened the door of the Porsche and lowered herself, with great care, into the driving seat. Her companion settled in beside her with equal caution. Then, as the engine roared into life, they both gave a cheery wave and were gone in a cloud of dust.

· · ·

The woman in the passenger seat said, 'I just cannot believe that we won't see her again.'

Her companion nodded as she climbed through the gears. 'We've been friends for so long, for *decades*! And when I think of what we used to get up to...' She blew her nose and wiped her eyes. 'Nobody would believe it! It's only a couple of weeks ago that we were all together, reminiscing...'

TWO WEEKS EARLIER

Molly

When Molly and Eve arrived at Vanessa's imposing mansion on this, the first time since Vanessa had taken up residence there, the three women hugged each other. They hadn't met for months, so there was a lot of catching up to do.

'I cannot believe it's over fifty years since we three *first* met!' exclaimed Eve.

'And aren't we all still gorgeous!' Molly proclaimed, making the other two giggle.

'Well, come on in,' said Vanessa, leading the way up the steps and into an elaborate hallway and equally impressive drawing room.

Molly looked around in awe. What a stunning house, and how typical of Vanessa to live somewhere so elegant and beautiful! As was Vanessa herself – elegant and beautiful!

'Now, what are you having to drink?' asked Vanessa. 'I've several fizzies here: Moët, Bolly, Dom Pérignon?'

'That's some choice!' said Molly, wishing she'd dieted before leaving Italy.

'You didn't circumnavigate the globe as an air hostess for all those years without developing a taste for some decent bubbly,' Eve reminded her.

'True. I'll have the Bollinger then please, Vanessa.'

Vanessa, wearing designer jeans and a cashmere sweater, her figure still slim and svelte, her hair expensively coiffed and coloured, poured out the champagne.

'Wow, Nessa, how on earth do you manage to look so fabulous at seventy!' Eve asked, plainly conscious of her chubby tummy and thighs.

Vanessa shrugged. 'Just luck, I guess. And you both look terrific too, although I have to say,' she added as they toasted each other, 'that I thought you were both a bit dull and boring-looking when I first set eyes on you.'

'*What?*' Eve nearly choked on her drink. 'At the air stewardess interview?'

Vanessa nodded.

'Well, I spent ages getting ready and thought I looked pretty good.' Eve sounded incredulous.

'Me too!' chorused Molly.

'First impressions aren't always accurate of course,' Vanessa conceded.

At times, Molly wondered how they'd managed to stay friends for all these years in spite of Vanessa's sometimes acerbic comments. It was Vanessa, of course, who'd come up with 'the sunshine club', to describe their early flying days, even though it wasn't always sunny, at home or away, but they'd remained friends through thick and thin and, Molly felt sure, would continue to do so.

As they sipped their champagne, the three of them appeared to be reminiscing about that very first meeting.

1964

CHAPTER ONE

Vanessa

Vanessa glanced at her watch. How much longer, for God's sake, before they came to a decision? She hoped and, to be honest, *expected* to be chosen of course, but you could never be sure.

Well, if Skyline didn't want her, she'd apply to one of the American airlines because both Pan Am and TWA were currently recruiting British girls. She wouldn't mind in the least being based in New York or somewhere.

She looked round at the others and decided that the competition wasn't that stiff really, so she'd probably be OK. Some of the others were lighting up cigarettes, and she wondered if she dared. Perhaps not, just in case someone came out of that room and wanted to shake her hand. It paid to be optimistic.

Vanessa was sitting directly opposite the untidy-looking Scottish girl, her red hair all over the place, and wearing a *tartan* skirt, of all things. Unlikely she'd be chosen. Likewise, the Irish-looking one. *Was* she Irish? She didn't have an Irish accent, but she did have an Irish name, along with the blue eyes and the black hair. Pretty little thing, but far too short.

She cast her eye round some of the others. There were a fair few miniskirts, which probably wasn't a good idea. She was glad she'd worn her pale-blue shift dress, which came to the knee, and showed off her long, slim, tanned legs (thanks to two weeks on the Côte d'Azur). Vanessa reckoned her chances were pretty good.

She was about to find out because the door had opened and one of the inquisitors had emerged, all smiles.

Molly

Molly was wearing three-inch heels, in an attempt to reach the lower height limit, but it hadn't worked of course, because that hateful woman on the selection board, Judy Somebody-or-Other, had made her take them off and then appraised her for several minutes before saying, 'Hmm.'

Well, that was that. No chance of being selected now, although she wondered why she had been asked to stay behind in this hot, stuffy waiting room with all these others. At this rate, she was going to miss the bus back to Bristol, and then she'd have to wait hours for the next one. She wondered if it was OK to be Irish; not that she had a bog-Irish accent or anything because the family had left Ireland when she was three years old and, if she had any kind of accent now, it was most likely a West Country one.

Without a doubt, Molly reckoned, they'd be choosing that tall, ice-cool blonde with the posh accent, and a couple more who didn't have a mass of black curly hair. She quite liked the look of the Scots girl in her Black Watch tartan skirt and with her red hair in a state of collapse, who was frantically picking at her nails.

Molly sighed. What on earth would her parents think if they saw her here at Heathrow Airport? She hadn't told them a thing, because she wasn't sure if they'd get all excited or whether they'd try to stop her. She'd borrowed her sister's tweed skirt for the occasion because it covered her knees and so, when she sat down, she wouldn't show too much leg. Looking around at the others, she noticed that several were wearing these new miniskirts, which showed a great deal of leg and *thigh*! Molly didn't think she'd ever want to wear one of them because you wouldn't want to look like some sort of 'floozie', which was a favourite word of her mother's.

Well, there was no chance whatsoever that she was going to be selected and, if she dashed out now, she might just catch that bus.

Just then, the door opened from the inner sanctum where their fate had been decided.

Eve

Eve was feeling sick. She was quite sure she hadn't got the damned Skyline job, so what was she going to do now? And why was she, along with this group of a dozen or so other women, asked to stay behind when, according to the blurb, they only wanted *three*? Apparently twenty-seven had already been selected, and they needed thirty. As if the interview hadn't been bad enough, was this laid on as further torture?

She looked round in awe at the others, all in their finery, hair and make-up immaculate. Her own attempt at a chignon had been somewhat less than successful, and wisps of her red tresses were escaping round her neck. She couldn't see anyone else covered in freckles either. No matter how good her French was, they were not going to be choosing *her*. They definitely *would* be choosing the tall blonde in the blue dress, with the immaculate hairdo and the cut-glass accent. Eve didn't fancy the little Irish girl's chances though, as you were supposed to be a minimum of five feet six, and she definitely wasn't.

Eve badly wanted a cigarette and noticed that a couple of the girls were already puffing away. *No*, she thought, *I'll wait until I get out of here. It might not go down too well with the selection board, who just might be watching us through a one-way mirror or something*. You could never tell, and she wouldn't put it past them, because they were so *awful*. The questions they asked! The way they made you walk round the room, studying you like you were in the ring at a cattle market! And they had deliberately tried to rattle her, but she had been ready for that.

She'd read an article written by an air hostess who'd written that the interviewers had tried very hard to upset her because, if she couldn't cope with them, it was highly unlikely she'd be able to cope with an irate, unreasonable passenger. She'd remained calm apparently and got the job. Easier said than done when your mouth was so dry that you could hardly speak, and you had to keep remembering not to pick at your nails.

Eve fiddled nervously with the locket she always wore. It was obvious she wasn't going to be chosen, and she was about to get up and leave when the door to the boardroom opened and out came two of the torturers, smiling away.

'We have made a decision,' one of them said.

Eve stayed seated.

'We've now chosen the three ladies who will complete our course,' he said cheerfully, looking around, 'but please don't be discouraged if you haven't been chosen this time, and do please try again. It was a very difficult choice, but we have finally decided on Miss Muir, Miss O'Hara and Miss Carter-Flint. Would you three please come into the office.'

CHAPTER TWO

Vanessa

Vanessa was relieved and pleased but noticed the other two looking quite shell-shocked as they were each given a copy of Skyline's Rules and Conditions of Employment.

'Congratulations, ladies! My name's Ed Wilkins and I'm the personnel officer who will be dealing with new aircrew. Don't forget, though, that you still have to get through the training and our very strict safety courses. You will each receive a letter of offer of employment in the next day or two, and I wish you the best of luck. I shall be in my office if you need any further information now.'

Vanessa decided she'd better take charge because the redhead seemed to be in a state of complete shock and the dark-haired girl looked as if she was about to burst into tears.

'Look,' she said, 'I'm Vanessa Carter-Flint, and I don't know about you two, but I could *murder* a drink! And we *do* need to celebrate!'

The redhead nodded. 'I'm Eve Muir and I certainly do need a drink!'

The little dark-haired one finally found her voice. 'I'm Molly – Molly O'Hara. I've missed my bus home, so I'd love to join you for a drink.'

Vanessa picked up her coat and bag. 'Follow me, ladies, because I know a reasonable pub about five minutes away. You two got wheels?'

Both shook their heads.

'OK then. My car's a two-seater, but I think I could squeeze in an extra small person,' Vanessa said, grinning at Molly.

As they walked towards the car park, a Skyline jet, with its distinctive dark-blue tail and large gold 'S', was coming screaming into land over their heads.

'Oh my God,' Eve said. 'I cannot believe we're actually going to be working on those things!'

'Neither can I,' Molly agreed. 'I thought I wasn't tall enough.'

'Well, rules are made to be broken,' Vanessa said as she squeezed them into the front of her blue Triumph Spitfire. Molly had probably been chosen because she had such a curvaceous little figure, Vanessa reckoned, and most of the selection committee were horny old men. She shut the door and they roared off to the pub.

The Flyer was a not-very-exciting pub of 1950s vintage, with a violently patterned carpet, mock beams and nicotine-stained walls. There was a jukebox in the corner playing the Beatles' 'I Want to Hold Your Hand'.

'My treat,' said Vanessa as they got to the bar. 'So what would you like to drink?'

'I'd love a gin and tonic,' Eve said without hesitation.

Molly looked confused. 'Maybe just an orange juice, if that's OK?'

'Sure you wouldn't like some gin in that?'

'Oh my goodness, no,' Molly replied.

The jukebox was now playing Roy Orbison's 'Oh, Pretty Woman', which was Vanessa's favourite song at the moment, so she took that to be a good omen.

As she ordered the drinks, including a gin and tonic for herself as well, she heard Molly ask Eve, 'So what made *you* want to become an air stewardess?'

She saw Eve hesitate for a moment before replying, 'I needed to move on.' Then, presumably seeing their slightly mystified faces, she added, 'I guess I just want to see the world and get paid for it, like everyone else. I've been staying with a friend at Earl's Court ever since I got back from Paris.'

'What were you doing in Paris?' Vanessa asked as they carried their drinks to a table near the window.

'Looking after a couple of precocious, spoiled French kids for the best part of a year,' Eve replied. 'The idea was to improve my French. I'm probably going to go home to Scotland now until we start our training. I need to make peace with my mother, if nothing else. And then I suppose I'd better find somewhere to live round here.'

Vanessa decided not to pursue the matter further. She wondered what the problem with the mother was. 'Here's to us,' she said, raising her drink. They all clinked glasses. 'How about you, Molly?'

'I'm back living with my family in Bristol, since I finished my nursing training in London a couple of months ago. I was planning to start my midwifery until I saw the Skyline advert in the paper.' She sipped her orange juice and laughed. 'It'll just be my luck if someone gives birth on one of my flights. I suppose I'll need to find some lodgings somewhere near the airport, won't I?' She turned to Vanessa. 'What about you?'

Vanessa gave a long sigh. 'I'm living with my mother and my latest stepfather in Guildford at the moment, which is not ideal.' She pulled a face. 'I think I'm going to look around for some-

where to rent now that I'm about to have steady employment.'
She hesitated, wondering if she was being too hasty as she
hardly knew these two, but a flat on her own would be expensive. She took a deep breath. 'If I found a flat somewhere around
here, would you two consider sharing with me?'

'Oh, that would be great!' Eve exclaimed. 'I'll need to find
somewhere and I can't do much if I'm in Scotland.'

They both looked at Molly.

'Likewise,' she said. 'I wouldn't have a clue where to start.'

'Leave it to me then,' said Vanessa, getting out her diary.
'Let's exchange addresses and I'll contact you both if I find
something.'

As she scribbled down their addresses, Vanessa reckoned
she wouldn't be sharing with them for long anyway, because she
was hoping to be snapped up by some globe-trotting millionaire.
The sooner she got to work in the first class section, the better.

CHAPTER THREE

Molly

Molly's parents were extremely dubious about the whole thing.

'You're over twenty-one, so I suppose we can't stop you,' Jack O'Hara said, 'but I'm not at all happy about this flat-sharing business, and neither is your mother. Is there not a nice hostel around there for young ladies on their own?'

'No, there isn't, Dad,' Molly replied. The nurses' home had been restrictive enough, she thought, but if her dad had his way, she'd be incarcerated somewhere with a load of nuns watching her every move.

'Are those planes safe now?' her mother asked anxiously. 'I've just been reading about that terrible crash—'

'Mam!' Molly shouted. 'Don't you know there are more accidents on the roads every *day* than aeroplane accidents in a *year*?'

'Yes, dear, but you have a better chance of coming out of a car accident alive,' her mother said ominously.

'Well, I'm quite prepared to take my chances,' Molly said.

For goodness' sake, she thought, *it's not like I'm an only one! They've got plenty of reserves! Four brothers and one sister!*

The sister was called Siobhan, she was two years older than Molly, they shared a bedroom and, for some reason, they'd never really got on. Siobhan was a hairdresser, man-mad, and Molly was quite sure she wasn't a virgin. Molly considered herself a prize-in-waiting, but not until her wedding night of course. During her time in London for her nursing training, plenty of the fellows had tried to seduce her, and some had come very close indeed to succeeding, but Molly was still intact and that was the way she planned to stay until she met The Man. She could tell that Siobhan was green with envy though, but all her older sister said was, 'It was probably my good tweed skirt that got you the job!'

The O'Haras had come across from Ireland and rented a house, this very same house, in a not-very-salubrious area of Bristol, into which they packed too many children into too few rooms. Molly had decided early on that she wanted to make something of her life and not finish up in a dead-end job like most of her siblings. She'd hoped that being a nurse might lead to better things, and it was beginning to look as if she might be right. It had seemed to be an advantage at the interview. She'd loved London and St Thomas's in particular, where she was an immediate hit with the patients, due to her cheerfulness, her repertoire of jokes and her ability to imitate to perfection the senior staff, matron included.

But Molly had dreams of emigrating to the USA one day. She'd spent a large part of her youth in the local Odeon, where she'd fallen madly in love with Gregory Peck and Tony Curtis. Perhaps The Man might be American and drive one of those amazing chrome-clad Cadillacs. She might even meet one on the plane, because, for sure, they weren't thick on the ground around Bristol. Come to think of it, she hadn't met him in

London either. But he must be out there *somewhere*. Most of all, she wanted to make her parents proud of her.

Her three older brothers had all left home, but Connor was still there. He was Molly's twin, and he worked in Barclays Bank, which made the parents very proud. They'd even moved their bank account there. He was the only one of the family who seemed genuinely pleased for her.

'Good for you,' he said, sounding wistful. 'Sometimes I wish I was a girl because that job sounds *amazing*!'

'But, Connor,' Molly said earnestly, 'they have stewards on board as well, so why don't you apply? I'll probably be able to let you know when the next intake will be.'

'Mmm,' said Connor, suddenly sounding doubtful.

What is it with this family? Molly wondered. Why were they so afraid of venturing outside their comfort zone?

Molly had been at home a week when Vanessa's letter arrived. It dropped through the letterbox on Wednesday and, by Saturday, Molly was on her way to the flat in Bellingham Road.

Would she mind sharing a room with Eve? Of course not! She'd never had a room to herself in her life, and anything would be better than sharing with Siobhan, who snored like a steam train. She hoped Eve didn't snore so loudly, or at all, but she did have a collection of earplugs, just in case.

Eve

Eve was apprehensive about meeting her mother again after such a long time: two years and three months, to be exact. A great deal had happened in that time. They had written to each other occasionally, always on general topics of interest, but never about 'it'. Like 'it' hadn't happened at all. Not once had Aileen Muir come down to see her daughter in London at that time. She'd visited Calum in Edinburgh plenty of times though. He'd always been the favourite, and now he'd hit the jackpot by qualifying as a *doctor*, no less. Aileen was in her element. But, of course, Edinburgh was a lot closer than London, so maybe that was why she hadn't visited, Eve thought wistfully.

She was now rapidly running out of money and so her journey to Inverness had to be on the overnight sleeper from Euston, sitting bolt upright in a carriage with a couple of giggling girls and a middle-aged man who smelled of sweat. She'd only been able to doze intermittently and she got off the train with a crick in her neck.

Aileen, looking older and greyer than when Eve had last seen her, was waiting on the platform as the train pulled in. They embraced a little awkwardly and then chatted about nothing in particular on the drive to Strathcannon in Aileen's Morris Minor. Aileen only became animated when they passed what had once been a field and was now a building site.

'Will you just *look* at all these houses they're putting up!' Aileen ranted. 'I do not know why planning permission was ever granted! It's not as if we need another housing estate round here. We sent in lots of objections, but a lot of good *that* did!'

'That field was always a bit of an eyesore anyway,' Eve said, 'and people do need somewhere to live.'

Aileen sniffed but said nothing.

It wasn't until after lunch, as they were sitting drinking tea by the Aga, that Eve imparted her news.

'An *air hostess*! Oh my goodness!'

For once, Eve could see that she'd done something right.

'You'll go all over the *world*! I mean, anybody who's anybody flies on Skyline, don't they?' Aileen was studying her daughter in amazement. 'I bet lots of girls applied for that!'

'Rumour has it there were several thousand,' Eve replied,

smiling inwardly at her mother's glee. 'They only interviewed a couple of hundred and then accepted only thirty of us.'

'Oh my!'

Eve knew the news would be all over town in a matter of days. At long last, Aileen Muir had a daughter to be proud of, something to brag about at the church, at the WI and at the countless coffee mornings she hosted for every charity under the sun. More reflected glory! A doctor and an air hostess!

It all helped to compensate for the scandal of Aileen's untimely widowhood when, ten years previously, Jim Muir had wrapped his car round a tree, in the company of Jessie Grant, the barmaid from the Royal Hotel. Jessie had escaped with just a broken leg, the one Jim had been groping, which, according to the police, was probably the cause of the accident...

Eve was only half listening as her mother went on and on about Mrs This and Mrs That, how the council were allowing all this building to go ahead and how she'd sent in letters, signed by all the ladies at the Conservative Club.

'Mum,' Eve interrupted after a good ten minutes, 'I know you're a pillar of respectability round here, but I'd really like to talk to you about—'

'Paris?' Aileen asked, loudly and hopefully.

'No, not Paris, Mum – you know what I want to talk to you about.'

'Oh no, no,' Aileen said hurriedly. 'I've had trouble enough living down the disgrace of your father's transgressions, and I've no wish at all to hear about yours. More tea?'

'No thanks. Look, I'm feeling a bit tired after being up all night, so would you mind if I went up and took a nap for an hour or so?' Yet again Eve felt deflated and annoyed. Surely, after all this time, she and her mother could talk about things?

'Of course. But perhaps later in the week, you might like to address the Women's Institute about how you were selected for this job. Out of several *thousand*! I mean, it's like being a *model* or something! So glamorous!'

'It may appear glamorous, Mum, but I'm told it's very hard work.' Eve suddenly thought about Vanessa. 'I'm also expecting a letter soon about flat-sharing with two other girls.'

'Flat-sharing? What's wrong with where you are now, in Earl's Court?'

'Nothing wrong with Earl's Court. I'd just like to be closer to the airport. We have to do standby sometimes, in case a crew member goes sick or doesn't show up, so every minute would count.'

After a week, Eve was relieved and delighted to hear from Vanessa. She'd found a flat and hoped that Eve wouldn't mind sharing a room with Molly.

Eve didn't mind at all. There had been no change in her mother's attitude, which had put considerable strain on their relationship. She'd be glad to get away.

Vanessa

Vanessa had refused to be rushed as she gave each room of the flat at Bellingham Road a thorough examination. Mr West, the short, balding landlord, was two steps behind her and plainly irritated. She had an inkling that he'd put the rent up the moment he got wind of the fact that his tenants were going to be stewardesses. Vanessa disliked him intensely, but she did like the flat.

The living room was spacious, the kitchen and bathroom adequate, and there was a single and a double bedroom. It was also on a nice tree-lined road which was not under the flight path. Everything seemed reasonably clean, but she examined the gas cooker in minute detail, ignoring the increasingly exasperated Mr West sighing loudly in her wake.

Fifteen pounds a week! Vanessa tried haggling, but the wretched man wouldn't budge an inch. Afraid of losing the place, she decided not to push him too far.

'I'll take it on condition you put a decent fridge in the kitchen,' Vanessa said at last. 'That thing will hardly hold a pint of milk.'

Grudgingly, he acquiesced, keen to escape.

Vanessa had another look at the single bedroom. She could just about get most of her stuff in there. She hoped the other two wouldn't mind sharing, but too bad if they did. Anyway, one or both would be away half of the time.

An hour later, she rolled to a halt in her Spitfire, with much crunching of gravel, outside the front of Kershaw House, and eased her long frame out of the car. As if on cue, her mother, Hermione, clad in her usual uniform of twinset, tweed skirt and double row of pearls, appeared from behind the imposing front door.

'Nessa darling, *do* move that thing round the back. James should be home quite soon, and you *know* how he likes to park there.'

Bloody James, Vanessa swore under her breath. She didn't think a great deal of her latest stepfather.

She slammed the door as she got back into the car and roared round to the rear of the house. *The sooner I get out of here, the better*.

She encountered her mother again in the kitchen. 'I have some news for you,' Vanessa informed her. 'You and James can have this sprawling house and parking spaces all to yourselves, because I'm moving into a flat.'

Hermione's eyebrows shot up to her hairline. 'And how exactly do you intend to pay for *that*?'

'With my salary. I've found a rather nice job.'

'A job? Do you mean more *modelling*? It's hardly a regular salary, for goodness' sake!'

'I'm going to be an air stewardess with Skyline, and I start training in two weeks' time.'

'An *air stewardess*?' She sniffed.

'An air stewardess, Mother,' Vanessa said matter-of-factly and waited.

Hermione's hand flew dramatically towards her heart. 'But, darling, that means you'll have to *serve* people... like a *waitress*!' She practically choked on the words.

Vanessa smiled inwardly. This was exactly the reaction she'd expected.

'Thing is, I'll be serving champagne and caviar, and flying all over the world.'

'But you can fly anywhere in the world if you want to *anyway*,' Hermione said, looking genuinely puzzled. 'You could sit in a nice, comfy first-class seat and have someone serve *you* with champagne and caviar!'

'On *your* money!'

'James's actually.'

'Even worse! I don't want to be beholden to anyone, particularly *James*. No, Mother, I'm going to explore the big, wide world – and get paid for it!'

Hermione sighed. 'Each to his, or her, own, I suppose.'

In spite of her mother's disparaging comments, Vanessa began to feel excited and impatient to discover what adventures might lie ahead.

CHAPTER FOUR

Molly

'Get a move on, Miss O'Hara!'

Molly noticed Len Morris, the training steward, studying his watch as she rushed from the galley clutching two lunch trays. The other would-be stewardesses sat patiently waiting for their lunch in the mock-up of an aircraft economy cabin. Each day, two girls had to serve 'drinks' and lunch to the other twenty-eight, as opposed to the hundred-plus passengers on the real thing.

Today was Molly's turn and she was paired with a dozy girl called Pat, who was having major problems removing the hot meals from the oven and placing them on Molly's trays.

'What are you two *doing*? You've got a bunch of starving passengers out there!' the steward shouted.

Finally, Molly emerged to deliver the trays shakily onto the pull-down tables. It had *looked* easy, and perhaps it wouldn't be so awful if you didn't have a training steward breathing down your neck. She rolled her eyes as she placed Eve's tray down in front of her.

'You're doing fine,' Eve said comfortingly.

'Keep smiling, Miss O'Hara!' ordered Len when she returned to the galley. Molly was well aware that he was studying her cleavage with interest as she bent down to remove two further trays from their stowage. 'And I think the lady in 15A is ready for another glass of wine!'

Molly and Pat had already done a drinks order prior to serving the meal, writing down each request next to the appropriate seat number, before returning with *empty* miniature bottles and mixes, served on silver trays.

'Finish serving the meals first,' Len instructed, 'before you fetch 15A the wine. And don't forget,' he added, 'that you're going to be doing this on an aircraft flying at around five hundred miles per hour – and often through turbulence.'

Molly wondered fleetingly if she'd chosen the wrong job. There was *so* much to learn! She'd known nothing about wines: red, white, pink or Champagne, far less knowing what to serve them with. And *cocktails*! *Fortified* wines, for goodness' sake! Silver service and special meals: vegetarian, kosher... Her parents would not *believe* this. They did visit the local pub occasionally; a beer for Dad, a small sweet sherry for Mam! For sure, Mam would never have known she was quaffing a *fortified wine*.

The lady in 15A was Vanessa. As Molly finally delivered her empty miniature wine bottle, Vanessa muttered, 'God, don't I wish they were real!'

Eve

On Monday mornings, the inaptly named Joy Fuller, the chief training stewardess, came swanning into the classroom, and they all had to stand up. She then gave each trainee the once-over, concentrating on hair and general grooming. She was a thin, frosty, formidable woman, herself groomed to perfection of course. Vanessa had immediately renamed her Joyless.

'Long hair,' Joyless said, looking round with disapproval, 'must be put up in an *immaculate* manner while you are on board. If you can't manage that, then it must be cut. It must never touch your collar, *never*.' She then walked round the classroom, stopping to unravel any tight curls which had been lacquered into submission but which didn't fool her. She tugged at Eve's inexpert chignon. '*That* wouldn't last *five minutes* on board,' she snapped. She then glared at the locket Eve always wore. 'And *no* jewellery! You may wear a plain wristwatch and pearl stud earrings, but *no* chains and *no* necklaces of any sort!'

'Can you imagine flying with a miserable old trout like that?' Vanessa asked Eve after Joyless had made her exit. 'She looks like she's constantly sucking lemons. Do you think any man's ever got *near* her?'

'Apparently, I hear she was quite a girl in her time,' Eve said, 'but perhaps she was jilted or something?'

'Wise guy,' muttered Vanessa.

The following Monday, Joyless appeared with a heavily made-up representative from one of the top cosmetic companies. Mrs Marx was the wrong side of fifty, plastered in foundation and dramatic eye make-up, and deep-fuchsia lipstick. Brandishing what she labelled 'my box of tricks', she called for a volunteer to be made up and was met with complete silence.

'Come along, ladies!' she trilled. 'A volunteer please!'

Everyone was studiously avoiding eye contact and, with the lack of response clearly irritating her, she homed in on Molly, who was in the front row.

'*You*, young lady! Come up here please!'

Eve watched Molly reluctantly positioning herself in the

chair, in front of the mirror which had been set up on the raised podium for the occasion. Then Mrs Marx got to work. In a very short time, Molly's natural look had been completely transformed – and not for the better.

'It's made her look ten years older,' Eve whispered to Vanessa.

'Like a bloody tart,' Vanessa whispered back.

'Now,' said Mrs Marx, plainly pleased with her handiwork, 'I hope you've all followed each step of the make-up process and made a note of the products used.' She seemed completely unaware of the disbelief on the faces of her audience. Hardly anyone bought any of the products and, as soon as it was diplomatic to do so, Eve accompanied Molly to the ladies' room to scrub it all off.

'Your passenger could die at any moment, Miss Carter-Flint! You'll need to give him more puff than that!' the first-aid instructor sighed loudly.

Vanessa blew lustily into the dummy's mouth and was gratified, at last, to see the damn thing's chest rise.

'That's better! Now, tilt his head back, pinch his nose and *keep blowing*!'

Vanessa looked at the dummy with distaste. If she ever had to provide such treatment, she hoped he'd be good-looking.

'Where exactly would you find the first-aid kit on our Boeing 707s, Miss Muir?'

Eve fingered her locket nervously. 'Er, I think it's in the cupboard behind the fire extinguisher?'

'You *think*? While *you're* thinking, this poor passenger is bleeding to death! Ensure you can locate all the safety and medical equipment with the *speed of light*, Miss Muir! Now, how about showing me the lifeboat stowage? Do not forget that the test is next week, and if you don't pass, you don't fly!

Molly was struggling to release the chute on the passenger door in the mock-up. Finally, after much effort, it ballooned out into space and made contact with the ground below.

'Come *on*, come *on*!' roared the instructor. 'Get a move on! Shoes *off*! Jump on the chute. Never mind your bloody handbags! Get down that chute 'cos there's a blazing aeroplane behind you and this is life or death!'

'Does it matter I can't swim?' Molly asked anxiously as she struggled into her life jacket at the local swimming pool.

'Stop worrying,' Eve said, tying the tapes of her own life jacket carefully round her waist. 'You're wearing a life jacket so you're not going to drown. Just paddle across and get yourself into that life raft.'

The large yellow raft was bobbing about on the water, only a few girls having succeeded in heaving themselves inside so far. At best, in a life jacket you could only paddle towards it and then, having got there, it was far from easy to hoist yourself up and into the raft without the whole thing capsizing. With difficulty, everyone, including a spluttering Molly, was finally hauled into its overloaded yellow interior.

Vanessa clambered across to sit next to Eve and Molly, causing the raft to lurch around alarmingly. 'Can you imagine,' she asked haughtily, 'doing this in the mid-Atlantic in a Force 9? It's a complete waste of time! Thank God I wore my waterproof mascara!'

Vanessa swore loudly as she almost dropped the large red extinguisher. Then she regained control and aimed the nozzle at the base of the fire, which was raging in a trough in front of her.

'Explain to me what you're supposed to be doing,' shouted the instructor.

'I'm trying to put out a bloody fire!' Vanessa snapped.

'What sort of fire?'

'It's a fabric fire,' she said through gritted teeth, 'and so I'm using a water extinguisher, OK?'

'Good.' The instructor turned his attention to Molly, who was staring at another fire, in another trough, with some trepidation. 'What exactly are you waiting for, Miss O'Hara?'

Molly struggled with the extinguisher for a moment before getting into position and aiming it at the base of the evil-smelling blaze.

'I'm putting out an electrical fire with a CO_2 extinguisher,' she chanted wearily.

Clad in boiler suits and wellington boots, they all completed their day at the fire compound by crawling through a smoke-filled tunnel.

'This,' the instructor said cheerfully, 'is a burning aircraft and you are in danger of losing your lives! You keep your heads down, and you move fast – *very* fast!'

Several trainees had to be helped out on the verge of choking, and most of them had blackened faces and streaming eyes.

Vanessa rubbed her eyes, wondering if the mascara was still there. 'Do you know what?' she remarked to Eve and Molly. 'I could be modelling lovely clothes in a nice warm studio somewhere! So, tell me, what the hell am I doing *here*?'

Eve squeezed her arm. 'Only a few more days to go and we'll get our wings. And the smart uniforms, so don't despair!'

A grimy and exhausted Molly joined them. 'Don't get carried away,' she said with a grin, 'because you have to do all this safety training every year!'

Eight weeks. Eight weeks of rude instructors and kindly instructors. Two girls in floods of tears before they finally walked out. Sea survival. Arctic survival. Desert survival. Air sea rescue. Breathing, bleeding, emergency points of the body, heart attacks. Cocktails: Manhattans, Martinis, Bloody Marys, pina coladas... Endless criticism. What would they have done without each other, to moan and groan and console? That was surely when the bond was formed.

The group photograph was impressive. Twenty-eight beautifully groomed ladies in their glamorous royal-blue uniforms, hats at a jaunty angle, gold wings and buttons glinting in the sunlight. It was the week before Christmas, which they could all spend with their families and then, come January, off they'd all go! They'd survived the training! With mounting excitement, the three hugged each other.

The chief training steward cleared his throat. 'Ladies, you've done well over the past weeks. You've had to learn a great deal and, believe me, there's a lot more to learn once you get airborne!' He smiled beatifically. 'It's damned hard work on board a full aircraft, but I have no doubt you'll be a credit to the excellent reputation we have here at Skyline. And you'll doubt-less be delighted to know that you'll see me, or one of the other training stewards, on board from time to time, checking on the service with our eagle eyes! So, for now, I wish you well, good luck and have a happy Christmas!'

CHAPTER FIVE

Eve

'The first thing you do, darling,' said Bob, who was the steward in the rear galley, 'is forget all that crap they told you at the training school. We've got a full load of punters out there and, if you're going to fanny around with every little detail, we ain't never going to get it done.' He tapped the side of his nose for emphasis and lit a cigarette. 'Got it?'

Eve got it. Such was her initiation as Skyline Flight 101 to New York climbed steeply and bumpily through the heavy January clouds.

'He's a bit of a rough diamond, but he's OK really,' said Jenny, her co-stewardess in the rear cabin, as they undid their seat belts. Bob was already in the galley. 'He's off the boats, you see.'

'The boats?' Eve asked.

'Yes, you know, the *Queen Mary*, the *Queen Elizabeth* and all that. We've got quite a few of them off the boats. Now, grab your notebook and take a drink order, starting at the front. You do one side; I'll do the other.'

The first rule to be broken was that you began work while the seat-belt sign was still on, because the moment it was switched off, half the passengers would be up, out of their seats and cluttering up the aisle. It was difficult enough having to deliver the right drinks to the right passengers, without having to squeeze past these people and prevent everything slithering off the tray.

'Bloody nuisance they are,' Bob commiserated, through a cloud of cigarette smoke, each time Eve came back for a refill. He was not at all keen on the people who provided him with a living and rarely left the galley.

As Eve cleared up some empty miniature bottles and glasses and made her way up the aisle, Jenny said, 'Bob likes you to save the little bottles, because he fills them up with booze from first class and sells them again. Makes him a few quid on the side and most of them do it.'

This had certainly *not* been part of the training, Eve thought. This trip was already proving to be quite an eye-opener. Furthermore, the chief steward on board, George, was devoting all his attention to the handsome young man in 15C instead of supposedly helping deliver the meal trays.

'George is lovely but camp as a row of tents,' Jenny informed her. 'If he gets his wicked way with 15C, you won't see him for dust in New York.'

Eve was astounded. She knew, of course, that homosexuality existed, but it was against the law and very much frowned upon at home. Whatever next?

After the meal trays had been collected and brought in, the bells began to ring.

Ding-dong! 'Can I have another drink please?'

Ding-dong! 'When is my kosher meal going to be ready?'

Ding-dong! 'Can you do me another bottle for my baby?'

Ding-dong! 'My little boy's just been sick...!'

Ding-dong! 'Have you got a copy of *The Times*?'

And so it went on.

'Is that Greenland down there?'

As far as Eve was concerned, it could be Timbuktu, because she didn't have time to get anywhere near a window. She hardly sat down for the whole eight hours, except to quickly gobble a crew meal while sitting on an upturned storage box in the galley. This was because Bob had covered the crew seats with his bar boxes while he tried to balance what he'd sold with the money taken. On top of that, it took time to work out how much was for Skyline and how much he could pocket for himself.

They then served afternoon tea before landing at the newly named Kennedy Airport. More trays, more tea, more coffee. And passengers wanted to talk, because they were bored stiff with sitting in an economy-class seat with no entertainment whatsoever, so they stood in the aisle or chatted while they queued for the toilets. Bob reckoned they should all be deep-frozen at check-in and only thawed out at their destination.

As the toilets were almost permanently occupied, Eve had little opportunity to either freshen up herself or tidy up the interiors, as they'd all been instructed to do. George had peeled himself away from 15C for a moment to ask Eve how she was coping. 'You go down the front, love,' he told her, 'and get five minutes to yourself.'

Eve hadn't yet dared venture through the curtain which separated the rear cabin from the holy of holies – first class. It was like stepping into a different world, with its large, comfortable seats, leg rests, starched white table linen, silver, crystal, fine wines and a general air of gentility.

'Yes, of course you can use the loo!' The first-class stewardess, Maggie, was just emerging from the flight deck. 'Fancy some smoked salmon while you're here?'

· · ·

Every bone in Eve's body ached as she fell into her seat in the crew bus at Kennedy Airport. There was snow everywhere, piled up in gigantic mounds, but no sign of the famous Manhattan skyline. It was icily cold, and it was only two o'clock in the afternoon, instead of being seven in the evening, as it would be back in England, although it felt like midnight to Eve.

During the long drive to the city centre, most of the crew dozed off. Eve, however, was far too excited in spite of her fatigue. Here she was in *America*! Unbelievable! She gazed out the window of the bus at the sprawling suburbs, the gaudy flashing lights, the brownstone apartment blocks with 'Renting Now!' painted on the sides, and the enormous cemetery that seemed to go on and on.

'Dead centre of New York, darling,' Bob informed her, lighting yet another cigarette. 'Everyone's dying to get in there!' There were groans from around the bus; apparently someone said this every trip.

Then, suddenly, out of the window, Eve could see the famous skyline, like black upturned icicles towering against the leaden sky on this cold winter's day. Manhattan! Oh wow! Eve felt a thrill of excitement. What would they say in Strathcannon if they could see her now, driving through the Midtown Tunnel into the Downtown area! Yellow cabs, sirens wailing, snow banked up against the sidewalks (mustn't call them pavements!) and clouds of steam rising from the vents.

Now they were on Third Avenue and heading towards Lexington Avenue, where the Plaza Hotel was situated.

The Plaza housed many Skyline crews as well as those from other European airlines, and the lobby was full of royal-blue uniforms due to several crews coming and going. Everyone seemed to know everyone else.

'What was the weather like in London?'

'We're just heading for San Francisco.'

'Just got in from Kingston – what a change in temperature!'

Someone spied Bob, who, as usual, had a cigarette dangling out of his mouth. 'How are you, Bob? Still doing more fiddling than the Philharmonic?'

Eve stood back a little uncertainly and then realised that the captain of her flight, resplendent with his four gold rings, had approached her.

'Hi,' he said, 'you must be our new lady?'

'I'm Eve Muir, sir.' She had been told that the captain should always be addressed as 'sir'.

'Oh, just call me Dave! And do I detect a Scottish accent? Yes, I thought so! I've always fancied red-haired Scottish lasses! I'll see you in my room for a drink in half an hour or so, OK?' He gave her the number.

Eve was somewhat shell-shocked until Jenny reassured her that it wouldn't be a personal invitation because everyone on the crew would be meeting up for drinks in the skipper's room. 'Some skippers are more sociable – and randy – than others,' she told Eve, 'and a few are downright horrible! But most are OK. Dave there's a bit of a lad though. You got your key? OK, now tell the bellboy which case is yours and he'll bring it up to your room. And whatever you do, *don't* go falling asleep! Have a shower, watch telly, *anything*! Fall asleep now and you'll be wide awake at two in the morning local time, and what are you going to do *then*?' What indeed? 'See you later – bring a glass!'

Her head in a whirl, Eve made her way up to the twenty-second floor in one of the lifts. The room was large and luxurious, with an enormous bed. Eve had never seen such a huge bed, and no bed had ever looked more inviting. She'd never been on a twenty-second floor before either, but she was disappointed that the view from the window was only that of another building close by.

She unpacked, showered, let her hair loose, changed and tried to watch a strange soap, called *Dark Shadows*, on the TV.

After a requisite time, she picked up a glass, as instructed, and headed towards the captain's room.

The captain had an even larger room and it was filled to capacity with not only her crew but with what appeared to be several others, parked on the bed, the floor and every available space. She looked for some familiar faces through the haze of cigarette smoke.

Bob, his customary cigarette dangling from the side of his mouth, was the self-appointed barman. 'What's your poison, love?'

Eve stared in amazement at the array of Scotch, gin, brandy, rum, beer and mixers on the dressing table. She had heard about room parties, but nevertheless nothing had prepared her for the noise, the laughter, the jokes and the amount of alcohol being imbibed. 'Oh, gin and tonic please.'

'Brought a glass? Good girl! Don't suppose you brought any booze off, did you?'

Eve shook her head. 'Should I have done?'

'My fault – I should have told you. Get yourself a flask so you can always bring something off. All free for first class, darling; all free for us! See what I mean?' More nose-tapping. He handed her a stiff gin and tonic. 'Checked the library yet?'

'There's a *library*?'

'Yeah, up there.' Bob pointed to the hatch in the ceiling, just inside the door. 'That's where you'll find some interesting books, *I* can tell you!'

Eve looked mystified. 'Why would you look for books up there?'

'*Dirty* books, darling. Some of them businessmen, and some of our lot too, buy them dirty books over here. But they can't take them home, can they? Can't have the missus coming across them in the suitcase! So up in the hatch they go!'

Eve nodded and made her way nervously across the room. She saw Jenny, long blonde hair down to her waist as opposed to the demure chignon she had on board. Everyone looked so different out of uniform.

'Hi,' said Jenny, 'and don't *you* look lovely with your hair down! There's no sign of George, so I reckon he's having his wicked way with 15C. Oops, here comes Dave...'

The captain had edged his way towards Eve. 'This is our new lady!' he called out.

Lots of faces turned towards her, wishing her luck and raising their glasses.

Eve was aware that the captain was sitting uncomfortably close, but there was nowhere she could move to.

'Are you ready for a refill?'

Eve had only had a couple of sips. 'Not yet, sir, I—'

'*Dave*! Call me Dave! I'll top it up anyway!' With that, he took her glass and headed towards the loaded dressing table. He returned with it filled up to the brim. 'Tell me about yourself, Eve. What have you been doing up to now?'

She was aware that he was definitely edging closer than was necessary. She cleared her throat. 'Well, sir, er... Dave, I've been in Paris for a year polishing up my French.' *Don't ask me what I did before that.*

'Oh, very good, very good. *Très bien!* Now, whereabouts in Scotland do you come from, my dear?'

'Oh, a village called Strathcannon, near Inverness.'

'I think I might have been golfing somewhere near there. Do you play golf yourself, Eve?'

'No, I don't.' She wondered if she should add that she was saving golfing for when she was middle-aged but then decided it might sound rude. She took an enormous gulp of her drink.

A tall very thin man had come up alongside the captain.

'Ah, Clive, trying to get in on the act?' call-me-Dave asked cheerfully. Then, turning to Eve: 'This is our first officer, Clive.'

Clive grinned sheepishly and asked a few general questions as to how she was enjoying the high life. Then he shouted,

'Shall we all go to Joe's? Great steaks, and not too far to go in this bloody weather.'

Shouts of agreement followed.

'Drink up!' ordered Dave. 'We'll all get our coats and meet up downstairs.'

Joe's Bar was two blocks away, which was far enough in the icy evening air. Some fresh snow had fallen since their arrival and, despite her warm coat, Eve was shivering. And she used to think Strathcannon was so cold!

They entered a cavernous, dimly lit and crowded establishment with a bar at one end from where some scantily clad waitresses, in fishnet tights and not much else, were busily dispensing drinks.

A suitably large table was found to accommodate the dozen or so crew members who'd decided to venture out, Dave sitting himself next to Eve. Then one of the fishnet girls, with a mass of peroxide blonde curls, approached their table. 'You guys just got in?'

'Yeah, Bonnie, how are *you*?' Dave asked, patting her bottom.

Bonnie appeared to be just fine and went off to get their order of steaks and Budweisers.

'Best steak around,' Dave told Eve.

'I honestly don't think I could manage a beer after all that gin,' Eve said uncertainly.

'Don't you worry, because I can help you with that,' said Dave with a wink.

Eve couldn't believe the size of the steaks or the equally large salads. She'd never had iceberg lettuce before and it was nothing like the little, boring dark-green things that her mother hauled out of the garden each year. And such a variety of dressings: Caesar, Thousand Island, blue cheese, Italian... and not one bottle of salad cream in sight! Without doubt, this was one of the best steaks she'd ever tasted, and Eve surprised herself by eating it all.

By now she was feeling relaxed and not a little tipsy and had even got used to Dave flirting with her non-stop.

'Shall we have a wee dance?' he asked in what he considered to be a Scottish accent.

Eve could see no escape, and everyone was chatting away to everyone else, so she got up to dance with him. The jukebox had been playing some rock music, but now it was 'Mack the Knife' by Bobby Darin, which slowed the tempo down and gave Dave the excuse to clamp himself ever closer. She was becoming increasingly fed up of being monopolised by him and longed for an opportunity to chat and get to know some of the others. Was there a diplomatic way of getting rid of a captain? she wondered. Nobody had advised her on *that* in the training school either.

When the song finished, she managed to free herself and head back to the table. 'I'm becoming very tired,' she said and caught Jenny's eye as she sat down.

'We'll walk back together,' Jenny said, plainly aware of Eve's problem.

However, Dave wasn't put off so easily and followed close behind.

'Grab your key and get into the lift quick!' Jenny advised.

They managed to lose Dave at this point, and it was with great relief that Eve got to her room, shutting and locking the door behind her. She'd hardly got her coat off when the knock came.

'Who is it?' she asked, leaving the chain in position and peering out nervously into the corridor to see Dave standing there, with two glasses and a bottle of brandy.

'A wee nightcap?' he slurred hopefully.

'No thank you, and goodnight, *sir*!'

He wasn't giving up. 'I just need to make sure your room's satisfactory, Eve, you being new and all that.'

'My room is perfectly fine!'

'You know I have to do a report on you?' He was beginning to sound belligerent now.

Eve knew that the chief steward had to do a report on her, but the captain...? Surely not?

'I'm sorry, I'm tired. Goodnight!'

He went away eventually, leaving Eve feeling slightly concerned. Was this wretched man blackmailing her to get his evil way? They hadn't covered blackmail in the training school either.

But right now, Eve was too tired to care.

'I can't believe an old captain would act like that,' Eve said to the other two girls in the coffee shop next morning, as she got to grips with her first New York breakfast of eggs sunny side up and corned beef hash. 'I mean, he must be in his *fifties!*'

Maggie laughed. 'Oh, lots of them are like that,' she said between mouthfuls of pancakes and maple syrup. 'Dipstick Dave is one of many.'

Eve giggled. 'Dipstick Dave?'

'I'll leave it to your imagination to work out why he gets called that.'

The waitress had come round again to fill up the coffee mugs. Eve was impressed because they certainly didn't do that at home. She was loving the food here, the size of the portions, the free coffee.

She also loved strolling along Fifth Avenue and gazing up at the incredible height of the Empire State Building. She'd been advised to save the sightseeing for when she had a complete day off in New York, but, on this occasion, they were flying home tonight so she'd need to take it easy in the afternoon. There was always time for shopping though. They passed the Empire State Building and headed towards Macy's department store.

'Just for a look,' Jenny said, 'because we're searching for bargains, and that means Korvettes!'

After a quick look round the amazing Macy's, they walked back to the bargain store, Korvettes, where Eve was awestruck with the huge selections and the low prices. In the household department, she spent most of her meal allowance on some beautiful blue-and-green patterned towels, which would brighten up that austere bathroom in Bellingham Road. Then she fell in love with a sundress and wondered if she was crazy in view of the weather outside.

'That is *beautiful*!' Jenny enthused. 'Keep that, along with your bikini, in the bottom of your suitcase at *all* times. You just never know when you might get called out, even here, to replace someone who's gone sick, and you don't want to find yourself in Barbados with a load of winter clothes, now do you?'

Eve would have been thrilled to find herself in Barbados with *anything*.

The night flight back to London was an hour shorter than the one coming over, due to the prevailing winds. After everyone was served dinner and duty-free goods, there was little time for lights out and sleep before dawn came up and they began preparing to serve breakfast. They did have a couple of comparatively quiet hours, during which Dipstick Dave sauntered through the cabin, his four gold rings on display.

'How are you coping, my dear?' he asked Eve, who was trying to ignore Bob and Jenny giggling behind the galley curtain.

'Fine, sir. Fine thank you.'

'I'm sure we'll fly together again sometime and perhaps get

to know each other better,' he said with a definite gleam in his eye before retracing his steps back to the flight deck.

'Don't reckon he gets much at home,' Bob snorted.

'And you should see his snooty wife,' Jenny added. 'Face like a fortnight of frost and looks down her nose at cabin crew – if only she knew!'

CHAPTER SIX

Vanessa

'What an experience!' Vanessa poured herself a hefty gin as she regaled Eve with a blow-by-blow account of her first trip to the Middle East.

Vanessa hadn't been too impressed at being rostered to the Gulf as she'd rather hoped for a trip back to Nairobi, where she'd grown up. Instead, she got sent to the middle of nowhere with a full load of passengers, most of whom were men heading out to the oil rigs. They'd be working in remote areas and alcohol was forbidden, so they intended to make the most of the flight.

'They were completely smashed by the time we were halfway there. You'd think they were camels storing alcohol in their humps for the dry months ahead! Two passed out altogether, half of them were incapable of fastening their seat belts and most of them were trying it on, every chance they got!' Vanessa took a large gulp of her gin. 'It was even worse coming back because these oil blokes hadn't had a drink, or seen a woman, in months! I can't *begin* to tell you! They don't tell you how to deal with lecherous or drunken men in the training school, do they?'

Eve laughed. 'Makes my New York trip with Dipstick Dave seem quite mundane!' Eve was enthralled. 'They don't teach you how to deal with randy captains either! There's an awful lot they don't tell you at the training school! Now, what was the name of the guy you met?'

Vanessa sighed. 'Abdul. I mean, yes, he was tall, dark and handsome and he was obviously loaded. Everyone is a cousin, or a second cousin twice removed, of the sheikh, you see. But first, let me tell you about visiting the sheikh's palace, because you've never seen anything like it! Marble walls, floors, ceilings, all adorned with chandeliers, glitter balls, indoor fountains, outdoor fountains in the floodlit gardens, all of which are gold. Gold *everything*! No sign of the sheikh himself though. And there was *gallons* of the finest vintage champagne! *Gallons* of the stuff! Abdul kept topping up my glass, and I got more than tipsy, I can tell you.'

Eve shook her head, laughing. 'What happened then?'

'You should have seen the loo! All mirrors and soft pink lighting, lovely French soap, fluffy towels. And gold taps of course!'

'Go on!'

'Abdul is waiting right outside the door and he takes me to this amazing buffet. The skipper and the rest of the crew are already there of course, stuffing themselves silly and topping up their glasses. There's caviar, the lot! But, to be honest, I'm feeling pretty exhausted by now. I mean, it's a long drag out from London and it's late. So taxis are summoned. Abdul says he'd like to say goodnight and, let's face it, he's very attractive and I'm very tipsy, so we're smooching away behind a pillar while the skipper keeps clearing his throat and looking at his watch.' Vanessa drained her glass. 'I think I might need another one of these.'

'Come into the kitchen for a refill while I make us some omelettes,' Eve said, agog. 'I think we could both do with something to eat.'

They moved into the kitchen, and Vanessa refilled her glass while Eve cracked eggs.

'Well, next day, we're all out by the hotel pool, because we're desperate to get a bit of sun before coming back to *this*.' She waved her hand at the rain-lashed window. 'I'm wearing my bikini, the pink one, and floating around in the pool because it's so warm and lovely. This time of year's OK out there, you know, but it's unbearably hot in the summer, they tell me. Anyway, I hear this voice.'

'Abdul?'

'Abdul. Standing by the pool, he leans over the edge to tell me I've got a beautiful body. Then he asks if I'd like to do some shopping? He knows some wonderful shops, and he can barter for me. Well, Eve, *who* doesn't like shopping?'

'Who indeed?' Eve said, a dreamy look in her eye.

'So I agree. And he's got this fantastic Mercedes, all air-conditioned with the most incredible soft, white leather seats. Off we go to the gold market, and he asks me what kind of jewellery I like.'

'Oh wow!' said Eve, one eye on her omelettes. 'So what did you say?'

'Well, what kind of jewellery *don't* I like? I mean, *what* a question! But I wanted to be honest, so I told him that I don't much care for yellow gold. Ah, he says, he knows just the place where I can find gold in just the colour I like, so back to the Merc we go and end up at this fantastic apartment, a penthouse with views over the rooftops to the desert. More champagne! And then he brings out this gorgeous pair of pale gold earrings. They're for me, he says. I can't possibly take them, I tell him. He tops up my champagne, and one glass led to another. I had the devil's own job trying to keep him at arm's-length, I can tell you!'

'Did you succeed?'

'With great difficulty!'

The kitchen was filling with smoke, but Eve didn't seem to care. 'What happened then?'

'Mercifully, the telephone rang, and he ended up on some long, drawn-out business call. When he came off the phone, he seemed to be much calmer. Told me he'd fallen in love with me at first sight, and he was prepared to wait!'

'Wow! What about the earrings?'

'In my bedroom! I'll show them to you in a minute. Finally, I had to remind him that I needed to get back to the hotel, as the crew would be wondering where I'd got to, and we had to be up at three in the morning to fly back home. He only wants to come *with* me, but I managed to put him off.'

'Will you see him again?' Eve seemed gobsmacked.

'Probably not, unless I go there again. He was very attractive and I could be persuaded next time.'

The omelettes were burned to a cinder, and Eve, completely caught up in Vanessa's story, ditched them. 'Wouldn't you be worried about getting pregnant?'

'Oh, I've taken care of that. I've been on the birth control pill for a couple of years now,' Vanessa replied airily.

'But how do you manage to get it if you're single? I mean it's only for certain married women, isn't it?' Eve seemed quite shocked.

'Oh, you just have to find the right doctor. You have to pay of course. I can give you his name and number if you want.' Vanessa saw Eve had that faraway look in her eyes and that she was fiddling with that locket of hers, which was a nervous habit. Perhaps Vanessa shouldn't have suggested that. Perhaps she shouldn't have told her about Abdul either.

After a moment, Eve said, 'This is some job, isn't it?'

'It certainly is.'

'Sorry about the omelettes, but I'll make us some more!'

'I wonder where we'll go next?' Vanessa said. 'Have you had a roster yet?'

Eve shook her head. 'No, but I hope it's somewhere sunny. New York was freezing!'

'It's always sunny above the clouds,' said Vanessa, 'so we'll think of this job as our little sunshine club.'

CHAPTER SEVEN

Molly

Molly had never been abroad before, a fact she'd kept to herself. She was in awe of Vanessa, who'd spent her childhood in Africa, and also of Eve, who'd spent a year in Paris. It wouldn't do for them both to think that she was so completely unworldly and that she'd only flown once in her life, to Dublin, to see relatives. She kept her brand-new passport out of sight and wondered at times if perhaps she should kick it about a bit to make it look more well travelled. She'd be whole lot happier when it contained a few exotic stamps and visas.

When she'd got her roster for Nairobi, she was beside herself with excitement and couldn't wait to phone home.

'Nairobi? In Africa? Oh goodness, Molly, watch out for all those lions!' her mother had said.

'Well, they'll just have to subdue their hunger pangs until I get there!' Molly had said, laughing.

It was with mounting excitement that Molly boarded the Boeing 707, resplendent in her new blue uniform, with her new

Globetrotter suitcase, new cabin bag and the new passport. It didn't boost her confidence, though, to discover that the girl she'd be working with, Cindy, was at least five feet ten. But Cindy was a sweet girl, and very helpful, and Molly soon forgot about the height difference. And then there was Martin, who she fancied at first sight.

The first thing Molly had to do was demonstrate the safety equipment to a full load of economy-class passengers. They'd practised this in the training school of course, but she felt desperately self-conscious as she stood in the aisle and tried to do everything in time with the steward at the front on the public address system.

It was going well: she got the life jacket over her head, pulled the tapes down firmly and tied them in a double bow at the side of her body, and demonstrated how to inflate it. Then the steward added, 'There is a whistle for attracting attention,' and, when Molly went to lift the little white whistle out of its pocket, she found herself brandishing a Tampax for all to see. There were snorts of laughter all round, and Molly thought she might die of humiliation as, pink-faced and flustered, she managed to get it back into the pocket and carry on with the demonstration.

Who would play a trick like that? she wondered. It turned out to be the steward in the front galley who, a little later, gave her a friendly wink and said, 'We do some rotten things to new girls!'

As she walked back through the cabin, several people applauded, most were smiling and one said, 'That was the best demonstration I've seen in a long time!'

'It was a put-up job,' Molly informed him, poker-faced.

Dinner went well. Both Martin and Cindy congratulated her on being so efficient and assured her that no one would have guessed it was her very first trip. There followed a very long night with the lights dimmed and blinds down, to supposedly encourage sleep. Some passengers did sleep but most wanted drinks, or to chat as they went to the toilets, which were alongside the galley. Nevertheless, it did give Molly a chance to get to know Martin. She loved his sense of humour, the jokes he told and the coffees he made her.

'You have to buck these up a bit,' he said, sloshing brandy into the cups.

She wasn't used to much in the way of alcohol and wondered if she'd lurch drunkenly down the aisle, but, in fact, it made her feel very good indeed, as well as making Martin appear even more devastatingly handsome. In the training school, they had been told that crews were forbidden to drink alcohol on board, but apparently rules were meant to be broken.

Shortly after they served breakfast, the chief steward came back and informed her that the captain wondered if she'd like to sit up on the flight deck for the landing into Nairobi.

The flight deck! The *captain!* Molly could hardly contain herself.

The captain was probably much the same age as her father, and he was charming. As was the first officer. As was the second officer. As was the engineer.

Molly had only seen flight decks and cockpits in the cinema, and now here she was, strapping herself in to the empty 'jump seat' directly behind the captain, while they all asked her how she was getting on, and did she think she was going to enjoy this job? Molly, who was in seventh heaven, said she thought she was going to enjoy the job very much indeed.

The chatter ceased as the crew concentrated on the final stages of landing, and Molly looked down at her first sight of Africa, at the red earth and flat grasslands of Kenya.

'We're coming in over the game park,' the second officer whispered to her, 'so you might see some animals.'

The early-morning sunshine was dappling the ground below with gold as Molly looked out in awe, and then she saw zebras, running away from the sound of the aircraft overhead. And then a solitary elephant!

I'm really, really in Africa, she thought, hugging herself in delight. Then she saw the long strip of runway ahead, and gazed out of the front as they made the final approach and then touched down, the engines roaring into reverse thrust.

Molly thanked the captain profusely then hurried back to the rear while the aircraft was taxiing round. Then they finally came to a stop and flung the door open.

The heat! Even in the early morning, it was like stepping into an oven as, after the passengers had disembarked, Molly descended the steps to be greeted by smiling Kenyan faces.

Everything was fascinating as far as Molly was concerned: the ride into the city, the hotel room, the pool, the friendly staff.

'The euphoria will wear off, Molly,' Martin told her with a smile. 'Next time we see you, you'll be a hardened old bat like the rest of us!'

Never, Molly thought.

'I'll see you by the pool later,' Martin added, 'but try to get a few hours' sleep now.'

Sleep? Impossible! How could she sleep when she had this luxurious hotel room all to herself, never having had any room all to herself before in her entire life? She thought about Vanessa then, and how she had been brought up in this incredible part of the world. Sometimes it was hard to appreciate the magnitude of the differences in their backgrounds and upbringing.

Molly showered then lay spreadeagled on the king-sized bed and, after a few further moments marvelling at everything, immediately fell asleep.

. . .

The pool was blue and inviting, the sun was hazy and most of the sunbeds already occupied by chattering crews when Molly, in her demure one-piece, finally got there.

Martin had saved her a sunbed next to his. 'Fancy a dip?'

Molly was embarrassed. 'Would you believe I can't swim?'

'Well, you can still have a dip, and I can show you how to float.'

Feeling self-conscious amongst a bevy of bronzed, bikini-clad women, Molly followed him across to the steps, where she cautiously lowered herself into the water. They splashed about for a while before Martin showed her how to float, supporting her body from beneath. This gorgeous man was actually making contact with *her bare skin!* Then he swam off to do some lengths of the pool while Molly watched him admiringly from the side.

He had such a beautiful, toned body, some manly dark hair on his chest, and her preconceived ideas about The Man were rapidly being turned upside down. She wondered if it was at all possible he might fancy her too. Even if she was pale, and a bit chunky, and wearing this awful bathing suit? She was definitely going to have to do some work on herself, and the first thing was to get a tan and then a bikini.

'Have you got some suntan lotion on?' asked the first steward – the one who'd replaced the life-jacket whistle with the Tampax. 'You can *fry* out here! Just because it's hazy doesn't mean you can't burn. Don't forget we're bang on the equator and at a high altitude as well.'

Molly looked around at everyone plastering themselves with all manner of oils and prostrating their gleaming bodies under the sun. Heedless of the fact that most of the others had basic tans to begin with, Molly did the same, and then she fell asleep.

It was later, after she'd showered off the oils, that she realised she was a very bright pink, and sore in places, particularly on her shoulders. She looked at herself with horror in the mirror. Martin would *never* fancy her now.

Martin and Cindy accompanied Molly to the game park the following day. Molly was well covered up and doused in calamine lotion but was aware that her nose was already beginning to peel. She was surprised to see that Martin had brought along a couple of cigarettes in the pocket of his shirt, because he didn't smoke.

Then she discovered the reason. At the entrance to the park, tethered to a post, was a large male chimpanzee smoking a cigarette. He looked hopefully at all arriving visitors, but only the regulars knew of his addiction and came prepared. He greedily grabbed at the cigarettes proffered to him by Martin. Privately, Molly thought it sad that the poor animal should spend his life tethered and chain-smoking, although she had to admit the chimp seemed happy enough.

Then, in company with three Americans and two Germans, they were ferried around in a zebra-striped Volkswagen minibus, raising clouds of red dust when they motored off. As they bumped along amongst the stunted trees and shrubs, they managed to see elephants, giraffes, zebras, impalas and – joy of joys – a cheetah racing away at an unbelievable speed.

'You are so lucky,' Martin said. 'I've come here several times and never seen a cheetah until now.'

Her bright personality and sense of humour endeared Molly to the crew in the same way as she'd previously charmed her patients. They teased her mercilessly about her red skin, they insisted she drank gin, which she'd found to be very palatable with orange juice, and they told some very risqué jokes, most of which she understood.

Ian, the first-class steward, had a repertoire of these. On the crew bus going back to the airport in the evening, he asked Molly if she knew of the Fakawee tribe. No, Molly told him, she'd never heard of them.

'Ah well,' he said, 'the thing is, they're very short. Not one of them more than about four feet tall, and they live in the long grass, so, when they want to find each other, they have to jump up and down, yelling, "Where the Fakawee?"'

Molly managed to keep smiling, although the return flight was quite uncomfortable, with her bra straps rubbing on her sore, burned shoulders and her face shining like a Belisha beacon. She felt a little sad because she would have liked to fly with Martin for*ever*, but you rarely flew with the same people twice.

'Not all crews are as delightful as us,' he teased her, grinning. 'You can get some unpleasant types, believe me, and some who don't get on with each other, but they are the minority. Never forget that it's temporary, and you'll get a much nicer bunch next time. Just pray that you don't get a lousy crew on a two- or three-week trip, like Sydney or round the world.'

Molly would have loved three weeks anywhere with this gorgeous man. She was also a little disappointed when he didn't arrange a definite date as they parted company in London. But he *did* have her phone number, and he *had* said that he'd take her to a concert, so that would have to do for now. He hugged her, kissed her on the cheek (she'd hoped for the lips) and said how much he'd enjoyed flying with her.

Never mind – she'd taken a couple of photos of him in the game park, which she fervently hoped would come out OK.

Vanessa was ironing her uniform blouses when a bright-pink Molly staggered through the door, dropping avocados and pineapples in her wake.

'The bottom's fallen out of one of the boxes,' she wailed, 'and the taxi driver wasn't happy at having to load this lot in and out. The sooner I get a car, the better! But, oh, I *loved* Nairobi!'

'Have you emptied the market?' Vanessa asked as she abandoned the ironing and helped Molly to pick up the stray fruit. 'And,' she added, 'you've caught the sun, haven't you? You look like a little lobster!' She sniffed the fruit. 'Oh, how good it is to smell properly ripened pineapples again! How on earth did you manage to bring all this lot back?'

'All the crew bring loads of stuff back. You go to the market, buy what you fancy, get it labelled and delivered to the hotel later in the day, and then the captain authorises it all to go on board. Isn't it wonderful!'

'Did everyone bring back all this stuff?' Vanessa asked.

'Oh yes, and one of the stewards brought back twice as much because, would you believe, he sells it to the local greengrocer.'

Vanessa returned to her ironing. 'Nothing surprises me about this job! And you enjoyed Nairobi?'

'Oh, I did!' Molly kicked off her high heels and unbuttoned her uniform jacket. 'And I think I'm in love!'

'You are *kidding*!' Vanessa laid down the iron and stared at Molly in astonishment.

'No I'm not! He was the steward I was working with, and he was just *gorgeous*! Tall, lovely brown eyes, great sense of humour!'

'Molly, a *steward*, for God's sake!'

'What's wrong with being a steward? And Martin – that's his name – trained as an accountant but found it very dull, so he applied to Skyline. He's a dab hand with currency transactions.'

'Well, well. And are you seeing him again?' Vanessa asked.

'I hope so. He loves music, and so do I, so we thought that, once we know our schedules for the next few weeks, we'll make a date to go to the Albert Hall. I've never been to the Albert Hall, and I'm *so* excited!' Molly's eyes were shining in anticipation.

'Good for you. You certainly haven't wasted any time! And you liked my lovely Kenya?'

'Nairobi's beautiful, and the people are so friendly. We even went to the game park, which was fantastic, and had a drink in the New Stanley. There wasn't time for much else.'

'Now tell me,' Vanessa said, switching off the iron, 'did he have his wicked way with you? Did you *do* it?'

Molly looked horrified. 'Of course not! Martin is a *gentleman*! But if he turns out to be The One, then we will, when the time is right.'

'But you're twenty-*two*, Molly! Don't you want to know what it's all about?'

'Well, I admit I don't go to church as often as I should, but I am a Catholic, Vanessa, and I don't believe in sex before marriage. We'll see what happens with Martin. Where's Eve?'

Vanessa glanced at her watch. 'About halfway to Karachi, I should think. And I'm off to Toronto tomorrow morning, so you'll have the flat to yourself for a day or two. It could be a real little love nest! Anyway, see how much of that stuff you can get in the fridge so there's some left when we both come back.'

After she'd unloaded her fruit and vegetables, Molly said, 'Do you know what? I think I'm going to *love* this job!'

'Just don't go falling in love every trip,' Vanessa advised, 'and try not to have your skin peeling off!'

'I won't. Anyway, how was your trip to the Gulf?'

'Oh, you know, quite interesting,' Vanessa remarked offhandedly. 'Very hot.'

'Well, never mind. Maybe your next flight will be more exciting. You might even meet someone like Martin.' She gazed out at the flakes of snow swirling past the window. 'It's almost as if we've joined some sort of sunshine club, isn't it?'

CHAPTER EIGHT

Eve

Eve had been amazed at how much money she'd brought home after her New York trip. She hadn't realised that they'd be given allowances for breakfast, lunch and dinner at each stopover. The generous amounts were calculated on what you'd spend if you ate in the hotel, which, of course, crews never did. They were experts at finding diners, 'greasy spoons' and restaurants where good food was available at low prices and so pocketed most of the allowances. Eve had arrived home with a wad of dollars, much to her delight. And that was *after* she'd done her shopping.

Karachi was an exception. Skyline House was a two-storey rambling edifice, erected by the airline at a time when the local hotels were not considered to be of a reasonable standard. And *free* food was available, round the clock, which meant no allowance was given. This lack of allowance did not endear the place to many of the crews, although it *was* one stopover where everyone ate three meals a day, with snacks in between.

Eve had blown some of her own money on a very elegant

onyx lamp from the market in the city. It would look great in the sitting room at Bellingham Road and, eventually, in her own home.

As Eve was tanning herself by the pool in the afternoon, the cats began to arrive. There were grey cats, black cats, ginger cats, white cats, cats of every hue and description, all thin, bony and noisy.

'Where have they all come from?' Eve asked Linda, one of the other stewardesses, who was sunbathing next to her.

Linda looked at her watch and yawned. 'They've come for their cake,' she said, ''cos it's five to four.'

On the dot of four o'clock, a procession of bearers in pristine robes appeared, carrying trays laden with silver pots of tea, china cups and saucers, and plates heaped high with bright-yellow cakes.

Few of the crew members lolling round the pool ate the offerings, and the cats waited expectantly, edging ever closer in the hope that this unloved delicacy would be chucked in their direction.

'How on earth do they *know* it's four o'clock?' Eve asked, mesmerised, as she watched the cats gobbling the cake which had been tossed onto the grass nearby.

Linda shrugged. 'No idea, but they come every day. Cats aren't daft.'

When Eve stretched out her hand to stroke one of them, Linda added, 'I wouldn't if I were you! They're feral and full of mange and fleas.'

Huge quantities of beer and smuggled-in spirits were consumed in the evening prior to dinner. The dining room was vast, with starched white tablecloths, silver cutlery and whirring overhead fans. Menus were typed out daily and placed on each table, where they rested against glass vases of plastic flowers.

Curry was becoming very popular at home, and Eve had sampled some in a creamy sauce with bits of chicken and raisins floating around in it. This was to be Eve's first experience of *proper* curry, and she was advised that if she really wanted to sample the real McCoy, then she must eat the *bearers'* curry, which was much hotter than the stuff they served in the dining room.

It took much wheedling on the part of the first officer, who was sitting next to her, to persuade the bearer to bring them some of the special curry. After a great deal of head-shaking and dissent, the bearer finally capitulated and Eve had her first taste of the famous dish.

With the first forkful, Eve thought her head might blow off. After a few more forkfuls though, she decided she was coping pretty well and, although it was without doubt the hottest curry she'd ever tasted, it was also the most delicious.

The flight, which was heading back to London, proved to be another eye-opener for Eve. In her limited experience, passengers were mostly middle class, well dressed and articulate, but the joining passengers in Karachi were anything but. Most of them apparently were immigrants who were extremely poor and few had ever seen a plane before, far less a toilet.

When they changed crews at Beirut several exhausting hours later, Eve wasn't at all sorry to be handing over to another crew.

Beirut, in the early-morning sunshine, was glamorous and beautiful, its white buildings stretching back from the blue of the Mediterranean to the backdrop of snow-capped mountains. It had become a banking haven, and a favourite haunt of the jet set with its sophisticated French character. French and Arabic were the two main languages, and the city boasted an eclectic mixture of people of all cultures, mosques and churches co-existing peacefully.

It was also pleasantly warm after the extreme heat in Karachi, and Eve was advised by the crew that she could ski up in the mountains and then come down to take a dip in the sea, all on the same day. Not that any of them appeared to be in any way sporty, being more interested in shopping.

'I buy all my shoes and bags here,' the other girl told Eve. 'You wait till you see the selection and the great prices!'

Eve treated herself to two pairs of shoes, one black and one pink, both paid for out of the allowances for food, but found some of the other goods on offer more fascinating: leather pouffes, camel saddles, folding chairs, brass, copper. *One day*, she vowed, *I'm going to open a little homeware shop and import this sort of stuff.* She'd also have onyx lamps from Pakistan, and sumptuous towels from New York!

That evening, they had dinner in the hotel, and Eve sampled hummus and all different types of olives, plus an array of Lebanese delicacies which she'd never even heard of. After-wards, some of the crew were heading for the casino, but Eve decided she'd save that for another time, as they had a 6 a.m. call in the morning for their flight back to London.

This flight had come from the Far East, and most of the passengers were businessmen and expats. The trouble with expats was that they were unaccustomed to looking after their own children, having always had an amah for that, and so hadn't much clue what to do with them when they screamed – which is what the baby in 15A was doing, at the top of his little lungs.

Eve picked him up and cuddled him. Much to her delight, the little chap stopped crying almost straight away, and she was permitted – by the grateful mother – to hold on to him for as long as she liked.

Eve hoped nobody would see that her eyes were filled with tears.

They'd taken her baby away when he was just two weeks old. Eve had known it was coming of course, the inevitable parting. She'd seen so many of the other girls in the home handing over their babies for adoption, but nothing could have prepared her for the anguish, heartbreak and gut-wrenching awfulness of it all. She'd called her tiny dark-haired son Robert. All she had of him now was a photo, which fitted inside her locket, and a curl of his black hair. How would she ever cope with the fourth of June each year, his birthday?

She'd been assured that his adoptive parents were lovely and so grateful. Apparently, they were about forty and unable to have children of their own, and they lived somewhere in Sussex.

'Will you go home to Scotland?' the matron had asked as she handed Eve a cup of tea and tried to console her.

'Definitely not.' Eve could still recall the look of horror on her mother's face when she'd broken the news of her pregnancy. She'd known she was going to have to put some space between them for a while.

Eve's first year in London, 1962, had been wonderful. She'd met Costa in the first month, while he was on holiday from university. He was half Greek and a law student.

There was just the one time that they'd run out of sheaths and, of course, it only took once. Then he'd mysteriously disappeared.

The bump not yet discernible, she'd ventured home for a few days at Christmas.

'Are you dead set on bringing further disgrace to this family?' Aileen had ranted. 'You certainly *are* your father's daughter! And what about the father? Done a runner, I suppose? Well, there's no way you're bringing an illegitimate baby up here!'

But Aileen wasn't without compassion and, as Eve had got ready to leave, she'd pushed a bulky envelope into her hand. 'There should be enough there to get you through the last few months, but you'll need to find a home for unmarried mothers and get this baby adopted. The church has some places, I believe.'

The months ahead were spent as 'Mrs' Muir, complete with a Woolworths wedding ring. The secretarial agency she worked for asked no questions and sent her to a different office each week. How *sad* that she was widowed so young, they said. Eve became expert at describing the various types of demise that might have affected her imaginary husband.

Then, afterwards, she'd had the desperate need to get away. So she'd spent the year in Paris, looking after precocious seven-year-old twins. They were old enough not to stir her emotions too much, which was why she'd chosen them.

It was on the ferry coming back to Dover that she'd picked up the crumpled newspaper that had been dumped on the seat beside her and seen the Skyline advertisement. It was the fourth of June, and somewhere in England, a tiny, dark-haired boy had been celebrating his first birthday.

As far as Eve was concerned, it was an omen. She was twenty-two years old and looking for a complete change in her life.

Eve had thought long and hard as to whether to tell Vanessa and Molly about her past. The only people who knew about the baby were her mother and Nadia, who'd been a stalwart friend and flatmate.

There wasn't a day when Eve didn't think about her little son. He was her first thought in the morning and her last thought when she drifted off to sleep at night, and she sometimes fantasised about him during the day as well, when she was accused of having that faraway look in her eyes.

She didn't know why she didn't want to share her secret, except that she just wanted to hug her few precious memories of him close to her heart. He'd be eighteen months old now, probably talking and walking too. Did he still have that thatch of dark hair? She hoped he'd inherited Costa's olive skin and not her freckles. Just so long as he hadn't inherited Costa's irresponsible nature.

Eve fondled her locket for the umpteenth time as they landed in London. She'd had to buy a long chain which hung low and out of sight, so it was invisible when in uniform. There was no way she could ever take it off, despite the many reprimands in training about wearing jewellery.

One thing was for certain; she didn't intend to have any more children. Eve wasn't exactly sure why, but only that, in some strange way, it wouldn't have seemed fair to have given Robert away and then keep his siblings. Not that *he'd* ever know of course, because he had another family now, but *she'd* know. It didn't make a great deal of sense to Eve and so she could hardly expect any prospective husband to understand either; marriage was out of the question. She wasn't sure she could ever trust a man again. Her father had led them all a merry dance with his affairs, and then Costa, who she'd really thought had loved her, had abandoned her when she'd most needed him. Men were not to be trusted.

She'd still like sex though, so she decided a visit to Vanessa's doctor had to be a priority. She had to make sure that there would never be a repeat experience.

CHAPTER NINE

Vanessa

It was May and Vanessa, just back from New York, was lunching at an Italian restaurant in Soho with her friend, Barty. The Barty Collins Model Agency had snapped her up after she'd completed her course at the Lucy Clayton Modelling School three years previously, and she and Barty had become good friends. He was attractive, witty and patently homosexual, and she loved him to bits. On a couple of occasions, when he'd driven her home to Kershaw House, she'd even introduced him to her mother and stepfather.

In fact, Barty was the only person she'd ever confided in about the ups and downs of her childhood years, and her rocky relationship with her mother.

Because Barty understood.

Vanessa's father, Eddie Carter-Flint, had absconded with a dancer when she was still in her infancy and was killed shortly afterwards in the war. Hermione's second husband, Charlie Patterson, had whisked his new wife and tiny one-year-old step-daughter off to Kenya, where he owned several thousand acres near Lake Naivasha. Home became a rambling bungalow with a houseful of staff and a very vibrant social life, which the gregarious Hermione took to like a duck to water. The infamous Happy Valley set catered well for her insatiable appetite for socialising – and for men.

Vanessa had been reared by the staff and had rarely seen her mother. She loved it there, running around barefoot, riding her horse bareback and being thoroughly spoiled by the staff, whose children she played with.

Hermione had become seriously worried, on the rare occasions when she directed her attention to her daughter. 'She's becoming a little wild,' she'd complained to Charlie.

The solution was obvious. At eight years old, Vanessa was sent to her mother's old boarding school, Willowdene in Hampshire. She still shuddered at the thought of that long flight, as an unaccompanied minor, from Nairobi to London. She was the only child on board and wept for the entire journey in her too-large grey uniform. And when she arrived in London on an overcast grey September morning, she was then transported to the enormous grey stone pile that was Willowdene and introduced to the grey-clad thin-lipped headmistress with her grey, corrugated-iron hair. Vanessa had loathed grey ever since.

But she was a survivor and having taken stock of her situation had decided to make the situation work for her. Being tall, naturally blonde and beautiful undoubtedly gave her an advantage because she wasn't academically gifted. But people were attracted to her, and she soon had a dedicated following amongst the other girls in her form. They were overawed when, as a young teenager, Vanessa would sneak out late at night to meet up with boys from the local college. Somehow or other she never got caught and managed to earn an early reputation as a femme fatale. Every school holiday, she would fly home to Kenya and return suitably bronzed.

Then Charlie, who she adored, inexplicably flew his light

aircraft into the side of Mount Kenya one calm, cloudless day. There was much gossip and many theories as to how this could have occurred amongst Hermione's set, although it caused only a brief pause in her socialising.

Before the year was up, James Farrington had appeared on the scene. He'd gone to Nairobi on a business trip, where he came across Hermione in the renowned Muthaiga Country Club, sipping cocktails with a gaggle of aristocratic expats. He'd bedded her after a couple of days and proposed within the week, and thus Hermione was transported back to England again, much against her will.

'Oh, James, the *awful* weather!' she'd wailed.

However, eventually she was persuaded that, being close to London with its theatres and galleries, life might just be about bearable, so she had upped sticks and decided to become a leading light at the Surrey tennis clubs and dinner parties.

Vanessa, in the meantime, was about to leave Willowdene with the minimum of academic qualifications and was thus persuaded to move into Kershaw House with her mother and new stepfather. She wasn't particularly keen on her mother, and she loathed both James and Kershaw House.

'I'd like to join the Lucy Clayton Modelling School,' Vanessa had informed them shortly after she'd moved in, having seen an advertisement in the local paper.

'Why would you want to do that?' Hermione had asked.

She was finally persuaded to cough up for the course when Vanessa explained it was a finishing school for young ladies, where she'd receive instruction on the finer points of etiquette, not least about how to get out of a sports car without showing her knickers.

After the course, when she'd joined Barty's agency, she'd get regular modelling jobs for a couple of weeks, and then nothing for the next couple of weeks. The money was good but not good enough to pay the rent for a suitable flat, and she didn't want to be further beholden to her stepfather. Somebody called Jean Shrimpton seemed to be getting all the best jobs, and now someone called Tiggy, or Twiggy, or something, was getting in on the act. There was work of *a kind* of course, if she didn't mind advertising washing-up liquid or indigestion pills. But Vanessa had an image to maintain, and she most certainly *did* mind.

It was while she was scanning the 'Models Wanted' column in the *Evening Standard* that her attention had been caught by a large box advertisement. Skyline, the country's favourite airline, were looking for air stewardesses.

There and then Vanessa decided that this was the job for her. Not only that, she knew she'd look stunning in that blue uniform.

She and Barty had finished their meal.

'So how goes it in the big wide world?' Barty asked, dabbing his lips with a napkin. 'Met any interesting men yet?'

Vanessa hesitated. 'As a matter of fact, I have met someone, Barty, but I've not told anyone.'

'Why's that? Is he married or something?'

His perception never failed to amaze Vanessa. She didn't reply.

'So he's married.' Barty sighed. 'Honestly, Nessa, with your looks, couldn't you find yourself one nice single bloke amongst all those pilots and passengers?'

'I didn't exactly *plan* this,' she snapped, 'and neither did he.'

'Please don't tell me your eyes met across a crowded room!' Barty groaned, lighting a cigarette and then studying her through the smoke.

'*Of course* not!' Vanessa retorted.

But that was exactly what had happened.

.   .   .

Vanessa had been looking forward to the trip, which gave her two whole days off in New York, which was a rarity. She'd spent the first one doing the Circle Line boat trip round Manhattan and, on the second, she'd planned to go to the top of the Empire State Building then make her way to the shops along Fifth Avenue. She wanted to visit Macy's, and Korvettes, which Eve had waxed lyrical about. She might even make it to Bloomingdale's as well.

When she'd got back to the hotel and the phone rang, she'd assumed it was one of the other stewardesses. Instead, it was the duty officer at Kennedy Airport.

'I'm sorry, Miss Carter-Flint, but we're going to have to roster you down to Barbados tomorrow morning. A Miss Davidson on that crew has just reported sick and we need to replace her urgently. We don't have time to fly someone out from London to replace her, but we do have time to send someone out to replace you.'

Vanessa had mixed emotions. This scuppered her New York plans, but, on the other hand, how could anyone *not* want to go to Barbados? Fortunately, she'd heeded advice and had some hot-weather gear in the depths of her Globetrotter.

While she'd been mulling this over, the phone had rung again. It was Hal, the chief steward on the following day's Barbados flight, confirming that she was replacing Mandy Davidson ('silly cow's been eating some dodgy seafood') and would she like to join her new crew for a drink that evening?

She'd spent some time ringing up everyone she could find on her original crew, and bidding them farewell, before she presented herself in Hal's room, glass in hand, at the appointed hour.

The other five cabin crew and four flight-deck crew had been there already, all regarding her with interest. As she'd introduced herself and glanced around, her eyes had locked with those of a particularly attractive man on the far side of the room. They were very blue eyes, set in an attractive tanned face, and topped with silver-grey hair. Prematurely grey, she'd thought, because he couldn't be much more than forty. She'd realised then that her heart was hammering in a strange way as the man stood up, tall and lean, to shake her hand as Hal introduced them. 'And this is our skipper, Johnny Martell.'

His gaze was steady as he squeezed her hand and Vanessa had felt herself colouring. *Damn*, she'd thought, *I never blush!*

She'd picked up her drink and moved away to join the other two girls, not daring to look in his direction. But every inch of her body had been very aware of his presence.

As was normal, several members of another crew had joined them, including the steward she'd flown with from London. Everyone squeezed up to make room and, somehow or other, she'd found herself next to Johnny Martell. Had they gravitated towards each other without even realising it? Afterwards, she was never quite sure.

He'd insisted on refilling her glass, his hand lingering just a second too long. The din of conversation had reached a crescendo, and it was all they could do to make themselves heard. When the noise had abated slightly, he'd asked, 'Have you been to Barbados before?'

Vanessa had liked his voice. She'd shaken her head. 'I've only been flying for a few months.'

'Then you must let me show you the island, as we have a day off down there.' He'd smiled. 'You'll love it!'

She'd wondered if he could hear her heart thumping. This was *so* ridiculous! And he was of an age where he was bound to be married. Vanessa didn't have a high opinion of married people who had affairs, but, regardless, there was little question that she and this man were going to be making love. She hadn't doubted it for one minute and, from the look in his eyes, neither had he.

When they'd all ended up in the Chicago Diner on Third

Avenue, she hadn't been the least bit surprised to find that he was sitting next to her, where the very brush of his arm was sending her aquiver.

Later, when she'd got back to her room, she'd expected the phone to ring. And it had.

'Fancy a nightcap?'

Vanessa had known what that would lead to, and they had an early-morning call.

'Could we save that for Barbados?' she'd asked.

'Probably very wise,' he'd said, and she'd been able to tell from his voice that he'd been smiling.

Afterwards, she'd wondered if she should have taken him up on his offer, because she could hardly sleep a wink.

As they'd jetted towards Barbados, Vanessa had been able to think of nothing or no one other than the handsome man at the controls of the plane. They had a full load of very demanding passengers and her feet had hardly touched the ground for the entire flight. At least being busy hadn't allowed her too much time to think. She'd got goosebumps each time she'd heard him speak on the PA system, informing the passengers where they were and how far they had to go. She'd been exhausted by the time they'd begun the descent and had finally collapsed onto the crew seat just before Hal had appeared from the front to tell her that, 'The skipper's wondering if you'd like to go up front for the landing seeing as you've not been to Barbados before?'

Wouldn't she *just*!

As Vanessa had settled herself into the jump seat immediately behind him, she hadn't known whether to concentrate on the blue sea beneath them or the back of his well-shaped head. Eventually though, the view had won, as they flew lower and lower over the impossibly turquoise sea and palm-fringed white sands of this fabulous island, followed by the reverse roar of the engines as her hero had eased the aircraft, with barely a bump, onto the runway at Seawell Airport.

The Dolphin Beach Club, on the west coast of the island, was like something out of a film, Vanessa had reckoned. The beautiful air-conditioned rooms looked out over gardens full of tropical blossoms, towards the pool on one side and the sea straight ahead. With its white walls and furniture, cool marble floor and colourful tropical prints of the curtains and bedcover, it was one of the most gorgeous rooms Vanessa had ever seen.

She'd opened the sliding doors to the garden, but the blast of heat had caused her to close them again quickly. A dip in that fabulous sea was needed before she got ready for the evening ahead. Vanessa had dug her white bikini out from the bottom of her Globetrotter.

It was like walking into a warm bath as she'd waded through the shallows, her feet sinking into the soft white sand. It had turned cooler as she'd got into the deeper water, and she'd swum lazily backward and forward, then floated for a while. Paradise! There had been a few other swimmers bobbing around here and there, but no sign of any of the crew, and she'd secretly enjoyed having some time to herself. She had a feeling she wouldn't be alone again for some time.

Vanessa had taken great care with her appearance. She'd donned a long silk kaftan in vibrant blues and greens and, with her blonde hair loose on her shoulders, she'd known she was looking as good as she could. She'd even chosen her bra and pants with particular care, anticipating how the evening was likely to end.

They'd all met up on one of the terraces, close to the pool

with lanterns in the palms overhead. Steel drum music had competed with the continuous chirping of the tree frogs and, to complete the scene, there had even been a full moon overhead.

Johnny Martell, looking smooth, debonair and very tasty in a blue open-necked shirt (the same colour as his eyes), had stood up as she'd swanned towards the group. Everyone had been knocking back rum punches laden with fruit but deceptively potent, which was probably how the drink had got its name because it certainly delivered a punch. There had been a great deal of laughter and joke-telling going on as they'd topped up the rum and planned what to do the following day: swim and sunbathe in the morning, then a trip on the *Jolly Roger* sailing ship in the afternoon, where the rum was on tap.

Johnny had sat down next to her, as she'd known he would. She'd noticed the other two stewardesses exchanging looks, but she hadn't cared.

'You can do all that stuff next time you come here,' he'd murmured, 'but I've already hired a Mini Moke for tomorrow, and I'm going to show you the island.'

She'd held his glance for a moment then nodded.

They'd eaten from the Caribbean buffet, comprising of all manner of local delicacies, including flying fish and dolphin fish. 'No,' Johnny had told her, 'not the nice dolphins you're thinking about – these are actual fish.'

There had been a cabaret and, inevitably, limbo dancing, where, naturally, the well-fuelled crew had joined in, and the front galley stewardess had won the competition with an amazing display of back-bending control.

Inevitably, Vanessa and Johnny had danced together, their bodies intertwined. Nothing needed to be said, until Johnny whispered, 'I'll go up to my room in a minute, but give it ten minutes or so before you come, to avoid the inevitable gossip.'

Vanessa had nodded mutely, noting his room number.

He'd had one of the finest suites in the hotel, complete with a comprehensive bar. As he'd poured her a rum with ginger ale, he'd said, 'Tonight is very special, and I don't want you to be drunk.'

Later, Vanessa could only remember having a couple of sips of her drink before they could resist temptation no longer and, tearing each other's clothes off, made mad, passionate love. She'd never, in her wildest experiences, known anything like it. She couldn't believe that she could want this man, whom she'd only met the previous day, quite so much and quite so often. She'd never known such ecstasy as her body climaxed, time and time again.

They'd made love in the morning, and again later in the day on the beach at Cattlewash, on the east coast of the island, where the Atlantic exploded onto the rock-studded beaches.

She'd nuzzled his ear. 'I've got sand in my fanny.'

'I'd better check that out straight away,' he'd said.

It had been a magical day from start to finish as, in their Mini Moke, they'd driven along the narrow roads through fields of sugar cane and stopped at the colourful little chattel houses, where children and chickens had scattered in every direction as they approached.

They'd found deserted beaches, green hills, sugar-cane plantations and old plantation houses. They'd explored the wild Atlantic coast at Bathsheba, at Sam Lord's Castle and the Crane Hotel, which looked down over the most wonderful palm-fringed beach, all the time revelling in each other's company: touching, kissing, laughing and, of course, knowing that the day must end. Perhaps because she'd known that their time was so limited, Vanessa considered this to be the most wonderful time of her life.

They'd found a restaurant on the way back, near Bridgetown, because neither of them had wanted to be with the rest of the crew. 'Let them talk,' Johnny had said, holding her hand across the table.

Vanessa had been determined not to go down the 'how long have you been married' path, but she couldn't stop herself.

'How long have you been married?' she'd asked.

'Eighteen years,' he'd replied, 'and I have three children.' He'd regarded her steadily as he spoke. 'Susan is sixteen, John Junior is thirteen and Julie's just nine.' He'd paused. 'There's no competition, Vanessa. The feeling I have for you is something quite, quite separate. Bryony's a wonderful and loyal wife, and I love my kids to bits. I don't intend to hurt them, and I need you to understand that.'

Vanessa had understood. But she was looking into a future very far from what she'd ever anticipated.

She'd been none too pleased to find Molly in the flat when she'd returned to Bellingham Road. She'd dreamed of some quiet time to herself to mull over every minute of that heavenly day.

'Hi!' Molly had said. 'How was Barbados? Lucky you!'

'Ah yes, Molly, it was great – amazing in fact!'

'Oh good. Well, you must tell me about it sometime. But, before I forget, a man rang up for you. Abdul? Anyway, I've left his number beside the phone.'

Vanessa had rung Barty the following day.

'Barty, I need you to be my beau tomorrow because Abdul keeps ringing me from the Grosvenor House Hotel. I've agreed to have coffee with him because he was very kind to me, but I'm going to have to tell him that I have to go because I'm lunching with my boyfriend. That's *you*, my treasure!'

'Darling girl, I'm *incredibly* busy! Do you really expect me to just drop everything and come to your rescue at such short notice?'

'Yes,' Vanessa had said, 'I do.'

CHAPTER TEN

Molly

It was July before Molly found herself rostered for a trip to the Far East, giving her two whole days off in Singapore and a day off in Delhi, both on the way out and on the way back. But the icing on the cake was that – against all the odds – she was rostered again with Martin.

She'd seen him twice since the Nairobi trip, when he'd taken her to the Albert Hall. She'd waited for weeks and weeks for him to call, by which time she'd convinced herself that he'd forgotten all about her or changed his mind. When he finally rang, he'd said, 'They're playing some popular classics, and I'm sure you'd enjoy it.'

Molly agreed, whether she liked the classics or not, because she finally had a date with this gorgeous man.

'You're looking very pretty tonight,' he'd commented as they had sipped drinks in the bar before the concert.

Molly was relieved he'd noticed because she'd spent hours trying to decide what to wear, discarding outfit after outfit before finally opting for a blue wool dress which she fancied might accentuate the blue of her eyes. Vanessa had lent her some fabulous gold earrings, saying, 'Don't even *think* about coming back here if you manage to lose these!' Then she'd back-combed and sprayed Molly's wayward curls into a sleek bob, although minutes later it was doing its best to curl again. Eve had done her eyes, using discreet amounts of blue eyeshadow, and she'd shown her how to use mascara. She had to spit into the little block of Max Factor, then rub the brush into it to get the required amount with which to coat her lashes. When she'd surveyed herself in the mirror afterwards, Molly had never felt so glamorous and sophisticated in her whole life.

'If he doesn't fancy you tonight, I'll eat my hat,' Eve had said confidently.

He'd collected her in his car and driven to Hounslow, where he had parked and they took the Piccadilly Line into town because, he'd said, it was well-nigh impossible to park anywhere in Knightsbridge.

Molly had been overawed to finally set foot inside the Albert Hall. Martin was such a font of knowledge, whispering in her ear details and comments about the various composers. Even if she'd have preferred sweet nothings, she'd been impressed that he took his music so seriously. She'd kept her hand available, in the hope that he might want to hold it, but he didn't. Well, it wasn't the cinema after all, and perhaps people didn't do things like that in the Albert Hall.

When, at the end of the evening, he'd dropped her off at Bellingham Road, having declined her offer of coffee because he had to get up early 'for another bloody Lagos tomorrow', she'd had to make do with a quick hug and a peck on the cheek. 'That was fun and we must do it again,' was his parting shot, but no definite date for their next outing had been offered.

Nevertheless, he'd eventually phoned and taken her to her first opera. 'You'll love *Carmen*,' he'd assured her, 'not too high-brow.' Again, they'd had a few drinks, and the outing had finished with a quick cuddle and a peck on the cheek. Molly had hoped for more passion and decided that the blue eyeshadow and Max Factor eyelashes weren't quite doing the trick. Well, now she was going to be with him for ten whole days, and she was determined she was going to come back a happy and fulfilled woman.

Her co-hostess at the rear galley was Helen. Helen was besotted with the first officer, to the exclusion of everything else, such as work. At every opportunity, she found excuses to 'pop up front' and, when she did condescend to do some work, she floated around in a dream-like trance. This meant that Molly and Martin were rushed off their feet, which left little time to flirt.

After a long and exhausting meal service, Helen deigned to bring in a few trays. As the lights dimmed, in the hope that some of the passengers at least might take a nap, Helen asked, 'OK if I take my break now?' at the exact moment that the first officer was making his way to the back. The two of them then settled themselves in the back row.

Molly, from the galley, studied the first officer in the dim light. 'Don't you think he looks a lot *older* than her?' she asked Martin.

'Yes, he does,' Martin agreed before asking, 'Shall we have some of our brandy coffees?'

'Yes please.' Molly continued sizing up the romantic duo. 'Do you think he might be *married*?'

'Very likely,' he replied, pouring what looked like half a gallon of Courvoisier into her coffee.

Molly was genuinely horrified. 'That's *awful*! How *could* she?'

'Quite easily by the looks of it.' Martin grinned as he handed her the coffee cup. 'Get that down you!'

She had a sudden awful thought. '*You're* not married, are you?'

'You're joking – of course not! Do I *look* married, for goodness' sake?'

'No,' Molly replied, gazing at him. Then she wondered why she was asking all these silly questions; she mustn't appear too eager.

'I've had a few relationships, but I haven't even come close to getting tied up,' he added with a yawn. 'Trouble is, as I'm sure you've found out, you're never at home long enough, or regularly enough, to establish relationships. And it's almost impossible down the routes as you're never with the same people twice. Rarely anyway.'

Well, now's your chance, thought Molly as she knocked back her fortified coffee. It was strange really how he didn't seem to have the faintest idea that she fancied him.

Delhi came as a bit of a shock to Molly. She'd never seen so many imposing buildings alongside such abject poverty, although she had been warned. The heat was oppressive, and the stench from the sewers was, at times, overpowering.

Since Helen had disappeared to goodness knows where, probably bed, with the first officer, Molly was glad to have Martin to herself as he steered her firmly, by the arm, towards the famous Cottage Industries. This was the place to buy beautiful silks, cottons and handicrafts, but, nevertheless, even there it was hard to ignore tiny children, dressed in rags, who followed her everywhere. Some, who couldn't have been more than four or five themselves, were carrying babies in slings.

Molly felt guiltily relieved to get inside the Cottage Industries, where she bought a length of beautiful patterned silk, which, Martin assured her, could be made into a dress when they got to Singapore, and then to return to the air-conditioned opulence of the Oberoi Hotel, where elegant women in beautiful saris mingled with debonair men in expensive Western suits. It was difficult to accept that just a few yards separated the two very different worlds of India.

Most of the crew had already been to the Taj Mahal, but Molly knew it would be the highlight of her trip, and she was beside herself with excitement, particularly as Martin offered to take her. The engineer, whose name was Geoff, decided he'd like to go along too, much to her disappointment. Never mind, she and Martin were about to visit this wonder of the world!

'Bloody hell, does he think he's at Brands Hatch?' Geoff asked as the driver narrowly missed cyclists, pedestrians, tuktuks, trucks and carts piled high with all manner of goods and humanity, endless potholes and, not least, wandering cows. Molly spent most of the four-hour journey to Agra with her hand over her eyes, desperate for Martin to hold her hand, and not just for love but because she was terrified.

But never, for the rest of her life, would Molly forget the beauty of the Taj Mahal, that ultimate shrine to love. She stroked the walls in awe and was mesmerised by the perfection of the sun shining on the white marble, inset with semiprecious stones. They took countless photographs of each other with the Taj in the background. Geoff obligingly took several of herself and Martin, who had put his arm around her for the occasion. She'd have them developed and have the best one framed, to be placed on her bedside table, wherever she might be. She felt her eyes fill with tears at the wonder of it all.

'It does bring tears to the eyes,' Martin remarked, 'because of its beauty. Tears aren't just for sadness.'

Molly loved his sensitivity and perception. She was going to be gazing at these photographs, along with the ones from the

Nairobi game park, for years to come. But was this relationship doomed to exist only in a photograph album?

It was a long day. And it was on the return trip to Delhi, fortunately only with an hour or so to go, that Molly began to feel unwell. The pains in her stomach worsened with each mile, and she was beginning to feel nauseous. By the time they finally drew up at the Oberoi Hotel, she just had time to dash to her room – and the toilet.

She was furious that she'd managed to get the dreaded 'Delhi belly' in the mere twenty-four hours since they'd arrived. She, who was known to have a cast-iron stomach and could eat *anything*!

Molly spent what was left of the evening alternately rushing to and from the toilet or comatose on the bed. She certainly didn't want Martin to see her in such a state, but he duly appeared, clutching some tummy-settling pills.

'We all get it,' he said consolingly. 'You'll be OK in a couple of days.'

For once, she was glad he didn't hang around to see her grey face and tangled hair. Was it the ice cubes in the drinks or the salad garnish which she'd had with her curry, both of which she'd been told to avoid? *Ignore advice at your peril*, she thought, recalling the severe sunburn she'd experienced on her first trip. Why did she think *she* was the exception to every rule?

Finally, the chief steward appeared and notified the doctor, who, having seen it all before, duly arrived with a large syringe and some evil-tasting medicine. On no account was she going *anywhere* the next day, he declared firmly. After he'd gone, Molly wept with misery. She felt like death, she wasn't going to Singapore and Martin would be leaving without her. She'd be stuck here in this hotel room – beautiful though it was – where she wouldn't know anyone, feeling like death.

.   .   .

Molly felt slightly better the following morning after a restless
night of tramping in and out of the bathroom. Then Martin
appeared in uniform just before the crew – *her* crew – were due
to be picked up for the leg to Singapore. She had *so* wanted to
go to Singapore! When would she ever get the dress made,
because how long would it be before she got rostered out here
again? She would certainly be starving herself next time she
came to Delhi.

'Don't worry,' Martin said cheerfully. 'There'll be another
crew in later, and next thing you know, you'll be flying back to
London as a passenger, which *can't* be bad! God only knows
who's replacing you.' He deposited six bottles of ginger ale on
her dressing table. 'Helps to settle the tum.' He grinned. 'I'll
ring you when we're all back in London, and perhaps we can go
to the theatre or something? Or the ballet? You'd *love Swan
Lake!*'

After he left, Molly could only think how he'd seen her
looking a complete mess, and then tortured herself with the
knowledge that this could be his lasting impression of her. Was
her replacement a beautiful, golden-skinned, sari-clad, dark-
eyed beauty? Probably. And how many other lovely girls would
he fly with before she set eyes on him again? She began to feel
sick again at the very thought.

The doctor called later in the morning and pronounced that she
was recovering well and would be able to travel home very soon.
The incoming crew had been told she was here and had duly
called to check on her progress, and to invite her to join them
for a drink and a meal. Molly's stomach did a somersault at the
very thought.

She didn't meet them until she was ready, in the lobby, with her suitcase packed, for the trip home. However, she did feel considerably more cheerful when, after take-off, the crew upgraded her to first class, which was half empty. Her appetite hadn't fully recovered, so she had to decline most of the tempting food and drink on offer, but in the comfort of her luxurious seat, her feet propped up, and covered in a cashmere blanket, Molly slept most of the way home.

CHAPTER ELEVEN

Vanessa

It was shortly before Christmas when Molly brought up the idea of having a party. She said she'd been mulling it over for ages and, on one of the rare occasions when the three of them were all in the flat at the same time, decided to test the reactions of the other two.

'We've been here in Bellingham Road for nearly a year now,' Molly said casually as they lit up after-dinner cigarettes, 'and I was thinking it was high time we had some sort of thrash.'

'That's not a bad idea,' Eve agreed, inhaling deeply, 'and maybe that way we'll be able to get a look at this man of yours.'

'What do you think, Nessa?' Molly asked.

'Mmm,' she replied, 'depends on how many people you were thinking of inviting?'

'How about we each make out a list of people we'd like to invite, and then we could take it from there?' Molly suggested.

Vanessa didn't reply.

Eve, however, was enthusiastic. 'Well, we're all due to be

away for Christmas, so why don't we all request to be home for New Year?'

Molly, plainly encouraged, suggested, 'Perhaps a little bribery is called for? Anyone going to Nairobi in the next few weeks? A nice box of pineapples for the roster staff perhaps?'

'I am,' Eve confirmed, 'and it's certainly worth a try. I like the idea because it's a Hogmanay party, and I could get my mother to send down some real haggis, and I'll find some bagpipe music or something.'

'Great idea!' Molly said with enthusiasm.

Vanessa groaned audibly.

Vanessa wasn't a party animal at the best of times, unlike her mother. And since she'd met Johnny, she'd lost most of her enthusiasm for even general socialising. She found it hard to believe that she'd fallen hopelessly in love with a married man; *she*, who turned heads wherever she went and could have her pick of the bunch. She accepted the fact that he'd never leave his family, but she knew he loved her.

They'd recently snatched a couple of wonderful days, and even more amazing nights, together in Kuala Lumpur and were now trying to wangle Christmas together in Toronto. She'd informed Rosters that she had an aunt in Toronto who she'd *adore* spending Christmas with, and so could she please be on the Toronto flight on the twenty-third of December? Vanessa didn't have an aunt anywhere, but never mind.

Johnny lived in Dorset, which didn't help. However, he did have to do standbys every so often, near to the airport, in case someone was sick or didn't show up at the last minute. On those occasions, Vanessa desperately wished she had her own flat, but she always joined him at the Horizon Hotel, on the airport perimeter, and prayed he wouldn't get called out. Her whole life was now spent in anticipation of their next meeting, and she'd been aware for some time that Eve suspected something was going on.

'Are you OK, Nessa?' she asked one day as they were about to have a lunchtime sandwich at the flat. 'It's just that you've been a bit remote lately.'

Vanessa, who rarely wept, was mortified to find her eyes welling up. She desperately needed to confide in someone and she certainly couldn't confess all to Goody-Two-Shoes-Molly, who'd probably go to her grave a virgin.

'I don't mean to pry,' Eve said, looking horrified. 'It's got to bloody well be a man, hasn't it? Don't tell me he doesn't fancy you! We can't have another Molly on our hands!'

Vanessa smiled as she wiped her eyes. 'Yes, I've met someone. Crew. Married with three kids, and no intention of leaving them.'

'Oh, Nessa!' Eve pushed the sandwiches aside and offered her a cigarette. 'That is rotten luck. This job has a lot to answer for.'

'You hear of it happening to other people,' Vanessa said, flicking her lighter to their cigarettes, 'but I never thought it would happen to me. I always looked down on girls who got tied up with married men and thought they settled for that because they couldn't get a single man of their own. But that's not how it goes, Eve, and I wouldn't have chosen for this to happen in a million years.'

'So is he happily married? Or is that a stupid question?' Eve bit her lip and changed tack. 'How old is he?'

'He's forty.'

'*Forty*! That's *seventeen* years older than you!'

'I know, but I can't help that. Is he happily married? Who knows? He married young, when he was in the RAF, and so he's been married for eighteen years and says that he just jogs along. He adores his kids of course. In fact, I'm not even sure if I'd lose respect for him if he *did* leave them.'

Eve sighed. 'But it's a no-win situation for you, Nessa! After all, he's got the wife and kids ensconced cosily at home, and you to add a bit of excitement and naughtiness down the routes. I'm assuming he's flight deck? I can't see you going soppy over a steward somehow!'

'Yes, he's a skipper. I *can't* give him up, Eve! I'm not hurting his family, and I love him!'

'As long as they don't find out. And you're prepared to put up with this second-rate existence? To see him only when he can sneak away or you can fiddle a trip together?'

'Yes, I am.' Vanessa sighed. 'To change the subject, I'll go along with this party idea if only to get a look at this ridiculous steward of Molly's and perhaps have a word in his ear. I mean, she's such a pretty, amusing little thing and popular with everyone, so why does she have to fall for some weirdo like this Michael or whatever he's called?' She shook her head in despair.

Vanessa generally made monthly visits to Kershaw House, rationing herself to three or four hours at a time, which was as long as it took before she and her mother began to irritate each other. As this was a pre-Christmas visit, her mother had invited her to lunch. James, as usual, was out golfing somewhere.

'So where are you going to be for Christmas?' Hermione asked as she poured some Châteauneuf-du-Pape into Vanessa's crystal wine goblet.

'Toronto.'

'Not wildly exciting or conducive to the Christmas spirit, I would have thought,' Hermione said, studying Vanessa's earrings. 'Those earrings are rather nice, Nessa. Present from an admirer?'

'You could say that,' Vanessa muttered.

'I just did. Who is he? Is he *rich*?'

'Yes, he was rich, but he's very much in the past.'

'So is there anyone in the *present*?'

'No one you need concern yourself about, Mother,' Vanessa replied shortly. 'Anyway, what are you and James planning for Christmas?'

'A divorce probably,' Hermione snapped.

'*What*?' Vanessa almost dropped her glass.

Hermione sighed dramatically. 'Oh, we just seem to have drifted apart these days. He's so *dull*, Nessa! Only interested in his stocks and shares and his bloody golf! How I long for the good old days in Kenya! The *fun* we had! I'm tempted to go back, you know. However, I expect we'll join up with some of his equally boring friends at the golf club. I'd rather hoped you might have been able to join us, to chivvy things up a bit.'

Vanessa was extremely glad she was going to be in Toronto.

CHAPTER TWELVE

Eve

Eve bought her black Morris Minor from the local garage.

'Nice little runner,' said the salesman. 'Belonged to an old girl who popped her clogs a few months back. It's hardly been used.'

Just to be sure, Eve paid the RAC to give it a once-over, and they seemed to think it was a nice little runner too, which was just as well because it was a long drive up to Scotland.

She'd be spending Christmas in Melbourne and was rather looking forward to the anonymity of being on the other side of the world at what wasn't her favourite time of year. Like the fourth of June, it was a day to be endured, to try not to think too much of her little son growing up with his adoptive parents. Although she knew he'd been wanted and was doubtless being loved, it didn't fill the aching gap in her life.

Eve hadn't seen her mother for almost a year, about which she felt a little guilty until she reminded herself that not once had Aileen visited her in London during her pregnancy and the birth. She was rationing her time in Strathcannon to just three days, stopping off to see her brother in Edinburgh in both directions.

As well as being a qualified doctor, Calum had apparently also now met the love of his life. Some people's lives, Eve thought, seemed to run true to form and expectation. Her brother had done well at school, passed all his exams, gone to university and qualified with flying colours. He'd shared a flat with two other medical students, both of whom were also now engaged to very suitable girls and planning to marry next year. Long white dresses, marquees, champagne by the bucketful. No doubt, after a suitable period, there would be the pitter-patter of tiny feet on their expensive shag-pile carpeting.

No wonder Aileen was so proud of her future daughter-in-law, despite the fact they'd never met – so conventional, so satisfactory, unlike the wayward daughter chasing around London with a highly unsuitable type and getting pregnant to boot. Oh, the disgrace of it all!

'Bring your uniform with you,' her mother had instructed. 'I want to see you all dolled up.' Perhaps the new job might go some way to change Aileen's opinion.

Typical, thought Eve, *and she's probably already booked an appointment with the local photographer.*

Eve felt a great sense of achievement when she finally arrived in Edinburgh in the Morris Minor. She was pleased to see her brother, and he was delighted to see her, commenting that 'this flying business obviously suits you, because you're looking great!' She also met the tiny, dark-haired Sheena, who she liked immediately. They hoped to get married sometime in June, and Eve *must* come up for the wedding. In the meantime, they were going up to Strathcannon for Christmas, and what a pity that Eve wouldn't be there!

As Eve drove northwards through the Highlands, she felt a

great sense of relief that she wouldn't be part of the jolly Muir Christmas get-together. She wondered if she was weird, since almost everyone else on the planet wanted to be with their family over the festive season, while she preferred to be with a motley bunch of crew on the other side of the world.

As she drove up the A9, she was struck, as always, by the sheer beauty of her native land. The sun was shining on the heather-clad hills, which had turned from purple to brown, and on the blue-grey mountains, now topped with snow. Fortunately, the road wasn't too busy, because much of it was single carriageway and it was difficult to overtake. Stray sheep ambled across in front of her car from time to time, and there was deep snow up on Drumochter Pass, but otherwise the drive went smoothly.

'Now, what's this Sheena like?' Aileen asked as they sat with their after-dinner coffees.

'She's really nice, Mum, and I think you'll like her.'

'Oh, I'm sure I will, dear. She seems very suitable. Calum tells me she's from a Perthshire family, you know. Farmers. I'm hoping to meet them in the New Year.'

Eve was aware that she was being studied.

'What a pity that you won't be here for Christmas too,' Aileen said with a sigh. 'Oh, by the way, I've booked a wee session with the photographers in Durrow Road to get some nice pictures of you in that uniform. I trust you've brought it with you?'

CHAPTER THIRTEEN

Molly

Molly had saved hard all year, she'd passed her driving test at the second attempt and she'd just purchased a red Volkswagen Beetle from a girl she'd recently flown with. It was a lot of money, two hundred pounds, but it had low mileage and was supposed to be very reliable.

The others had planned trips home before Christmas and, as she'd only been back a couple of times in the past year, Molly decided such a visit was a priority before the festive season got under way. She was aware that her parents were desperate to know every detail of where she'd been – they'd wanted postcards from every stopover.

When she'd first parked her new red Beetle carefully in Bellingham Road, Eve had been away, but Vanessa was there and seemed suitably impressed.

'A very reliable little car,' she'd commented.

'I love it!' Molly had exclaimed. Then she'd remembered something. 'Talking of cars, there was a tall blonde stewardess on my last trip called Sue Watts – know her? No? Well, this Sue Watts only turns up at the airport in a sky-blue Cadillac! A *Cadillac*! Apparently, she'd met some guy down the Gulf somewhere with pots of money, and he fell *madly* in love with her! And he *bought* her the car! She told him her favourite colour was sky blue, and he had it sprayed specially. Not only that, he pays the rent on her *flat!* She must have been *very* naughty, mustn't she?'

'You could be right,' Vanessa had replied.

Molly felt quite exhilarated as she drove westwards along the A4 and, in places, on the new M4 motorway. It was due to be completed in the next year or two, so soon, she'd be able to use it all the way and cut her travel time. She was looking forward to three days with the family prior to being in Boston for Christmas and to getting the gossip – all the more so as she'd heard that Siobhan had moved in with a man, much to the displeasure of the O'Haras.

She was inordinately proud of her driving prowess as she navigated her way home without getting lost once, although she'd almost ended up in the centre of Bristol by mistake, before seeing the directional sign in the nick of time.

'Will you just *look* at her now!' Bridget O'Hara squeezed her husband's arm.

'Grand to see you, Molly!' He gave her a big hug. 'And what a lovely car! Aren't you doing well for yourself!'

It was Saturday afternoon and Jack O'Hara had a half day, all scrubbed up and clad in his best cardigan and grey flannels as if expecting royalty.

Molly duly admired the arrangements of postcards that her mother had stuck all over the kitchen door, even though several fell off each time the door was opened or closed and had to be painstakingly repositioned.

'Sellotape shares are booming,' Jack said as he replaced the Pyramids, with precision, above the Empire State Building.

'The neighbours can't believe you've been to all those places,' Bridget said, filling the kettle. 'Most of them have hardly been out of Bristol. You'll have to pop in to see them and show off that tan!'

'Tell me about *Siobhan*.' Molly was desperate to hear their reactions. 'What's this man of hers like?'

Bridget and Jack exchanged glances.

'We don't think he's at all suitable,' her father replied. 'He's a lot older than her, and he's a *chef*! A *cook*! I mean, what kind of job is that for a man?'

'And his eyes are too close together,' Bridget added.

'And he's got no respect for decency. There they are, living together! And he's a Protestant to boot!' Jack concluded.

Molly's twin, Connor, gave her a great bear hug when he got home. 'I really miss you, Molly,' he said. 'And I'm fed up at the bank, so maybe I will apply to be a steward. It must be great to see all those places – and get paid for it! I'm fed up here too, now that all the others have gone. Mum and Dad go on and on about Siobhan all day long, but I'm glad she's out of here, with all her moods and tantrums. That bloke is welcome to her. Anyway, what about you? No millionaire passenger whisked you away yet?'

Molly sighed. 'Those millionaire passengers are scarcer than hens' teeth,' she said, 'at least in the economy cabin. Now, we're having a party at New Year, so why don't you give yourself a break and come up for that?'

Connor brightened. 'You know what? I just might!'

CHAPTER FOURTEEN

Molly

'How was Melbourne?' Molly asked Eve when they'd all returned from their Christmas trips.

'Great!' Eve replied. 'Nice crew, glorious weather and Christmas on the beach! And such nice, friendly people! What about you?'

Molly's Christmas hadn't gone according to plan. 'We got to Boston all right, but an engine blew on landing. Turned out that major surgery was required, and they didn't have a spare engine over there, so the next day, back we flew on three engines – just us; no passengers of course. We had a skipper called Dipstick Dave; now why on earth would they call him that? I suppose he must tinker around with engines and things. Anyway, I slept most of the way home and spent Christmas with the folks in Bristol, much to their delight. Now, why is it that my trips never go as planned?'

Neither of them needed to ask Vanessa if she'd enjoyed her Toronto trip because she'd been walking on air ever since she got back and was sporting a beautiful gold, sapphire-studded locket and chain.

Molly had been told before Christmas, by Eve, about Vanessa's love life. She'd been very shocked at first, but then told Eve that she was actually quite jealous of Vanessa's happiness because she wanted to feel that way too. She said she'd almost written Martin off but still fancied him like mad, and he *was* coming to the party.

'This is his very last chance,' she said mournfully, 'and I'm going to have to pull out all the stops!'

They'd narrowed the guest list down to forty-five, which was as many as they could squeeze into the flat. Vanessa was asking several of her friends, of both sexes, from her pre-Skyline days, including Barty. Eve was asking mainly crew members with whom she'd become friendly during the past year, plus her ex-flatmate, Nadia. And, in addition to Martin, Molly had amassed quite a collection of friends since she'd started flying. And there was her brother, Connor, who was coming from Bristol for the occasion, along with another of her brothers, Fergal, who'd recently started up a joinery business in Chigwell. Both brothers had got themselves a room at the Mucky Duck, the pub at the end of Bellingham Road. Bearing in mind the anticipated decibel level, the girls thought it politic to invite the two guys in the flat upstairs as well.

It was shaping up to be a good party and New Year's Eve – 'Hogmanay,' corrected Eve – was spent cooking sausages, filling vol-au-vents and making salads. Eve worked out how to cook the haggis, and Molly was putting together a trifle, while Vanessa was making something called a Black Forest gateau, which, she told them, was the latest thing in puddings.

As well as the remaining Christmas decorations, there were garlands of tartan ribbon and next to the record player, alongside the Beatles, the Stones and the Mamas and the Papas, was a long-playing record of the massed pipes and drums of the

Scots Guards. Furthermore, each guest was requested to wear something tartan, however small.

There were squeals of laughter as everyone arrived sporting tartan shirts, ties, handkerchiefs and hair ribbons, and one flight engineer unzipped his flies so everyone could have a glimpse of his tartan underpants. Several of the girls wore tartan skirts, but Barty stole the show when he arrived wearing a Black Watch tartan kilt, which was far too short for him and exposed a pair of knobbly knees. He'd anchored a length of matching fabric to his shoulder. 'My plaid, darlings!'

'Where on earth did you get that lot?' Vanessa asked, giggling.

'A jumble sale – where else? You don't think I went to the Scotch House in Knightsbridge, do you? Now, I hope you've got some nice young men lined up for me?'

Molly had taken a great deal of care with her appearance. She'd bought a figure-skimming black dress from Selfridges at vast expense, but it was very, very flattering. 'You get what you pay for' was Vanessa's mantra, and she should know because she paid a fortune for everything. Molly had tied a tartan sash round her waist in order to fit the party theme, but she intended to remove it as soon as she could because she felt it detracted from her narrow waist.

Even Vanessa had said, 'Molly, you look fabulous! This man will ravish you tonight, but if he doesn't, I'll bet the others will!'

Martin had arrived wearing a very natty tartan waistcoat over his pristine white shirt, and Molly thought how handsome and distinguished he looked. Easily the most attractive man in the room! And he'd even brought a bottle of Chivas Regal, which gave her the excuse to give him a big hug before leading him into the room and introducing him all round.

Eve

Eve was pleased to see Nadia again. They'd always got on well when they'd shared the bedsitter at Earl's Court. It was Nadia who'd introduced her to Costa, Nadia's mother being Greek, as was Costa's. Eve knew that Nadia had always felt partly responsible for what had ultimately transpired, which was ridiculous. In fact, it had been Nadia who'd lectured her on the finer points of contraception, if only she'd listened. It was Nadia, too, who'd poured copious amounts of gin down her throat and ran her the scalding-hot baths, all of which had only produced awful hangovers and red, wrinkly skin. She'd meant well though, and, during the pregnancy, had been so helpful and supportive. Afterwards, when a very emotional Eve had needed somewhere to stay for some weeks before leaving for Paris, Nadia had come to the rescue again.

Nadia arrived at the party with a tartan scarf draped round the shoulders of her dress. As they hugged, she said, 'How about introducing me to one of those blue-eyed, strong-jawed pilots I keep reading about in the romance novels?'

'Nadia, if you find one, give me a shout!'

———

Barty was the centre of attention, as usual, entertaining the group who'd gathered round him. 'Isn't Vanessa looking just gorgeous!' he proclaimed. 'I could almost fancy her myself!'

'I think I'm much more your type,' piped up a short, bald steward.

'Well, you'll have to get in the queue, darling,' said Barty, casting his eye around the room. He grabbed Vanessa as she walked by with a tray of canapés. 'Nessa, darling, who is that *divine* creature over there?'

Vanessa followed the direction of his gaze. 'Do you mean Mr Tall, Dark and Handsome?'

'Yes, who *is* he?'

'That's Molly's friend. For God's sake get your eyes off him, because he's well and truly spoken for.'

'Oh, I don't think he *is*, darling. I shall make overtures in a minute. Now, tell me, how's the married lover these days?'

'Still married and looks like staying that way. I just live for our meetings. I'm trying not to even think of him tonight, because he's bound to be out partying with his damned wife. I know he'd love to be with me, Barty, honestly I do.'

'You poor darling,' murmured Barty, his eyes still firmly fixed on Martin.

Molly

Molly had been too busy as a hostess to give as much attention as she'd have liked to Martin. She'd spent ages passing round drinks and plates, and then clearing stuff away as well. Now they'd got to the stage where everyone was helping themselves to everything, and she found herself dancing non-stop. She'd danced a couple of slow numbers with Martin, who'd held her close and told her that she looked beautiful.

She came across Eve in the kitchen as she topped up her drink.

'What do you think of Martin, Eve?' she asked anxiously.

'He's very good-looking – I don't wonder you fancy him,' Eve replied.

At that moment, Vanessa came into the kitchen.

'What do you think of Martin, Nessa?'

Vanessa laughed. 'I think you should keep a tight rein on him!'

. . .

Midnight approached. The haggis had been eaten by the more adventurous guests, and Eve prepared to replace Adam Faith with the pipes and drums. The sound of music, laughter and chatter was deafening.

'We must be ready for "Auld Lang Syne" shortly,' Eve bellowed. 'It's coming up to twelve o'clock.'

Molly was looking around anxiously. 'Anyone seen Martin?'

'Probably in the toilet. I saw him heading in that direction a short time ago,' Vanessa said. 'Perhaps he had a few too many?'

'Oh no,' Molly said firmly, 'not Martin; he's very sensible.'

She checked her watch. Only three minutes to go until 1966! She looked round the crowded room once more before heading along the corridor towards the bathroom. Surprisingly, it was empty, but she could hear a faint sound coming from Vanessa's bedroom and wondered if he'd felt ill perhaps and decided to lie down for a little while.

Very quietly, she opened the door and peered in, her eyes slowly adjusting to the near darkness. The only light came from a street lamp several yards up the road, and so it took a minute or two to distinguish shapes.

There was *someone* on the bed – no, in fact there were *two* bodies on the bed, entwined together amid a sea of guests' overcoats.

Molly gasped as she deciphered Martin in his distinctive tartan waistcoat, and the other person, complete with mini-kilt and plaid askew, could only be Barty. They hadn't even noticed her.

In the background, combined with the sudden ringing in her ears, Molly could hear the strains of 'Auld Lang Syne'; 1965 was history.

CHAPTER FIFTEEN

2015

The reminiscing continued as they tackled their second large flutes of wine.

'Remember,' said Molly, 'that *awful* party at Bellingham Road!'

'You didn't think it was so awful when you were so determined to plan it,' Vanessa retorted.

'Well, it turned out to be horribly humiliating for me,' Molly said with a sigh.

'And it was the beginning of the end of our time at Bellingham Road,' Eve noted sadly, 'before we began to go our separate ways.'

'Before you decided to become a high-flying business-woman, you mean?' Vanessa reminded her.

'And you came back from New York determined to buy a flat, Nessa,' Eve remarked.

'Oh my God, New York!' Vanessa groaned. 'That was the weirdest trip back to London I've ever done!' She shook her head in belated disbelief.

'It didn't stop you though, did it?' Molly chimed in.

'No, it didn't. But what about *you*?'

'What about me?' Molly asked nonchalantly.

'Finding two blokes who fancied you! Or was it *three* after that Hawaii trip?'

Molly sniffed. 'Nobody's counting!'

'And I met George,' Eve added.

'He was a nice man,' said Molly.

'Unfortunately, "nice" isn't always good enough,' Eve said.

Molly grinned. 'Never mind – you got there in the end.'

'And so did you!' chorused her two friends.

'I did.' Molly grinned and took a large gulp of her Bollinger. 'In fact, I think we probably all got what we wanted.' She paused. 'More or less.'

'Not least because we supported each other along the way,' Eve added.

1971

CHAPTER SIXTEEN

Eve

Sometimes Eve wondered if they were all destined to be old maids. Vanessa and her captain had been going strong for six years, their passion still unabated, but it was a relationship that was going nowhere. Eve had given up lecturing her on the subject.

'I hate to use clichés,' Vanessa said, 'but absence really does make the heart grow fonder. And, of course, we're always at our best. I never have to wash his underwear or darn his socks. Do captain's wives darn socks, do you think? I certainly wouldn't.'

Molly, on the other hand, had finally surrendered her much-prized maidenhood to a handsome Australian Airlines pilot during a stopover in Honolulu. He'd chatted her up on Waikiki Beach and had been unable to believe that she was unable to swim and, even more incredible, that she was still a virgin. He'd decided it was his duty to do something about both those handicaps without delay, as it was a three-day stopover. By the end of the second day, Molly was able to float and do a couple of breaststrokes. By the end of the second night, after far too many mai tais, she was finally deflowered. Then he flew home to Sydney, and she headed west to Tokyo, never to meet again. She told Eve that she felt some relief at finally having made this great transition, and some guilt at breaking the pledge she'd made to save herself for The Man, if he ever appeared. She admitted that her ill-fated fling with Martin had left her devastated.

'I really was the little innocent,' she confided to Eve, 'and I had no idea that Martin preferred the guys to the dolls. I just never meet anyone I'd like to marry, and so when that gorgeous Aussie came along, well...! He was a great guy, so good-looking, and he was single, because I'd *never* do that with a married man.'

Privately, Eve wondered how Molly could be so confident about the pilot's marital status. 'What about that rich American you were once planning on?' she asked.

Molly shrugged. 'I thought that once I started working in first class, they'd be thick on the ground. The only ones I've come across are either old, overweight or married, and usually a combination of all three.'

Eve thought fondly of George, the thirty-five-year-old first officer she'd met on a Hong Kong trip. George was divorced with no kids or domestic problems. He was easy-going, unde-manding and satisfactory – if not exciting – in bed. Vanessa reckoned he was bordering on dull and that he would drive Eve mad eventually. But, of course, it didn't take much to drive Vanessa mad and, for the moment, he suited Eve very well.

She'd met him when, between Delhi and Hong Kong, he'd seemed to spend an unusual amount of time hovering around the front galley.

'Just like to stretch my legs occasionally,' he'd explained to Eve, 'because it gets very cramped up there.'

'No chance of getting cramp round here,' Eve had muttered. She'd been on her feet non-stop and was unloading caviar, smoked salmon and quails' eggs from the trolley, having served the first course of dinner to the first-class passengers.

He'd peered through the curtain. 'You've got a full load in there.'

'I *had* noticed,' Eve had said drily.

'No one famous?'

'No one I'd recognise,' Eve had replied as she prepared the trolley for the main course.

'Don't suppose there's any spare caviar going?'

It hadn't been a propitious start to their relationship. One of the many jobs the first-class stewardess had to do was feed the flight-deck crew, but *after* the passengers' meal service. The meal service could take forever; every table had to be laid up individually with crisp white cloths, silver and crystal glasses. Then there was course after course, silver-served onto china plates, wines offered and served. Sometimes the entire economy cabin had been fed and watered and they were still ploughing on with coffee and liqueurs. Then, just as everything was being cleared away, they had to start all over again with the flight deck. And that was in addition to their never-ending requests for tea and coffee. Crew meals were stored separately, but, of course, they much preferred the passengers' fare.

Thus Eve had been mildly irritated. 'Perhaps the skipper would like some?'

The captain and first officer had to eat completely different meals, because of the remote chance of food poisoning.

'No, I've already asked him,' George had said. 'He prefers the smoked salmon.'

As she'd spooned some caviar, chopped egg and lemon onto a plate with some toast, Eve had cast a sideways glance at him. Not bad. Tall, dark, thinning hair, blue eyes, nice smile. Probably married, she'd thought.

'Thank you,' he'd said. 'I'm doing the landing into Hong Kong and wondered if you'd like to come up front?'

'Oh, I *would*!' Eve loved Hong Kong, and the landing into Kai Tak Airport was something to behold. She'd been on the flight deck for landing there once before, when they approached from the sea. Due to lack of space, the runway was built straight out into the sea, and planes had to touch down at just the right spot to be able to pull up on time and not crash into the mountains of skyscrapers which seemed to be only yards ahead.

'We're coming in from the land,' he'd said, 'so that should be fun.'

Later, he'd turned and grinned at her before devoting his attention to what was considered to be one of the trickiest landings anywhere in the world. Approaching the runway from the land meant literally flying through part of Kowloon, the enormous aircraft weaving its way between apartment blocks and skyscrapers. Eve's heart was in her mouth, but George kept a steady course towards the silver strip of runway jutting out to the sea in front of them.

As always, the landing was perfect, and they stopped well short of drowning point. As they'd taxied towards the terminal building, Eve had reckoned that perhaps George had earned his caviar after all.

'So, how come nobody's snatched you up and taken you away from all this?' George had asked as he'd indicated Hong Kong's panoramic harbour. They were on the Star Ferry from Kowloon to the island, where they planned to take the tram up to the Peak to enjoy the fabulous view, before eating in a floating restaurant at Aberdeen Harbour.

'Mainly because I don't *want* to be snatched up and taken

away from all this,' Eve had replied. 'I love this job and coming to all these wonderful places.' She'd studied him for a moment. 'What about you? Wife and two-point-five kids at home?' For a brief moment, she'd felt the familiar ache in her heart for her own little boy, who was now – incredibly – nearly eight years old.

He shook his head sadly. 'Unfortunately not. We didn't have children, and then she absconded with our local dentist about four years ago.'

'Oh, I'm really sorry, George. I didn't mean to be patronising.'

He'd laughed. 'That's OK. I'm not in mourning. She lost her cheap staff travel, but she's got great teeth now!'

Six months later, George was cooking a meal for Eve in his mock-Georgian town house in Kingston-upon-Thames, when he suddenly asked, 'Would you consider moving in with me? I know there's not much point in proposing marriage to you again because you're such an independent hussy!'

Eve laughed. 'I promise to think about it, George.'

She doubted she'd give it much thought since she was still hell-bent on retaining her independence. Marriage certificate or not, she'd be as good as married to him if she moved in. She'd gathered from their conversations that the reason George hadn't had children was down to his ex-wife. Several times he'd assured her he was 'firing on all cylinders', which made her wonder, and worry, if he had ideas about starting a family. With her.

Apart from the fact that she wasn't madly in love with George, and certainly didn't want children, she still fancied herself as a businesswoman. She didn't want to give up flying, but she did still dream of having a little interior design shop.

She'd been in touch with Nadia, who was an upholsterer, and whose ambition was to open her own fabric shop, so perhaps between them they could make the dream come true. In the meantime, she continued to collect interesting knick-knacks on each trip.

CHAPTER SEVENTEEN

Vanessa

Vanessa and Johnny had managed to wangle two whole days together in New York. It was the sixth anniversary of their meeting, and so the timing and the location were perfect. They dined at the Top of the Sixes – one of their favourite restaurants, which was situated on top of a skyscraper (number 66) with stunning views of Manhattan by night.

Vanessa had taken great care with her appearance. Her blonde hair artfully arranged over her shoulders, and wearing an emerald-green silk minidress, she sighed with pleasure as she sipped her Cloud 66 cocktail.

Johnny squeezed her hand across the table. 'You are the most beautiful woman in here,' he murmured, 'by far.'

'You're such an old flatterer, but I love you.'

'I love you too. And less of the "old", if you please.'

'I was wondering,' Vanessa said, 'if you were going to be anywhere near Bahrain in six days' time? I've got my next roster already.'

He didn't speak for a moment. Then he cleared his throat.

'I'm afraid it's holiday time again, darling. Bryony's so keen to go to California and we thought we'd take the two youngest and hire a motorhome out there. You should *see* them – the motorhomes, I mean; they are *so* luxurious!'

Vanessa's evening was ruined. This was when it really hurt – she felt second-rate and insanely jealous of Bryony. Every year, at least once, they went on a holiday, which, of course, was a perfectly normal thing to do. Somehow or other she could cope with what she hoped was Johnny's humdrum life down in deepest Dorset, but holidays were something else. Holidays meant that couples had time to themselves, to revitalise and refresh their dreary marriages.

Johnny squeezed her hand again. 'I'll only be away for three weeks and then I expect they'll put me on standby, so we can have a few days together at the Horizon Hotel.'

'Unless it's like last time,' Vanessa said, hoping she wasn't going to cry, 'when they called you out after only four hours.' She'd been devastated, particularly as she'd phoned in 'sick' so she could be with him. They hadn't wasted any time and had made love shortly after she'd walked in the door, before the damned phone had rung and informed Captain Martell that he was about to fly to Sydney.

Back home, Vanessa faced the prospect of three whole weeks without her lover. There was no chance of even getting a glimpse of him down the routes, there'd be no love notes in her pigeonhole at the airport, and there would certainly be no phone calls. She tortured herself with visions of Johnny and Bryony making love in their bijou motorhome but then consoled herself with the thought that it might be nigh on impossible to indulge in much passion when two teenagers were within earshot.

Sometimes she fantasised that Bryony might die; a heart

attack perhaps, a car accident, even a trip on the stairs. Of course, then they'd have to wait a respectable period before he introduced her as the next Mrs Martell. But she was used to waiting. However, her imagination deserted her when she tried to contemplate moving to rural Dorset and coping with three stepchildren. She consoled herself by thinking that they were almost grown-up now and so she'd probably be able to persuade Johnny to move closer to London. Although Skyline were now considering allowing married stewardesses to continue flying, she'd want to be at home for him. But how did the saying go? If you marry your mistress, you create a vacancy? *No*, she thought, *with* me *in the marital bed, he wouldn't* need *any extra-marital activity*.

Sometimes Vanessa got angry. Why shouldn't *she* have a bit of hanky-panky as well? Goodness knows, she got enough offers.

The flight engineer on the Bahrain night stop was called Doug, and he was very attractive. She was confident that the feeling was mutual, and she made a point of flirting shamelessly with him at the crew party room in the hotel. Both of them had drunk far too much, as they discovered as they made their way unsteadily along the corridor.

He hiccoughed. 'Your room or mine, Veronica?'

'*Vanessa*, if you please. Mine.'

It had been a mistake. She'd faked an orgasm because no way could she get turned on with his *black socks*, which he didn't bother to remove. He just wasn't Johnny.

'How was it for you?' he asked.

God, he did *clichés* as well! Still, it was one in the eye for Johnny Martell and boring old Bryony!

'OK,' she replied, yawning.

.   .   .

The return flight to London was somewhat uncomfortable for them both. Doug was known to be a hit with the ladies, and Vanessa was aware that she'd dented his morale. She was polite as she served him his meal and refreshments but intentionally cool.

As she positioned herself on the crew seat beside the front door with a cold drink, Vanessa heard the first officer ask casually, 'How did you make out last night, Doug? She was coming on to you strong, but she doesn't look so friendly today.'

'Wouldn't recommend her to my worst enemy,' Doug retorted. 'Near enough frigid. Not what you'd expect at all.'

The first officer laughed. 'Well, none of us could work out why she was coming on so strong to you in the first place. No offence, old chap, but she's been Johnny Martell's bit of stuff for years! You must be the only person on the planet who doesn't know that!'

A bit of stuff, thought Vanessa. *Is that all I am?*

Two weeks later, she was back in New York. On her own. But Vanessa loved the atmosphere of the place: the wailing of the sirens, the food you couldn't get at home, the shopping, and the automatic responses of everyone: 'You're welcome!' 'Have a nice day!' Like they *cared*! Not that it mattered one iota. Sinatra was right when he called it 'the city that never sleeps' because it didn't.

She loved walking down Broadway, going to see the line-up of high-kicking Ronettes at Radio City; Times Square; St Patrick's Cathedral dwarfed by the skyscrapers all around; Fifth Avenue and shopping; the cosmopolitan atmosphere of Greenwich Village; and the shadier areas like The Bowery and Harlem. Most of all, New York was Johnny. Their place.

One of the other girls on the crew was called Barbara and,

in the absence of Johnny, she and Barbara had become quite friendly. It transpired that Barbara had a little flat in Twicken-ham, which she was about to put on the market, because she was getting married in a couple of months' time.

It sounded exactly right for Vanessa. Ground floor, two bedrooms and a tiny garden at the back. 'South-facing too,' Barbara added, 'so it gets the sun all day. You must come and see it when we get back.'

Vanessa had managed to save some money, and she was confident that her mother would help her out if necessary because it wasn't at all easy getting any kind of mortgage as a single woman, although she was probably earning more money than several of the men she knew.

Her *own* flat! She was becoming increasingly excited at the very thought. Then she wondered about Bellingham Road. How would Eve and Molly make out? Well, Eve had been making noises recently about renting a shop or something, and Molly would surely be able to find someone else to share with, if necessary. After all, they'd been together for more than six years, and it was time *somebody* made a move!

Nevertheless, the thought of them going their separate ways made her feel quite tearful. They'd always be friends of course; of that Vanessa was certain. But for now, the thought of a cosy little nest, with regular visits from Johnny, would be a dream come true. She couldn't wait to get back to London.

As Vanessa entered the first-class section of the aircraft at Kennedy Airport, she was surprised to see some passengers already on board. She hadn't realised it was a transit flight.

'Just come in from LA,' the chief steward said with a sigh, 'and it's a full load. Hope you weren't counting on any beauty sleep.'

Vanessa pulled back the curtain to survey the cabin. And there, in the front row, sitting comfortably with his feet up and reading a newspaper, was Johnny Martell. Next to him sat an attractive, dark-haired woman.

Bryony.

CHAPTER EIGHTEEN

Molly

Molly felt restless. She needed a break. She still had two weeks' leave yet to take, and she'd need to spend a few days of that at home in Bristol.

Eve had just come back from a two-week round-the-world and was still trying to adjust to all the time changes. She'd slept for almost fifteen hours, Molly reckoned. When she finally emerged into the living room, still in her nightie, she asked, 'Any tea going, Molly?'

'Well now, I'll consider making you a cup of tea if you'll consider something for me.'

'What's that?' Eve asked, yawning.

'How about a holiday? A change of scenery. A few days somewhere nice?'

Eve groaned. 'Molly, I've just got back from some of the most exotic locations on earth, so why do I need any more travelling – and at my own expense?'

Molly filled the kettle. 'We wouldn't need to go far.'

Eve looked out at the October rain lashing against the window. 'Please don't suggest anywhere in the UK!'

'I wasn't planning to. How about a few days somewhere in Europe? Paris? Or Rome?'

Eve yawned again. 'Well, I suppose I could manage that. I'm not sure I want to go back to Paris at the moment, but Rome might be good. I've only ever had a night stop there.'

'Me too.' Molly poured the tea. 'It's only a couple of hours away. Do you think Vanessa might like to come?'

'I doubt it, because her man is going to be on standby, I think. We can ask her. I'm warming to the idea,' Eve said as Molly placed the mug of tea on the table beside her. 'I might even agree to it if you could find me a biscuit.'

Staff travel could be tricky. Employees paid a mere ten per cent of the fare but only got on the flight if seats were available after all the commercial passengers had checked in. Fortunately, on Flight 807, to Rome, Bombay and Singapore, there was space. Not only that, but they both knew the chief steward and he just happened to have two seats free in the back row of first class.

'This is the life!' Molly exclaimed as they clinked champagne glasses.

'George wasn't happy,' Eve said. 'He wanted to come too. Said he'd hardly seen me lately. I had to explain it was a girls' trip, and that we'd still have a few days together when I get back.'

'I did think Nessa might have wanted to come,' Molly said.

'Well, you know Nessa. She's in a world of her own.'

The *pensione* on Via Nazionale was basic, clean, cheap and the owner was friendly. From their window, they could look up the street to the luxurious Hotel Quirinale, where the Skyline crews normally stayed.

'Makes you realise how lucky crew are,' Eve said, looking round the spartan little room as she hung up some clothes in the rickety wardrobe.

'And having your own bathroom,' Molly said with feeling as she left to head down the corridor, clutching her sponge bag.

It was late evening and they'd had a big meal on the plane, so they decided on an early night, all the better preparation for sightseeing the following day.

'I've only ever seen the Colosseum and the Trevi Fountain,' Molly said, studying the street map of Rome as they emerged onto the street the next morning.

'Me too. And the monument to Vittorio Emanuele, which is really impressive. You have to see *that*! Now, where shall we start?'

Like all good tourists, they started with the Colosseum and the Forum. The sun was shining from a blue, cloudless sky as they followed their guide, whose name was Giovanni, around. Giovanni, in turn, had his eye constantly on Eve as he verbally transported them back to the world of ancient Rome, with gory details of gladiators' wrestling with lions and the mass slaughter so loved by the first-century Romans. When he'd finished, and his band of followers had begun to disperse, he called to Eve, 'You like to have coffee with me?'

Eve laughed. 'No thank you.'

They'd arrived at the Pantheon and, as they gazed up in awe, Molly asked, 'How could they build something so perfect, in concrete, all those centuries ago?'

'Incredible,' Eve agreed as they tore their eyes away from

the roof and looked round at the statues, 'but I'll tell you what; I'm in dire need of a coffee. Shall we have one when we leave here?'

'Good idea,' Molly replied. 'There's a place directly opposite.'

Molly kicked her shoes off under the table.

'My feet are killing me already, and it's only day one!'

'No wonder; we've walked miles,' Eve said.

'*Grazie!*' Molly beamed at the waiter as he positioned their coffees on the table.

'You are English?' He appeared to be in no hurry to leave.

'Whatever made you think that?' Eve asked as, under her breath, she muttered, 'Not a drop of Anglo-Saxon blood in either of us!'

'I am called Bruno. One day I go to England.'

'Good luck with that, Bruno, and *arrivederci!*' Molly said.

Bruno made no attempt to move. 'You are here tonight?'

At that moment, a man sitting alone at a nearby table stood up and let out a torrent of Italian at the hapless waiter, who grudgingly retreated.

'I am sorry that he has bothered you,' he said in faultless English. He looked like a businessman in his beautifully tailored suit. He was also very handsome.

'Thank you,' Eve said politely, noting that Molly was openly admiring him.

'This is your first visit to Rome?' he asked.

Molly had found her voice. 'It's our first *proper* visit.'

Eve shot her an annoyed look as if to say – why encourage another lothario?

'There is much to see,' the man said. 'Where are you going next?'

'We thought we might head towards the Spanish Steps,' Molly replied.

'But,' he said, 'it is quite a long walk, and your feet are sore.'

He smiled at Molly and indicated the shoes beneath the table. 'It is easier by car.'

'Yes, I'm sure it is,' Molly replied, 'but we haven't got a car.'

'But I have!' He had the most disarming smile. 'I have a little business to attend to over there.' He indicated vaguely to the side of the Pantheon. 'It will take only ten minutes, so I should like to buy you both a drink while you wait, and then I shall take you to the Piazza di Spagna.'

'That would be lovely,' Molly cut in as Eve opened her mouth to protest.

'*Va bene.*' He stood up and summoned a grumpy-looking Bruno, who'd been scowling from the doorway. 'I am called Mario – Mario Bellini.' He held his hand out to Molly and gripped hers tightly.

'I'm Molly, and this is Eve.'

'Molly is such a pretty name,' he said, then added hurriedly, 'and Eve is too.'

As he strolled away to pay for their drinks, Eve nudged Molly. 'Honestly, Molly, you were complaining about all those lotharios and now *look* what you've done! You're *throwing* yourself at him!'

'I am *not!*' Molly said hotly. After a minute, she added, 'But you must admit he's rather gorgeous! And so nice! And, admit it, you'd quite like a lift to the Spanish Steps, wouldn't you?'

Eve

Mario reappeared after nearly half an hour, by which time Eve had become increasingly annoyed. Molly had had to continually persuade her to wait, much against her will.

'Is this an Italian's idea of ten minutes?' she'd asked Molly.

When he arrived, he was most apologetic. 'It was a business

appointment and they kept me waiting. I was so afraid you would be gone. *Andiamo!*'

His small Fiat was parked nearby in a no-parking area, which was full of cars and Vespas.

'It's no good having a big car here in the city,' he said, 'because it is so difficult to park, so I bring only the little one.'

Eve, squashed in the back, suspected she was about to become a gooseberry.

The traffic was chaotic, and both of them put their hands over their eyes as Mario navigated his way through with much hooting.

'Why do they bother painting those lines on the road?' Eve asked as she uncovered her eyes briefly before another car cut right across their path. Traffic zigzagged everywhere, at speed, horns blaring. 'It's a complete waste of paint, particularly on zebra crossings where nobody bothers to stop.'

Mario laughed. 'Ah, but there are not many accidents, you know. In Rome, it is wise to cross the road directly behind a nun. They will *never* kill a nun.'

They were too exhausted to climb up to the very top of the Spanish Steps and contented themselves with sitting halfway up, surrounded by baskets of flowers. In spite of herself, Eve was warming to Mario. He was charming and polite and obviously fancied Molly. Trouble was, at this rate she could see herself sightseeing alone over the next few days.

As if reading her mind, on the way back to Via Nazionale, Mario said, 'Tonight I would like to take you both out to dinner, to apologise for keeping you waiting this afternoon. I will come with my friend, Silvio.' He met Eve's eye in the rear-view mirror. 'Silvio is a gentleman, and I think you will like him.'

.   .   .

Both men arrived at the *pensione* that evening, Mario driving a smart black Alfa Romeo.

Silvio was taller than Mario, but not so good-looking. As they drove away, they wanted to know what these English ladies did for a living. Eve explained that neither of them were actually English, and that they flew with Skyline.

Both men appeared impressed to be escorting *British* air hostesses.

At this point, they were crossing the river.

'The Tiber?' Molly asked, clearly trying to remember her geography lessons.

'*Si*,' Silvio replied. 'In Italian, it is the Tevere, and now we are going to *Trastevere*, which means "across the River Tevere".'

The area they found themselves in was quaint, with cobbled streets and lots of flower sellers, bars, galleries and restaurants.

'Your turn,' Molly said, walking alongside Mario, while Eve and Silvio followed behind. 'What do *you* do for a living?'

'I work in the family business,' Mario replied, putting his hand under her elbow as she navigated the cobbles, 'which is wine. We have many vineyards, and we export our wine to shops and restaurants all over the world.'

'How interesting!' Molly exclaimed. 'Is your business in Rome?'

'No, no, we are in Frascati – just outside Rome. Many great wines come from Frascati. We also have vineyards up in Tuscany and my brother, Alessandro, looks after these.'

'Are you in the wine business too?' Eve asked Silvio.

He laughed. 'Sometimes, yes. I am in import-export, mainly export: wine, leather, pasta, anything. I, too, have my own business. Mario and I are friends since school.'

They'd reached the Trattoria Napoli, where there was much hugging with the owner, a short, portly man with a shiny bald head. Eve was fascinated; men just didn't go around hugging each other in the UK.

As they were directed to a table in the corner, Eve noticed Mario's dark eyes gazing at Molly with something approaching rapture, and she seemed equally besotted in return. Silvio was a perfect gentleman, which was fine, but there was no chance of any relationship there. *Apart from anything else*, Eve thought sadly, *I fear I might also have lost the ability to fall in love.*

The evening was enjoyable though. Both men were charming and humorous, and the meal was excellent, starting with *antipasti* ('appetisers' explained Mario as he demolished a plate of Parma ham, salami and olives). Then there was *il primo*, which was pasta in shapes they'd never seen before, served with a delicious sauce, followed by *il secondo*, delicately cooked liver in an amazing wine sauce, followed by *la dolce*, when both girls tasted tiramisu for the first time. Eve reckoned she must have put on pounds and wondered if she'd ever be able to get into her uniform skirt again.

Predictably, it wasn't proving easy to keep Silvio at arm's-length and Eve decided that, if Molly was going to continue seeing Mario, she would need to find something to do on her own.

Eve and Molly spent the following day together at St Peter's, while Mario had to work. They were both footsore after the long trek through the Vatican museum, culminating in the Sistine Chapel, where they got cricks in their necks gazing up in awe at Michelangelo's incredible ceiling.

In the evening, Mario was there with the Alfa Romeo at Via Nazionale to take Molly out, although he politely extended the offer to Eve as well.

'No thank you,' Eve said equally politely, 'I really fancy a quiet evening.'

Molly

As Mario held the car door open for Molly, he said, 'Tomorrow I must go to Milano for three days, so tonight I want you all to myself!'

'This city,' Molly said dreamily as they drove away, 'is like a giant film set! There's just one amazing sight after another, and I can hardly believe it's real. I love the terracotta and gold colours of the buildings, and the shutters on all the windows and everything! I just *love* it!'

'Good,' said Mario, 'because then you will come back. But, right now, we are going to Frascati, because I would like you to meet my family, just in case one day you might agree to marry me!'

'*Marry you?*' Molly's heart was thumping strangely, and she wondered if she'd heard correctly.

'I'm not asking you *now!*' He patted her knee as he steered his way round the chaotic Piazza Venezia with one hand. 'But I will come to see you in London, and I hope you will come to see me again in Rome, and then you will decide.'

Molly, in a state of shock, took a few minutes to find her voice. '*We* will decide, you mean?'

'No, *cara*,' said Mario. '*You* will decide. *I* have already decided.'

Graziana Concetti was small, buxom and elegant, in the style of many older Italian women. A Sicilian by birth, she had sharp brown eyes and greying hair, tied up loosely with tortoiseshell clips.

'Welcome!' she said as she led the way into the *salotto*.

Molly was aware that she was being scrutinised closely, not

just by the rather formidable *mamma*, but by a taller, younger version standing behind her.

'This is Mamma,' said Mario with a wave of his hand, 'and this is my sister, Donatella.'

Molly shook hands with them both, feeling distinctly nervous.

The *mamma* was now setting out some glasses. 'We will have some wine,' she said firmly.

Mario turned to Molly. 'Later, we will go to the restaurant of my friend, here in Frascati.'

They all lifted their glasses. '*Salute!*'

'*Cin cin!*'

Graziana placed her glass on the table. 'Mario tells me you are Irish?'

'Yes, I was born there, but we've lived in England since I was two years old. In Bristol. Do you know England?'

Graziana shook her head. 'No,' she said. 'One time I go to France, but never to England. My English is not good. So, you are Catholic?'

Molly almost choked. 'Well, yes, but—'

'*Va bene!*' said Graziana. Subject closed.

'Mamma!' Even Mario looked embarrassed.

Donatella, aware of some tension, stepped in diplomatically. She smiled at Molly. 'I do like your dress.'

'*This?*' Molly, still nonplussed, looked down at her red wool dress.

Donatella nodded. '*Si*, I like. Is from Mark and Spencer, no? One day I very much like to visit that shop.'

Later, in the restaurant, Mario said, 'I think my mother liked you.'

Molly was none too sure about that. She hadn't felt entirely comfortable in the older woman's presence, but, then again, it had been an unusual situation to say the least. Did it matter? Well, yes, it *could* matter because she was rapidly falling in love with Mario. Furthermore, she physically wanted him very badly! But *where*? Most definitely not in Mamma's apartment, nor in the room she shared with Eve. And certainly not in the back of a car, Alfa Romeo or not.

He appeared to read her mind. 'Molly,' he said, gazing into her eyes, 'I very much wish to make love to you, but we must wait until I come to London, no? I will be there on business in one month's time, and I will be in a hotel.'

Molly nodded. 'You must give me the dates so I can request to be at home.'

'I am looking forward to this so much,' he said later as he kissed her passionately outside the *pensione*.

'So am I,' Molly replied truthfully.

Eve

Eve spent the evening on her own, eating dinner in the *pensione* and then passed an hour or two drinking grappa and chatting with the friendly owners. They were thrilled to learn she came from Scotland because their elder son had gone there, to Glasgow, to open a café. 'Do you know him?' they asked. 'His name is Pietro—'

'Scotland is a big country,' Eve said, laughing.

She was glad of an early night and fell asleep almost immediately, only to be woken just after midnight by Molly, tiptoeing around the room and then dropping her hairbrush on the marble floor.

'Oops, I'm so sorry, Eve!'

Eve opened her eyes to observe Molly grinning from ear to

ear. 'You don't *look* that sorry; you look pretty damned pleased about something!'

Molly sat down on the bed. 'You aren't going to believe this! Mario took me to meet his mother, and he wants me to marry him!'

'*What!*' Eve was fully awake now. 'But you've only known him a couple of days!'

'Yes, but I'm sure he's The Man! I haven't agreed to marry him yet of course, but he's coming to London next month, and I shall try to get a trip here as well.'

Aware that she was probably in for a sleepless night, Eve hauled herself up to a sitting position. 'Tell me all!'

Molly didn't need asking twice. 'He lives at home with his mother and his sister. His father died some years ago. Did you know that Italian men live at home until they get married, even if they're quite old? Anyway, they have this enormous apartment in a beautiful old building in Frascati, stuffed with antiques and things. I liked the sister, but I'm not so sure about the mother. Graziana, she's called. Mario says she wants him to marry the daughter of her best friend, but he doesn't fancy the girl at all. I think it's been a bone of contention between them for some time.'

'But, Molly,' Eve said, smothering a yawn, 'you hardly know him! Please, please, take this slowly. I mean, it would be a complete change of culture for you if you did decide to marry him. Rome's lovely for a holiday, but would you want to *live* here? You'd have to leave all your friends and family, and learn Italian as well!'

'I've learned a few words already! *Ti amo* means I love you and *cara* means dear or darling. Isn't that wonderful! Anyway, he's off to Milan tomorrow for a few days, so I won't see him now until he comes to London. So, tomorrow, shall we go to the Trevi Fountain? No, wait, it's *La Fontana di Trevi*!

CHAPTER NINETEEN

Eve

'I've been to look at a flat in Twickenham,' Vanessa announced, 'and I'm thinking of buying it.'

Eve and Molly, just returned from Rome, looked at her in astonishment.

'I didn't think you'd find something so soon,' Eve said, hauling her suitcase along the corridor.

'You'll have to come with me to see it.' Then, as an afterthought, Vanessa added, 'How was Rome?'

'Rome was quite something,' Eve replied, grinning. 'And Molly's in love!'

'What, *again*?' Vanessa rolled her eyes heavenwards.

'What do you mean *again*?' Molly protested. 'It's a long time since I thought I was in love, but this is *it*!'

'Italian?'

'Yes, he's called Mario. He's *gorgeous*!'

Vanessa turned to Eve. 'What did you think of him?'

'Yes, he was nice – and good-looking. But I've told her to

take her time and think this through. She's only known him for
five minutes.'

'Nessa, you probably won't believe me, but it really *was* love
at first sight!' Molly sighed.

'Yes, I do believe you,' Vanessa said. She sounded a
little sad.

'Nadia, it could be perfect!' Eve exclaimed.

The shop in Chiswick needed only cosmetic refurbishment,
and the layout was ideal. It was a good size, there was a large
window for displays, and there was a room at the back which
could be used as a workroom cum storeroom.

'He wants to let out the flat upstairs as well,' Nadia
explained as she walked around with her tape measure. 'I think
he was hoping I'd be interested.'

'What's the flat like?'

'Two good-sized rooms, tiddly kitchen and bathroom. You
could make it nice – needs gallons of white paint. If I wasn't
moving in with Frank, I'd be very happy to have it. But I thought
of you straight away. I can get the key tomorrow if you want to
have a look at it. There's even a door directly onto the pavement,
so you wouldn't have to go through the shop each time.'

Eve was becoming increasingly excited. 'It sounds ideal,
and I'd love to see it.'

This could be the answer to all her problems. Nadia was
moving in with her fiancé, Vanessa was in the process of buying
a flat and Molly was possibly going to get married. They'd
already worked out the cost of the rent and the lease, and how
they could split it between them, but it signalled the end of the
happy years at Bellingham Road. It was inevitable, of course,
that this time had to come, but Eve felt great sadness at the
thought, alongside excitement at the prospect of her new life.

She would continue flying and looking out for items that would sell well in their shop. Larger items would have to be shipped back, and staff discount couldn't be applied for commercial purposes. She'd discovered she had a gift for haggling and spent most of her stopovers these days arguing over prices for brass lamps, wooden chests, carvings and household linens. She carried her camera everywhere and, while the newer members of the crew were snapping away at the local sights, Eve was photographing possible stock to show to Nadia when she got home.

Eve inspected the flat the following day. Both the main rooms were square, of ample proportions, complete with cornicing and Victorian fireplaces. The kitchen was tiny but adequate, the bathroom likewise. Nadia gave the toilet chain an experimental tug and it flushed noisily.

Noisy or not, Eve loved it all.

Nadia had already given in her notice at the upholsterers where she worked and spent most evenings in the shop wielding a paintbrush, while Frank, her fiancé, fitted shelving and lighting.

'We've got to get this place up and running within a month,' she told Eve as she washed out her paintbrush, 'so I can begin to earn some money again. I'm living on air at the moment!'

Between trips, Eve had taken the lease on the upstairs flat and was in the process of painting everything white, with the exception of the outside door, which was being painted pillar-box red. She'd need to get some furniture, but there were some good second-hand shops around. She travelled with the minimum of clothing in order to fill up her suitcase with items to sell. In the meantime, sewing machines and large bales of material were being stacked up in the workroom, ready to be unpacked.

Eve was aware that George was none too happy about this

arrangement. After all, he was offering her a roof over her head for free, in a very nice house, in a very desirable area. Of course, if she *wanted* to go ahead with this crazy shop idea, he'd support her in any way he could, even if she did decide to live in that scruffy flat above.

Eve felt sorry for George. He confessed that he really didn't understand women at all, not the ones he met anyway. And she guessed he was lonely, as most of his friends were now married, some for the second time, and they all had kids. It must be nice to have kids, he said, and why did he always fall for the wrong women? His ex couldn't, and Eve wouldn't. It was time to give him space to meet someone else.

Nadia, admiring Eve's blindingly white walls, asked, 'When are you planning to move in?'

'Well, I've given in my notice at Bellingham Road. Nessa's definitely buying the Twickenham flat, and Molly's dead set on marrying her Italian and will commute from Bristol until she does. She can do her standbys with me, because I'm putting a bed-settee in the sitting room.'

'And where does that leave poor old George?'

'In Kingston-upon-Thames.'

Nadia sighed. 'Oh, Eve, that man's crazy about you!'

'He knows the score. I've always been honest with him.'

'Perhaps he'd understand you better if you told him about what happened to you...?'

Eve fingered her locket. 'No way. As far as he's concerned, I'm just one of this rare new breed of women who want to be independent, which I am. And God knows I've told him that often enough.'

'But we could still run this business if you were living with George.'

'What's the point? I'll never marry him.'

Nadia sighed. 'OK, OK, but you still enjoy sex with him, don't you? Even if he's never going to be Mr Right?'

'Well, the sex isn't madly exciting, but then neither is George. He's never going to be Mr Right, but he's Mr *All* Right.' Eve sighed. She should have met somebody like George all those years ago. *He* wouldn't have disappeared and left her to give up her baby. She blinked her tears away.

CHAPTER TWENTY

Vanessa

Vanessa was on the phone. 'Barty, I'd really like you to come and see this flat I'm buying. I plan to be moving in at the end of the month.'

'All right, darling, but it'll have to be tomorrow because Martin and I are going to a wedding reception this afternoon. Wish it was ours! Do you think we'll ever be allowed to be married?'

'I doubt it. But maybe one day... Anyway, tomorrow afternoon's fine.'

Barty and Marty, love's sweet dream. Although Molly had taken some time to recover from finding them at the party years ago, even she'd had to concede they were ideally suited.

'What about lover boy?' Barty asked. 'Has he seen it yet?'

'Lover boy's in Tokyo, and no, he hasn't seen it yet.'

Vanessa sniffed as she hung up. Tokyo. She didn't care too much for the place, although she had to admit that the Tokyo Prince Hotel was the last word in luxury. The city was enormous, industrial and noisy, and devoid of charm as far as she was concerned. Apart from the nice hotel, its only saving graces were Noritake china and Mikimoto pearls, both highly coveted and fashionable at home. Hardly anyone spoke English, which made any form of haggling impossible and, strolling along the Ginza, there was absolutely no chance of finding anything in her size. She also found it disconcerting to be stared at by groups of tiny kimono-clad ladies, who, with hands over their mouths, would dissolve into giggles at her blonde hair and great height – a rarity in the Land of the Rising Sun.

No, Tokyo wasn't Vanessa's favourite stopover. Not somewhere she'd ever want to be with Johnny.

Barty arrived alone to examine the flat. 'Marty's had to go to Bermuda, poor lamb,' he said sadly as he examined the rooms and praised the tiny garden. 'Yes, I do like it, darling; it's very *you*.'

'It just feels right. Let's go and have a coffee at that little place down the road.'

He took her arm as they headed towards the café.

'I've had to pay full price for it because so many people were after it,' Vanessa said with a sigh.

'*C'est la vie*,' he replied as they sat down and ordered their drinks. 'Now, tell me how it's going with lover boy because I haven't seen you for ages, not since before your New York trip last month.'

Vanessa sipped her coffee. 'Johnny was on holiday in California with his wife and two of his kids, so I was on my own in New York, missing him like hell. It's *our* place, you see.'

Barty unwrapped a chocolate biscuit. 'I shouldn't be eating these because I'm putting on so much weight around my tummy.' He patted his considerable paunch. 'So go on, darling.'

'What I didn't know was that the flight we were working home on was in transit from Los Angeles.'

Barty flicked crumbs from his chin.

'There he was, in first class, with his bloody wife. The kids were down the back somewhere.'

'Wow!' Barty leaned across the table towards her. 'What about the *wife*? What did you think of her? And how did lover boy react when he saw you?'

'I don't know which of us got the biggest shock.' Vanessa was mentally reliving the horror of seeing them there. 'It took me a few minutes to regain my composure and get a good look at her. She was dark-haired, pleasant looking.'

'*Pleasant looking*? How dull! Was she a bitch?'

'No, damnit, she was really nice. I actually *liked* her! Johnny, of course, looked like he wanted to sink through the floor! Later, he got me on my own in the galley and was so apologetic. But it was hardly his fault; just a horrible coincidence.'

'Has this wife got a name?'

'Bryony.'

'*Bryony*? Not nearly as classy as Vanessa, darling!'

'There's nothing wrong with the name, Barty. She, too, stopped by the galley on her way to the toilet and chatted to me. How long had I been in New York? Did I like it? God, if only she *knew*! Then she wittered on about their holiday and their bloody wonderful motorhome. I could have *screamed*!'

'Have you seen him since?'

'Just once. You know, when I got home, I was almost ready to pack it all in. I really was. They were a nice, friendly, ordinary family.'

'That's it!' Barty exclaimed excitedly. 'Nice and ordinary! Lover boy needs passion and excitement in his life, and that's *you*! But it's you I worry about, Nessa. This thing has been going on for years and could go on to eternity. Bryony will become old and grey while you will age beautifully of course! Nevertheless, one day you *will* become old, like it or not, and what will you have? A part-time man, if he's still around. No kids. No grandchildren. *That's* what worries me, Nessa.'

'Goodness, Barty, you *do* have a heart!'

'I've known you a long time, darling. I always saw you as a jet-setter, snaring a rich husband, me visiting you on the yacht down in St Tropez! With your looks, you could marry *anyone*! Not mortgaging yourself to the hilt with a tiddly flat in Twickers, just so you can entertain lover boy! Can't you even begin to fancy anyone else?'

'Honestly, I did try, with an engineer who's considered to be very fanciable, but it was awful! Laughable!'

'That must have done no end of good to the poor man's ego!'

Vanessa shrugged. 'When I got back from New York, I was really determined to finish it. I could see how crazy it all was.'

'So is it all over then?' Barty raised an enquiring eyebrow.

'I stuck to my resolution for all of twenty-four hours until we met at the Horizon Hotel, me determined to end it all. But I couldn't, Barty. I just went weak at the knees, all resolutions gone!'

'You're such a silly cow! Another coffee?'

CHAPTER TWENTY-ONE

Molly

Molly was aware that their days at Bellingham Road were numbered. It had to come of course, the end of an era, but it wasn't going to be easy leaving the flat and their time there together. Molly felt a lump in her throat. There was no way she'd want to share that flat with anyone else, and so, with the prospect of marriage to Mario in mind, she'd commute home to Bristol, and do her standbys staying with Eve.

She set off for San Francisco, armed with a *Teach Yourself Italian* book. She'd invested in some tapes as well but could only play them in the flat when the other two weren't there because they said it drove them mad. Particularly Vanessa, who made it quite clear she thought this whole thing to be ridiculous. 'For God's sake, Molly, Italians lust after everything in a skirt!'

But Molly knew Mario was sincere. He'd even phoned her the night before she left on this trip and wanted to know the name of the hotel in San Francisco so that he could phone her there too.

Molly hadn't been to San Francisco before, and she loved

everything about it, particularly the cable cars trundling their way up and down the steep hills, Fisherman's Wharf, and the boat trip round Alcatraz Island. They even took a trip out to the Golden Gate Bridge, and she enjoyed herself so much that she studied very little Italian.

Nevertheless, everywhere she went, Mario dominated her thoughts. She dreamed of marrying him and living in Frascati, but not too close to Graziana though. Would she miss flying? Well, yes, of course she would, particularly when coming to places like this. However, she'd now had years of constant travelling, living out of a suitcase and not knowing where she was likely to be next week.

She did, though, enjoy working in first class and all the paraphernalia of the specialised cabin service: the film stars, politicians, television personalities. It wasn't just a job; it was a way of life and well paid too.

There was a full load of very demanding passengers on the long return trip to London, including some British diplomat or other and his wife in 4E and 4F, where the wife was knocking back champagne cocktails at an alarming rate. She was noisy and causing complaints from other passengers, so Molly did what she usually did in the circumstances and doubled the amount of brandy in the cocktails, which finally knocked Lady 4F out for the count.

After the meal service was over, the nice-looking man in 2B appeared in the galley and beamed at Molly.

'You girls sure do work hard,' he said. 'Do you get any rest?'

'Not much,' Molly admitted. 'I have to feed the flight-deck crew now.'

He seemed in no hurry to return to his seat. 'You told us you were Molly and, with those blue eyes and that black hair, I wondered if you might be Irish by any chance?'

'Well now, I might be,' Molly replied as she began to prepare the crew meals.

'I thought as much! Let me introduce myself; my name is Patrick Doyle.' He held out his hand and shook Molly's. 'My father came over to the States from County Wicklow when he was just eighteen.'

Patrick Doyle said that he could never sleep on planes, so would Molly mind if he stayed and chatted for a little while? Molly, who was practically ready to sleep standing up, stifled a yawn and said, 'Not at all.'

He was from Seattle, and he worked for Boeing. 'So I know what's holding this old crate together,' he said, waving his arm around in a proprietorial fashion.

She laughed obediently but reckoned he'd done well for himself, given his expensive suit and shoes.

'I come to London from time to time and I'd like very much if we could get together for dinner or something?'

Molly explained that she had a special friend from Italy arriving shortly, but perhaps the *next* time he was in London...? After all, he was a nice guy, and why not? She wasn't married yet!

It was the usual story; like London buses, nothing comes along for ages and then two come at once.

Molly had had her hair expertly cut at Vidal Sassoon's, she'd given herself a face mask, she'd shaved her legs and she'd varnished both her fingernails and her toenails. She'd also lost nearly half a stone, because she could hardly eat with the excitement and anticipation of Mario's visit.

Now she stood in Terminal 2, awaiting the arrival of the Alitalia flight from Rome, in her new, blue minidress, and her knee-high white boots – which were all the fashion – with a small suitcase by her side. She was going to be with him for three whole days.

Molly saw him the moment he emerged from the customs area. He stood out from the crowd: immaculately dressed, very handsome, very Italian.

As she ran towards him, he dropped his suitcase, hugged and kissed her.

'*Buongiorno, caro!*' Molly had been practising this.

'*Mamma mia!* And you are already speaking Italian!' He released her and picked up both cases. '*Andiamo!*'

He held her tight during the taxi ride into Central London. When they arrived at the Langport Hotel in Mayfair, Mario reminded her that she was his wife, because otherwise she wouldn't be allowed in his room. Molly, already nervous, felt sinful as she stood behind him, partially hidden by a potted palm. The receptionist only glanced briefly in her direction as she handed over the key.

The bedroom was large, complete with king-sized bed, a bar, a sofa and an en-suite bathroom. Molly suddenly felt desperately shy, wishing fervently that she was still a virgin. She had tried to keep herself intact for her future husband, but, oh goodness, what with those mai tai cocktails and that gorgeous Aussie hunk! But would Mario expect her to be a virgin? Probably all Italian girls were virgins when they got married.

They wasted no time. Molly felt pale and uninteresting next to this olive-skinned man with the black hair on his chest and his tummy. But he was a good lover – gentle and considerate.

'My lovely Molly,' he said as they sat up in bed afterwards. 'But you have not waited for me, no?'

'Mario, it was only *once*. And I am twenty-eight, and this is 1971!'

He nodded. 'I am sorry, *cara*, I should not have said that.'

'He married someone else,' she explained sadly, having decided Martin would suffice as the scapegoat if it was ever necessary, as it would hardly be in her best interest to mention a passing Australian pilot. And he was as good as married, wasn't he?

'Well,' he said, 'I am glad he did, because otherwise we would not be together, no?'

Not for the first time she wondered why virginity was so important to some men, when they spent most of their lives and energy trying to lure girls into bed and then expected the chosen one to be a virgin.

They were sipping mai tais, of all things, in the Beachcomber Bar of the Mayfair Hotel when Mario formally asked her to marry him.

She almost dropped her glass but then remembered how much the blue minidress had cost – she mustn't stain it. 'Oh, Mario! Why me, when there are so many beautiful girls in Italy?'

'Do not underestimate yourself, Molly. You are very beautiful, and it is you I would like to marry and to be the mother of my children.'

'What will your family say?'

'Molly, I have just asked you to marry me, not my family. Yes? No?'

'Sì, Mario, sì!'

This was when Mario produced the ring. It was a beautiful sapphire, surrounded by diamonds in an antique setting, and it was absolutely beautiful. Molly had never owned anything so lovely.

'Oh, Mario...' She was almost speechless. And it fitted too.

'I am so happy! I must telephone my family. My *mamma* will be pleased.'

'Then you must meet my parents too. Have you time to come to Bristol?'

'We can go and return in one day?'

'Yes, if we leave early.'

'Then we shall go on the day before I go back.'

Molly pinched herself. Was this *real*? What would Mam and Dad say?

CHAPTER TWENTY-TWO

Eve

The decision had been made. They'd rented the flat until the end of January, and even though both Eve and Vanessa would have moved out by then, at least Molly could remain there for the time being. In the meantime, Christmas was looming again.

Eve opened her roster. '*When* did you say you were going to Bombay for Christmas, George?'

George looked up from his newspaper. 'Leaving next Monday.'

'I'm on the same flight!'

'Well, that's wonderful! Christmas together! What are the chances of *that*?'

'A hot Christmas!'

'And a *dry* one,' George added, referring to the fact that alcohol was prohibited in Bombay, though many ingenious methods had been used to smuggle it in over the years. Bribes were usually attempted; a bottle of Scotch passed under the counter could result in the customs officer waving them through without as much as a glance at their luggage. This tactic didn't always work though, and an overzealous officer would go through everyone's luggage with a fine-tooth comb and confiscate every drop of alcohol – even that which had been decanted to look like something else, such as gin sealed into tonic bottles and Scotch into ginger ales bottles. Some enterprising crew member had found a gadget in New York which put an authentic seal onto mixer bottles, but eventually customs had got wise to that too.

Eve was pleased that George would be with her as it would take her mind off that little eight-year-old boy somewhere in England.

'It would be nice if you could manage to come home for Christmas now and again,' Aileen had said drily, unaware that Eve requested to be overseas each year.

She couldn't bear the thought of playing happy families in Strathcannon, particularly now that Calum and Sheena had produced a little boy, and Aileen, like most grandmothers, was besotted.

'He's so lovely – my first wee grandchild,' she'd cooed to Eve.

'Except he's *not* your first grandson,' Eve had snapped.

Her mother had reacted, as she always did when *that* was alluded to, by rapidly changing the subject. 'Did I tell you that old Mrs MacPherson died?'

The customs officer at Bombay Airport was in a benevolent mood. This was fortunate because the crew who'd arrived the previous day had had every ounce of alcohol removed from their luggage – and their bodies.

When Eve's crew arrived at the hotel, they were greeted warmly by the unfortunate chief steward from the previous day's crew.

'But you're OK if you drink gin,' he added, 'because there's an Aussie here with an inexhaustible supply.'

The Australian Airlines steward had flown in a couple of days earlier from London and strolled through customs with an enormous green hosepipe neatly rolled up in its box. 'Can't get a hosepipe for love or money in Oz,' he'd told the officer cheerfully, ''cos there's a drought. Got this one in London, 'cos there's never a drought there!'

The officer had stifled a yawn and ignored him completely.

'He's told me that he rinsed it out well before he filled it with gin,' the steward added, 'but I suppose it might taste a bit rubbery.'

The hotel laid on a special dinner on Christmas Eve. A couple of long tables had been arranged near the pool and close to the beach, each swathed in white tablecloths. For authenticity, there was plastic holly and some damp-looking crackers alongside each place setting. Beneath the tables, obscured by the cloths, were bottles of all shapes and sizes, plus a long green hose.

The waiters who served them studiously ignored all the under-table activity going on, and so it took very little time for two British crews and one Australian crew to become tiddly, particularly the gin drinkers.

George was wrestling with his meal. 'If this scrawny thing is a turkey, I'll eat my hat!'

'Probably be tastier,' Eve remarked. As she spoke, she felt something warm and furry on her sandalled feet and hurriedly pushed her chair back. 'What the...!' she yelled as the most enormous rat she'd ever seen made its way slowly and methodically under the table, checking for any dropped edibles.

There were further screams as everyone pushed their chairs back, causing one girl, who was sitting near the pool, to lose her balance in the furore and fall in. Immediately, some of the men jumped in too, to keep her company. In the midst of the laughter and the chaos, there were cries of, 'Bloody hell, mind the bottles!' The rat, in the meantime, had taken himself off.

'Just think,' George said with longing as they repositioned themselves at the table, 'we could be eating a nice fat turkey, beside a real Christmas tree and a warm fire, gazing out at the falling snow!'

Eve laughed. 'You old traditionalist, you!'

'Nothing wrong with that. And drinking some decent wine.'

'Here, have some more gin! I'm developing a taste for the slight rubbery flavour!'

They woke up late, and very hungover, on Christmas morning in George's room. It was the larger of their two rooms and boasted a sea view, although the turquoise sea and white sand belied the misery of the shanty towns just a few yards away. Like everyone, Eve had found it difficult at first to come to terms with the extremities of Indian life, but, eventually, she'd accepted it because there was so little she could do about it.

Eve sat up in bed and groaned. 'Will we *ever* learn?'

George grunted.

'Wake up, because Father Christmas has been!'

Rubbing his eyes and his head, George propped himself up on one elbow and was eventually persuaded to unwrap the box on his bedside table.

'Oh, Eve, these are beautiful!'

She'd had two silk shirts made up for him in Singapore on a previous trip, one in black and the other in cream.

He leaned over and kissed her. 'I shall wear one of these this evening.' He extracted a small, professionally wrapped box from his drawer. 'Santa hasn't forgotten you either!'

It was obviously jewellery and, for a moment, Eve panicked

that he might have bought her a ring. *Oh please*, she thought, *don't let's have that damned argument again today of all days*! Then her eyes widened with delight as she uncovered a sparkling pair of emerald earrings and a matching pendant on a gold chain.

She gasped. 'Oh, George, these are absolutely stunning!'

She leaped out of bed and donned her jewellery to admire herself in the mirror, trying to avoid looking at her bleary eyes and dishevelled hair.

'They must only be worn by someone with glorious red hair,' George said.

Eve kissed him. 'Happy Christmas, George! I shall wear these tonight!'

'Perhaps you could take off that locket of yours for once and wear the emerald instead?'

'I'll wear the emerald as well,' Eve said, fondling the tiny locket which she never took off – and trying very hard not to think of a little boy opening his stocking somewhere back home.

CHAPTER TWENTY-THREE

Vanessa

Vanessa positioned her new armchair in front of the window, next to the Christmas tree. It blocked the light, so she moved it back again, unwilling to obscure the view out onto her little garden. It was bare and lifeless at the moment, but she fully intended to pretty it up when spring arrived. She straightened her beautiful William Morris-patterned curtains, and then flicked at some imaginary specks of dust on the Habitat kitchen work surfaces.

Johnny was due any minute. They'd have about three precious hours together before he had to head home to Dorset to spend Christmas with his family. The brand-new sheets – poly-cotton from New York – were on the brand-new bed, just waiting to be christened. He'd just landed from a long Far East trip, so he'd be tired and she mustn't let him fall asleep after-wards, tempting though it might be.

She heard the doorbell ring and automatically lifted her hand to smooth her already immaculate hair.

She opened the door. 'Johnny.'

He took her in his arms then stood back and studied her. 'You look gorgeous as always! Now, let me see this pad of yours!'

Proudly, Vanessa showed him round her new domain, beginning with the bedroom. 'First things first,' she said, giving him a wicked grin. 'I've painted this room yellow because Eve, my interior design adviser, chose the colour and said it was just right for a north-facing room. And do you like my bed?'

'Do I like your bed? What kind of a question is *that*? You bet I do!' He produced a bottle of bubbly from his cabin bag. 'I thought this might help to christen it!'

'Oh, lovely! But first you must see my sitting room and my little garden.'

With childlike enthusiasm, she showed him round the little flat.

'At last I can imagine you at home now,' he said. 'This is delightful.'

She'd only taken him to Bellingham Road a couple of times when the others were away, knowing they wouldn't approve.

'Are you hungry, Johnny?'

'Only for you, my darling!'

They stripped off with practised speed and, clinging to each other greedily, fell onto the bed. They hadn't been together for some weeks, so their lovemaking was fast and desperate.

'Oh, Nessa, if only I could be here for longer and make love to you slowly and passionately, and then *sleep*! Please know, my darling, that I would if I could.'

They sat up in bed and drank the champagne. He had one glass because he had a long drive ahead of him, but Vanessa topped up her own several times.

'How about I give you a key so you can come here anytime?' she suggested.

'And what if I was to find you entertaining some young blade?'

She laughed. 'That is *so* unlikely! And why not do your standbys here?'

He thought for a moment. 'I don't see why not. It's close enough to the airport, and I can always say that a crew member is letting out a spare bedroom. Do you have a spare bedroom, Miss Carter-Flint?'

'Oh, indeed I do, Captain Martell! But you are *not* going to be in it!'

'I should hope not as I'm already becoming very fond of your yellow walls! Oh, Nessa, I *do* wish I could spend Christmas with you!'

They had managed to wangle a few Christmases together down the routes over the years, but not this one. Much as she loved her little flat, Vanessa hadn't relished the prospect of spending Christmas alone or, even worse, spending it with her mother and James, who now spent most of their time sniping at each other. So she'd requested to be overseas and was now rostered for a three-day trip to Miami.

As he departed, Johnny handed Vanessa a little box. 'Not, on *any* account, to be opened before Christmas Day. I hope you get a nice crew for Miami and only wish I was one of them.' He held her tight in his arms. 'Happy Christmas, my darling.'

Molly

Molly had decided, in the interests of economy, to move back to Bristol until such time as she got married after their lease expired on Bellingham Road at the end of January. She hoped not to be flying for too much longer of course. Now she was spending Christmas at home, much to her parents' delight. Mario had suggested she came to Rome, but Molly felt it was too soon for all that. Anyway, this was probably the last

Christmas she'd spend with her family, and there'd be plenty of them in Rome.

Mario's visit had been a great success. He'd had a long conversation with Jack O'Hara, after which Jack had pronounced himself well satisfied with Molly's choice of husband.

'Such a handsome boy, and Catholic too!' Bridget had said approvingly. 'Thank goodness you're doing well for yourself, and not like that silly sister of yours. She's still with that good-for-nothing, and now she's six months pregnant. All *he* does is fry chips and things all day long. And *them not married*! I'm so ashamed!'

The wedding was to be in Rome. 'We couldn't have afforded to do much here,' her father said sadly, 'and Mario says his family can afford to arrange and pay for everything. He said we only needed to get ourselves on a plane and get over there, and we weren't to worry about a thing. Sure, he's a fine fellow. And your mother's practically wetting herself at the prospect of going to Italy and already wittering on about what she's going to wear.'

Molly decided it politic not to mention that she was planning to meet an American for dinner and drinks shortly after New Year. She saw no reason why she shouldn't, as she'd then be able to tell Patrick that she was now engaged, and that it was unlikely they'd be able to meet in the future. But he was a nice man, even if she didn't fancy him *like that*.

She enjoyed Christmas, particularly as Mario phoned from Italy. 'We shall not be apart at Christmas again, *cara*,' he assured her.

In the meantime, her beautiful sapphire ring was greatly admired. Connor was delighted for her, and even Siobhan admitted it was quite pretty, as she and her bump arrived with the 'cook', as her father referred to him. He was a nice enough man and, from all accounts, a good chef, even if he did wear his hair long and chain-smoked all the time. But, hopefully, not when he was cooking.

Patrick was staying at the Dorchester in Park Lane and, shortly after New Year, he invited Molly to dine with him there. Molly, who'd never been to the Dorchester before – or any smart West End hotels for that matter until Mario came on the scene – was suitably impressed and dug out the blue minidress and white boots again, but with a warm coat.

The lights were low, there was background music, the food was delicious and Patrick was the perfect gentleman.

'The thing is,' Molly told him, 'that I'm getting married in the summer.' He hadn't appeared to notice the ring. 'To an Italian.'

Patrick sighed. 'Lucky Italian! Oh, how I wish I'd met you first, Molly!'

Molly didn't comment. Although she liked him enormously, even if she *had* met him first, she wouldn't have fallen in love with him – but she couldn't say that of course.

'You'll be living in Italy?'

She nodded. 'Yes, in Rome. Mario's in the wine business and lives in Frascati, which is close to Rome.'

'I sometimes go to Rome on business,' Patrick said, 'so perhaps we can meet up again one day and you can tell me how you're coping with life in and around the Eternal City? Even if you have a *bambino* under each arm!'

'Who knows?' Molly beamed at him.

CHAPTER TWENTY-FOUR

Eve

It was the thirtieth of January, and their last night together at Bellingham Road. Eve was moving into her flat the very next morning; Vanessa had already moved but had come back for the occasion; and Molly was flying to Cairo in the morning and heading home to Bristol when she got back, having already transported her belongings into the O'Hara attic.

Eve sighed. 'I can't believe this; seven whole years we've been here!'

Vanessa lit a cigarette. 'And only Molly's found a husband.'

Molly looked round the familiar room. 'We've been so happy here, and we've never really had a row, have we?'

Eve laughed. 'Just the odd argument.'

Molly appeared quite tearful. 'Promise me we'll always be friends.'

'Of course we will,' Eve said, 'so long as you remember to ask us to Rome now and again.'

'Oh, I do hope you'll come often. I'm going to miss you both so much!'

Vanessa topped up their glasses. 'You know, I'm probably going to miss you more than you'll miss me. After all, you're going to an exciting new life in Italy, Molly, and you, Eve, will be a high-flying businesswoman!' She grinned. 'And poor old George, of course, will still be hanging around!'

Eve gritted her teeth. 'If anyone else refers to him as "poor old George" just once more, I'll bloody well scream! He's not under any kind of contract, you know! He's perfectly free to find someone else if he wants to. I've always been completely honest with him.'

'Sorry, sorry!' Vanessa raised her glass. 'Here's to *lucky* old George then, and to lucky old Mario, because they've both found real treasures in you two.'

'Thanks, Nessa,' Eve said, raising her glass too. 'I'm sure you're going to be very happy in that lovely flat.'

There was a moment's silence.

Vanessa gave a little sigh. 'All on my own though.' She hesitated. 'I *know* you think I'm wasting my life. *Everyone* thinks I'm wasting my life. But if I can't be Johnny's wife, then I don't want to be anyone's wife. Now, to change the subject, I have some other news. Skyline have asked me to be their model for a new advertising campaign. Publicity, photographs, advertisements, that sort of thing.'

'Nessa, that's great news!' Eve beamed.

'And you deserve it,' added Molly. 'You'll be the beautiful face of Skyline.'

'Thank you, girls,' Vanessa replied. 'And every time you come back to the UK, Molly, we three are going to get together for a very long, very alcoholic lunch and catch up on what's happening in each other's lives!'

'I'll drink to that!' said Molly, topping up her gin.

'Now, what about this wedding, Molly? Any decisions yet?' Eve asked.

'I'm flying out to Rome for a couple of days next week on

my stand-off, and we'll make the arrangements then, I expect. We've decided to marry in Rome because Mario has countless relatives who will have to be invited, so it's easier for my family to go over there. I'm getting discount tickets for Mam and Dad, but the others are all working, so they can pay their own fares, although Mario had offered to help. I'm going to see the church in Frascati, to meet the priest and the rest of his family. And set a date. And while we're on the subject, I'd like you both to be my bridesmaids.'

Vanessa's eyes widened, and Eve burst into tears.

'Oh, Molly, what an honour!' Eve said. 'But what about your sister?'

'Well, Siobhan and I have never been that close and she's also likely to have just given birth. I suppose I'll have to ask Donatella, Mario's sister. I'm not altogether sure what I'm supposed to do as it's all a bit of a minefield!'

'Never mind, Molly – we'll be there,' Vanessa said. 'Sounds like you're going to need moral support!'

'And please don't put us in pink frills,' Eve added with a grin. 'I've never looked good in pink!'

Mario knocked back his espresso in one gulp and gave an exaggerated sigh. 'It's always the same in this family when there's weddings,' he said, 'all this arguing about who to invite, who not to invite.'

The wedding wasn't until the end of May, but Graziana's guest list had already reached frightening proportions. She rubbed her forehead. 'What about Zio Vincenzo?'

'Uncle Vincenzo is nuts,' said Mario, 'so *no*.'

Graziana sighed loudly and turned to Molly. 'You know we don't have bridesmaids in Italy—'

'We've been through all this already, Mamma!' Mario was

becoming increasingly exasperated. 'Molly wants bridesmaids, and that's *that.*'

Graziana wasn't done yet. 'And, Molly, you tell your friends in England, *no white*! Only the *bride* will wear white, as a sign of purity.' She looked doubtfully at her prospective daughter-in-law. 'And I hope they won't be wearing these skirts *above the knees*!'

Vanessa

Neither Eve nor Vanessa were wildly happy at the prospect of being bridesmaids, and so it was a relief when they were told that she was only allowed one, and it had to be her sister. Molly was sleeping on Eve's camp bed, and they'd got together in Vanessa's flat.

'It's not the thing apparently,' Molly said sadly. 'We just have a witness each, and I have to have Siobhan, and Mario has to have his brother, Alessandro. I'm sorry, girls, but there it is. I got quite exhausted arguing about it all, but, as the Bellinis are doing most of the paying, I had to go along with it.'

'Whose bloody wedding is this anyway?' Vanessa muttered under her breath to Eve.

Eve put her arm round Molly. 'Well, I'd love to have been your bridesmaid of course, but Nessa and I will be close by to give you all the support you need.'

'And we can choose our own outfits,' Vanessa said with obvious relief.

'Only the bride wears white,' Molly went on, 'no one else.' She grinned. 'Purity and all that.'

'We'd better find little black dresses then,' Vanessa said.

'In the meantime, will you come with me for my dress fitting?'

. . .

On a very cold February day, Eve and Vanessa shivered in the inadequately heated Belle's Bridal Boutique, while Belle went through to her workroom to find Molly's dress. She emerged several minutes later with the dress and directed Molly into the changing room.

'Why is it so *cold* in here?' Vanessa demanded haughtily. 'You can't have the bride shivering and getting double pneumonia before her wedding.'

Belle sighed and went off in search of a fan heater, which she plugged in alongside the changing room. With her toe, Vanessa pushed the heater inside, to where Molly was stripping off.

It was about five minutes before Molly emerged in her puritanical white, looking beautiful but apprehensive. The dress was floor length, had a square neckline and long sleeves. It was elegant and showed off Molly's light tan to perfection.

'Fab-u-lous!' Eve exclaimed.

Vanessa was silent for a moment. 'Molly, you look bloody stunning!'

As she drove back to Twickenham, Vanessa felt somewhat depressed. She'd never contemplated a white wedding for herself, unlike some girls who dreamed of little else. Nevertheless, seeing Molly looking so radiant in that dress, she'd felt some strange stirrings of envy.

She, Vanessa Carter-Flint, envious? Surely not! This was a completely new emotion. Underneath her cool, groomed, sophisticated exterior, was she becoming as potty as the rest of them?

She'd found her Mr Right, but, unfortunately, someone else had found him first. There would be no wedding, white or otherwise, for them. Not that marriage was so important; she'd have been quite happy to defy convention and 'live in sin', as they put it. After all, this was 1972 and attitudes were changing. What really hurt was that they could never openly be a couple, except in faraway locations where they were unknown. She could never introduce him to her mother, to her friends, as she so longed to do. Every meeting took weeks of planning, scheming, begging and bribing the rostering department. And how she would have loved to be with Johnny at the wedding in Rome!

The only time they were accepted, or at least ignored, was when the plane had climbed up through the clouds into the unbroken blue above. Convention could be left behind for the duration of the trip, in this cloudless no man's land. A sunshine club! But the time always came to descend through those clouds again, to face reality. Girls went back to boyfriends, fiancés and, in a few clandestine cases, husbands. The guys went back to girlfriends and wives. Vanessa went back to Twickenham.

She'd hardly got her coat off when the doorbell rang. Irritated, Vanessa opened the door to find her mother there, swathed in mink.

'Mother, what on earth...?'

'You wanted me to come to see your flat, so here I am.' Hermione swanned in without further ado.

'It's not like *you* to appear out of the blue.'

Hermione cast her gaze round the sitting room. 'This is quite nice. Have you got heating on? Is it warm enough for me to take off my coat?'

'Of course it is. Let me take your coat and I'll hang it up.' Vanessa disappeared briefly with the fur. 'So, to what do I owe the honour of this visit?'

Hermione sank into an armchair. 'Well, the fact is that I'm planning to leave James. We've just had the most awful row – you can't *imagine*!'

Vanessa sighed. 'I can imagine. You're always rowing.'

'I'm tired of it, so I'm leaving him, and he'll be free to live with his trollop.'

'His *trollop*?'

'I don't know her name, only that she's young enough to be his daughter. Aren't they *always*? It's been going on for years apparently, but the wife's always the last to know of course. How *dare* he make a fool out of me? I've been completely faithful to him for years and years, and don't think for one moment that I haven't had many propositions and temptations, let me tell you! I've always stuck with the boring old fool, and now *this*!' Hermione dug into her handbag, produced a cigarette, inserted it into an elegant holder and lit it.

Vanessa took a moment to find her voice. 'Drink?'

'Have you Scotch? Soda's fine.'

Vanessa got up to get the drink. 'Mother,' she said, 'this sort of thing happens all the time. And it's not as if you *loved* James.'

'That's not the point!' Hermione snapped.

No, thought Vanessa, *it probably isn't. The tables have turned; you're the one with the long history of straying.* She remembered only too well the gossip in Kenya as Hermione dallied from man to man.

'What sort of woman would set her sights on somebody else's husband?' Hermione asked. 'Tell me *that*!'

Vanessa handed her mother the drink and poured one for herself.

'A *trollop*, that's who!' Hermione went on. 'A trollop who can't find a man of her own!' She gulped her drink. 'Anyway, I shall need some temporary accommodation while I look around for something suitable. I *would* like to be back in London again.'

Vanessa was beginning to feel quite faint. 'Is that why you're here?'

'Well, you did say you had two bedrooms and, anyway,

you're *away* half the time. I've made it quite clear to James that I shall be leaving. I shall pay a generous rent.'

'But you *can't!*'

'Why ever not? I shan't interfere with your love life. And, Nessa darling, I hate to say it, but I did help you to *buy* this place.'

Vanessa was thinking rapidly. 'Yes, I know you did, and I'm truly grateful. It's just that I let out my spare room to crew members on standby and I can't now let them down. They come from all over the country, you see, and they depend on this.' She wasn't altogether sure that her mother believed her. 'Surely you can rent somewhere else? In Central London perhaps?'

Hermione narrowed her eyes as she drained her drink. 'Have you a secret lover or something?'

Molly

'But we *can't!*' Molly stared at Mario in disbelief.

'It's only until we find a place of our own, *cara*. This apartment is *huge*! There is room for us all, and Mamma won't interfere.'

Molly was in Rome to make final arrangements, and now Mario was telling her that they would be starting their married life in his mother's apartment.

'Surely there's *somewhere* we could rent?' she asked in desperation.

Mario shook his head. 'I have looked everywhere and there is nothing. I want us to have a beautiful place, Molly, and not take the first thing that comes along. And it will cost us nothing to live here, so we can save some money, no?'

Molly looked round in despair. Yes, it was certainly a large apartment. It was also drearily dark and filled to capacity with heavy, overly ornate furniture. Terence Conran, and Eve for that matter, could have a field day here. She suspected that Graziana had more than a little to do with this arrangement. Did she want to hang on to her precious son for as long as possible? Or was it because she wanted to keep an eagle eye on this foreign daughter-in-law who travelled the world, smoke, drank and wore a miniskirt? Molly suspected it was a little of both, but, with the wedding only a month away, she was in no position to argue. As soon as she was living there, Molly would devote every minute to finding a suitable apartment.

'But what about my *things*?' she asked. 'And our wedding presents?'

'No problem, *cara*,' said Mario. 'We will make ourselves a little apartment with the two bedrooms at the back, and the larger things can be stored until we move. It will be fine.'

There were five bedrooms in the apartment. At the moment, Graziana, Donatella and Mario occupied one each. You had to walk through the fourth bedroom to access the fifth, which was smaller, but Molly thought this smaller one could be their bedroom, and the larger one their sitting room. That left the kitchen, and she dreaded sharing a kitchen. Particularly with Graziana.

As if reading her thoughts, Mario said, 'It will be wonderful because Mamma can show you how to make all my favourite dishes!'

CHAPTER TWENTY-FIVE

Molly

Molly had never been afraid of flying. Never, for one moment, until she fell in love with Mario. Now life had become more precious, and more precarious, as far as she was concerned. She'd had seven happy years flying to incredible places, and she'd miss that. She felt sad too that she'd miss that special, unique camaraderie that existed between crews. Where else would a motley collection of people be teamed together and not only get the job done but, more often than not, have fun too. And make friendships. Affairs of course. Molly thought of Vanessa. A job divorced from reality most of the time, under a cloudless sky. A sunshine club.

But she was tired. The work was arduous, the hours long and the time differences hard to cope with. But now a new emotion had engulfed her: fear. Fear that the plane wasn't going to make it and she would be denied the chance of happiness with Mario. Suddenly, she was aware of turbulence and was white-knuckled on take-off and landing. To compound the fear, both Lufthansa and United Airlines had been hijacked recently, and an Alitalia DC8 had crashed near Palermo, killing more than a hundred people. *It must be my turn*, thought Molly. *Things have been going too well for me.*

Something else she'd really miss would be that first glimpse of home, particularly arriving back from the west on a cloudless summer morning, when they crossed the coast of Scotland, Ireland, Wales or Cornwall. The incredible green of the gentle countryside, the little fields, the familiarity of it all. Home. No place quite like it, no matter how great the trip had been.

Molly had never thought she'd be able to leave it all. Until she met Mario.

Her final trip was to Chicago, not one of her favourite places. They had a great room party though, the night before they left to come home, to celebrate her leaving and to wish her well. The captain was a lovely man and he even made an announcement on the return flight that Miss O'Hara was on her final trip and was going to marry and live in Italy. Applause all round, and several Italian Americans wished her well and asked where she'd be living in 'the old country'.

Shortly after take-off, the captain summoned Eddie, the chief steward, up onto the flight deck. He returned a few minutes later, ashen-faced.

'You OK?' Molly asked as she and Joe, the first steward, emerged from the galley area.

'Some nutcase has just been in touch with O'Hare Airport to inform them that there's a bomb on board this flight.'

'*What?*' Molly and Joe echoed together.

'Probably a hoax, but we've no way of knowing. It's due to go off on the descent, when we get to twenty thousand feet or something. And we've no idea where the bloody thing is likely to be. I think I fancy a drink.'

'You and me both,' said Joe, producing a bottle of brandy and three glasses. 'So what are we supposed to do now?'

'Not much. The skipper's trying to find out more from

Chicago, and the engineer's going to go down into the hold to check what he can. But there's no way we can check the cabin because we've got a full load and there'd be mass panic.'

Molly felt sick. She'd known, of course, that she was doomed now that she'd found The Man. Real love at last. But *never* to know wedded bliss. She knocked back her drink quickly, immediately feeling one degree better.

'Carry on as usual,' Eddie went on, 'and for God's sake don't let the passengers get wind of the fact that anything might be wrong. But keep your eyes open, both of you.' With that, he headed back into the economy cabin to spread the tidings.

Molly was trying hard not to cry. 'I'm supposed to be getting *married*!'

Joe put an arm round her. 'And my wife's about to have our first baby. C'mon, we've got to keep busy. It's probably a hoax anyway. And we've got a meal to serve. The last supper perhaps?' He laughed nervously.

Somehow or other, they managed to serve drinks and dinner to twenty first-class passengers, fortifying themselves with the occasional brandy.

'I have no intention of being blown up sober,' said Joe as the engineer lifted the hatch and lowered himself into the hold.

The captain was philosophical. 'Apparently, it's some weird group who want independence for Illinois or something, although what good blowing up a British jet would do, I cannot imagine. If this thing exists at all, it could be tiny.'

They served breakfast one and a half hours out of London. Molly's insides had been churning all night, but she managed, with difficulty, to keep her cool in the cabin. Then came that change in engine noise as the aircraft began its long descent.

Molly cleared away the stray cups and glasses that lurked around the flight deck as usual. 'Nice sunny morning,' the captain remarked cheerfully as he handed her a plate.

Everyone seemed to be calm. Molly, like all crew, had been

trained in how to cope in an emergency, but she was feeling sick inside. *I want to live! I don't want to die because some bloody lunatic wants bloody independence for bloody Illinois!*

Inevitably, the time came when everything was cleared and stowed away. Molly and Joe settled themselves in the crew seats by the front door, and the descent continued.

'How will we know when we get to twenty thousand feet or whatever it is?' Molly asked anxiously.

'When we hear the bang.'

'Joe, that's *not* funny.'

'We've got to try to make it funny, Molly. I'm as scared as you are, but there's nothing we can do. We can't stay up here forever.'

The flight-deck door was open for landing, and Molly could hear them making the usual checks. And then the engineer, much louder than normal, called out, 'Fifteen thousand feet!'

Molly squeezed Joe's arm. 'Did you *hear* that?'

He nodded mutely, and then they heard the sound of the undercarriage being lowered. 'We're OK, Molly. Don't cry!'

There were tears of relief as the aircraft touched down and the engines roared into reverse thrust. Molly composed herself in order to make the landing announcement, but the captain beat her to it.

'Ladies and gentlemen,' he said, 'we have just landed at Heathrow Airport, London. For your information, we did have a bomb threat on board this flight, which, mercifully, has turned out to be a hoax. Please do not be alarmed at the emergency vehicles you can see alongside as this is standard emergency procedure.'

Molly could hear the raised, panicking voices of the passengers as they digested this news.

'Although it appears to have been a hoax,' the captain continued, 'the authorities here wish to isolate our aircraft and, for that reason, we shall be parked some distance away from the terminal building, and we will be disembarking via the emergency chutes.'

The cacophony of voices had now reached fever pitch, and people were beginning to push their way through the cabins.

'Our cabin crews are trained to operate these chutes and get everyone out of the plane quickly and safely. Please do as you are instructed. Go to the nearest exit, leave all your personal belongings behind and jump into the chutes. Then, get as far away from the aircraft as you can, and buses will collect you. Your personal belongings will be returned to you later, when we know for sure that the plane is safe. Good luck, and thank you.'

Passengers were now jostling and pushing past each other to get out as Molly and Joe operated the chutes on the front doors of the plane. Fortunately, both floated down to the tarmac without a hitch.

Molly grabbed each passenger by the arm. 'Jump! Sit! *Quick!*' She was shouting herself hoarse. Predictably, some people were panicking, and some people considered it all a big joke.

Finally, both Molly and Joe were able to jump onto the chutes themselves, and the crew were united in a group some distance from the plane. Relief and exhaustion flooded Molly's veins. She was safe! And she'd managed to keep her cool. She'd often wondered how she'd cope in an emergency, training or not.

'You've all done a fantastic job,' the captain said, looking around. Then, turning to Molly, he added, 'A memorable final trip for you, my dear!'

CHAPTER TWENTY-SIX

Molly

'I've never seen you look so beautiful, Molly,' Jack O'Hara said proudly. 'You look like a model in that dress, and you seem so *tall*!'

Molly lifted the hem of her dress. 'Four-inch heels, Dad!'

'How on earth will you ever walk in them?'

'Goodness knows. I'll just concentrate on not tripping. Now, are we ready to go?'

The O'Hara clan had arrived two days previously and been warmly welcomed by the Bellinis.

'They're fine people,' Jack had pronounced. 'It's just that Italy's so far away.'

'Only a couple of hours' flying time, Dad. Less time than it takes to drive to London from Bristol.'

'Maybe.' Her father had looked doubtful.

Bridget, on the other hand, had been eager to look her best. 'I've spent months trying to find an outfit,' she told Molly. She pirouetted in a pale-blue suit. 'Are you sure this looks OK?'

'It's lovely, Mum. Stop worrying.'

'It cost an arm and a leg, and then I had to have it shortened. What do you think of my perm?'

Privately, Molly thought her mother's head looked like a grey chrysanthemum, topped with a blue pillbox hat which she was having great difficulty keeping in place on top of the bouncy curls. 'You look *great!*'

All her brothers had made the effort, and even Siobhan – minus the chef – had come too, complete with a tiny baby who was called Wayne. Just as well these Italians loved babies so much, particularly blonde ones.

Eve

Eve, dressed in emerald green, and Vanessa, in royal blue, were seated at the front of the church, just behind Molly's mother.

'Isn't this just the most beautiful church?' Bridget murmured, adjusting her hatpin for the umpteenth time as she turned round. 'Have you seen these frescoes?'

'Yes, lovely,' Eve agreed, enjoying the cool of the dark, ornate interior.

'She made me wear mascara,' Bridget went on, 'and I'm that frightened it'll run, because I'm bound to cry.'

'Don't you worry, Mrs O'Hara, because I have loads of tissues.'

'Just as well I made the effort,' Bridget said, sighing, 'because will you just *look* at these Italian women! I've never seen so much glamour in my entire life. Do you know, I saw an Italian film once, set in some village or other, and all the older Italian women seemed to totter around in black dresses and black stockings.'

'Not round here they don't!'

Then, as she watched a very proud Jack O'Hara walk his

elegant daughter up the aisle, Eve could hardly believe that all this was the result of a chance meeting over a cup of coffee, opposite the Pantheon.

―――――

Molly

Molly was concentrating on not tripping as she walked slowly up the aisle to meet her *fidanzato*. Although she'd hoped at one time that they might marry in the *duomo*, she'd come to love the church of San Rocco, with its beautiful twelfth-century bell tower and wonderful frescoes. She could see herself coming in here on her own in years to come. And there would, hopefully, be christenings and confirmations too!

'*Tu sei bellissima!*' Mario whispered as she arrived by his side.

―――――

Eve

No doubt about it, Molly looked gorgeous and Mario very handsome, and they made a stunning couple amidst a huge group of some of the most elegant people Eve had ever seen. The Italians certainly knew how to dress up for the occasion.

'Have you ever seen so many posers?' Vanessa asked as they grouped, and regrouped, for countless photographs.

Eve giggled. 'But they have so much *style!*'

She'd found parts of the ceremony confusing, as she hadn't been to many Catholic Masses, particularly with a mixture of Latin and Italian. The incense had been catching on her breath at times, and she'd had to concentrate on not coughing. But how beautiful everything was! And what a feast for the eyes, and the ears, and, indeed, all the senses, as opposed to the comparative austerity of the Church of Scotland! But how would Molly ever be able to understand this beautiful, melodic, crazy language?

And would I want all this? Eve asked herself, looking around. Most definitely not. *Just for a start*, she thought, *I shall not be getting married. There are quite a few fanciable men around though, and some of them have been looking at me! I suppose it's my hair.*

Vanessa

Vanessa was well aware of being admired and remarked upon. The men seemed mesmerised. *Well*, she thought, *I'm a whole lot taller than most of these women, and that Gianni – or whatever his name was – has done an amazing job on my hair.* She was enjoying the attention, and the only thing that marred her day was the absence of Johnny. If *only* he could have been there!

But would I want all this paraphernalia? she wondered. No, of course not. A quick trip to Richmond-upon-Thames Registry Office would fit the bill nicely. She was happy for Molly but didn't fancy the mother-in-law much. From what she'd heard, Graziana was a formidable woman who appeared to distrust everyone north of Sicily. That woman could be trouble. Mario's brother was a good-looking devil though! What was his name – Alessandro? She'd enjoy a nice little flirt with him if she could just get him away from that chubby little wife of his.

Then a worrying thought occurred to her. Why did she never fancy *single men*?

Eve

The reception at Susanna's, overlooking the lake at Castel Gandolfo, lasted for almost eight hours. There was course after course after course, and all delicious.

'We're never going to be able to fit into our uniforms after this lot,' Vanessa moaned as she sampled her third plate of pasta.

Eve sighed as she sat back in her chair. 'Just as well they're small portions. They're supposed to be *appetisers*, Nessa! We still have a fish and a meat course to come, not to mention the dessert – and the cake!'

They were seated opposite each other, Vanessa with Molly's brother, Fergal, on one side and an ancient uncle of Mario's on the other. The uncle spoke no English and sucked his teeth noisily after each mouthful. Eve had Molly's twin, Connor, on one side, and Silvio – of double-date fame – on the other. He was being very attentive in spite of being accompanied by a very tiny and very chic lady with hair hanging down to her bottom.

'She from Napoli and no speak English,' said Silvio as he explained the contents of each course as they were served. The fact that she was from Napoli seemed to give him licence to flirt as much as he liked. He also kept filling up her wine glass, causing Eve to wonder what his intentions were. In spite of their glamorous girlfriends and wives, both Vanessa and Eve were attracting admiring glances from most of the men present. Eve felt a little uncomfortable about this, but Vanessa appeared to be enjoying it.

Then came the dancing. Eve lost count of the number of men who wanted to partner her, and Vanessa danced with every man in the room, with the exception of Alessandro.

Molly

Molly and Mario flew to London the following morning, to connect with the flight to Barbados, where they would spend their two-weeks honeymoon. Molly had got discount tickets, the last she'd be entitled to, and Mario was paying for fourteen nights at the Dolphin Beach, where the crews stayed and where they got a further discount.

They'd had a terrific send-off from Frascati, with both families showering them with *coriandoli*, and even Graziana had kissed her fondly.

As they boarded the flight for Barbados, Molly could scarcely believe her eyes when she saw who the chief steward was.

'*Martin!*' she squealed.

'Well, I heard you were getting married,' he said as he shook hands with Mario. 'Now, come along, I've got two nice first-class seats for you!'

'He took me on my very first trip,' she explained to Mario as they settled themselves in the luxurious seats. She smiled to herself at the memory. 'We were both working down at the back then.'

'He seems very nice,' Mario said, 'and what luxury!'

Martin returned with a bottle of champagne and two glasses. 'Don't go spilling that now,' he said with a grin.

As they raised their glasses to each other, Mario said, 'How many more surprises have you got for me, *cara*?'

Molly turned and kissed him on the cheek. 'Just the one, *caro*! I think I may be pregnant!'

CHAPTER TWENTY-SEVEN

2015

'I hated the eighties,' Vanessa said sadly, 'because it was a time of great tragedy for me.'

'It wasn't *all* bad,' Eve pointed out.

'At least you and I were speaking to each other again!' Vanessa said.

'Do you remember it must have been at the beginning of the eighties that we made the pilgrimage back to Bellingham Road?' Molly asked, in an effort to change the subject.

'Sometimes,' Eve sighed, 'I wish we hadn't.'

'The pub was still there on the corner,' Vanessa said.

'That whole row of old houses had been razed,' Molly recalled, 'to make way for that awful office building.'

'Time moves on,' Vanessa said, 'and nothing stays the same. There were *huge* changes in my life.'

'There were huge changes in all of our lives,' added Eve.

'We live and learn,' remarked Molly, 'but I certainly won't be going back to Bellingham Road again.'

1982

CHAPTER TWENTY-EIGHT

Vanessa

Vanessa was exhausted. She'd spent the day freezing, on the steps of a Skyline 747, smiling until her mouth ached and waving manically, while Archie, the enthusiastic photographer, took photograph after photograph. The chosen ones would appear in the national press with some clichéd heading like 'Come Fly with Me'. They would, of course, look unposed and natural, and no one would know that she'd spent hours being shouted at, in a force-eight gale.

'Turn your head just a bit to the right, sweetie! To the left now... Keep that smile going! Don't forget to wave!' There was no doubt Archie was a fine photographer, but he was a bossy little man, full of his own importance, and given to sticking a finger up his right nostril when he was agitated, which was most of the time. Vanessa hoped never to set eyes on him again – unless perhaps he was working for *Vogue* or someone like that.

She'd done a great deal of publicity work for Skyline over the past few years, to the extent that she was being recognised in the street. 'Hey, aren't you that *Skyline girl*?' Girl, indeed!

Here she was pushing forty, for goodness' sake! She could see the fine little lines appearing round her eyes, and soon no one would want her to model anything, other than washing machines perhaps. Apart from the Skyline stuff, Barty had managed to find her some catwalk jobs and some photographic modelling for a mail-order catalogue. So far, Skyline appeared unaware of her other publicity work, which was probably just as well, since Vanessa had no idea if she was supposed to be doing that or not. She was a route stewardess now, supervising the cabin service, but she'd opted to cut down her hours. This meant that she normally only did a couple of short trips a month, or one longer trip. Nevertheless, she was now able to live comfortably on her slightly reduced salary, plus any modelling fees.

Then there was Johnny; dear, dear Johnny. He would only be flying for another couple of years before he finally retired. He should have been retired by now but had been granted a further contract because they were currently short of captains on the 'minis', most of the younger ones having transferred to the 747s. How would she ever cope if Johnny retired? What possible excuse could they have to see each other? After all these years, she still lived for their meetings. His libido showed no signs of diminishing, and she loved him as much as ever. She'd even turned down the opportunity of transferring to the jumbo fleet herself, because then there'd be no opportunity at all of flying with him.

As she got into her new yellow Triumph Stag, Vanessa decided she needed a tonic. She was feeling extremely tired and had begun to wonder if she was going to be one of those women who experienced an early menopause. She made an appointment with Dr Kyle at the Skyline Medical Centre.

· · ·

'Good to see you, Vanessa,' he said, several days later. 'What seems to be the trouble?'

She had rehearsed a list of all the little niggles which were plaguing her and managed to remember most of them.

The doctor studied her file. 'Let's give you a thorough check then. How long have you been flying now? *Seventeen* years! This job takes its toll on you girls, you know.'

An hour later, Vanessa got back to her car, where she sat in a state of complete shock. She was none too sure she was capable of driving home, but she was certainly going to need a stiff drink when she did.

CHAPTER TWENTY-NINE

Eve

Training stewardess Eve Muir looked at the sea of eager faces in front of her; girls and boys all determined to join Skyline's expanding 747 fleet. She could still remember how terrified she'd been when she'd begun her own training all those years ago, and she never wanted these young people to feel like that. The training was just as thorough now as it had been then, but it was more relaxed and enjoyable now. The 747 was a huge aircraft, and there was a lot to learn in eight weeks, particularly now that there was a business-class cabin wedged between first class and economy.

Eve enjoyed training. She only did, on average, two or three courses a year, ensuring that she was free on Saturdays to work in Elite Interiors. The rest of the year she flew as a route stewardess, checking on the standard of Skyline service worldwide. She could, within reason, choose her trips now, and she had generous time off. Nadia, now married with two children, could only work part-time in the shop, and so they had taken on Liz, who had turned out to be an absolute gem. According to Nadia, Liz could sell a freezer to an Eskimo.

The shop had expanded to twice its original size. When the estate agency next door had moved to new premises, they'd taken it over. Their interiors were known to rival John Lewis and Sandersons, for their extensive range of upholstery and imported accessories. Word had got around, and customers came from all over the place to look and, more importantly, to buy.

Eve still lived above the shop. Although she now had the wherewithal to move to something more luxurious, she never seemed to have enough time to do anything about it. Besides, it was so convenient – although the street had become busier and noisier than when she had first moved in.

Aileen had paid a couple of visits but hadn't been wildly impressed at having to sleep on a bed-settee in the sitting room, which had to be folded away every morning and made up again at night.

'Well, hardly anyone ever stays here,' Eve had told her mother. 'Just yourself occasionally, and Molly sometimes when she needs to escape from the Bellini clan.'

It had also been a huge relief to Eve when George had finally found someone he wanted to marry – and, more importantly, who wanted to marry him. She did miss him though, because they'd been together for a long time, but she had to admit she'd treated him like a pair of comfortable old slippers. Nice to come home to. No effort required.

When she'd started training cabin crews, she'd hardly set eyes on him for weeks on end sometimes, and it hadn't entered her head that he might get fed up sitting around waiting. George had put up with this for a few months, and then he'd done a Caracas trip with a lovely stewardess called Belinda. Belinda had been married to an insurance broker in Basingstoke, who, while she was on a ten-day trip, had found comfort in the arms of another lady after she'd come to get some quotes for insuring her new Ferrari. He'd been rather impressed with her and gone out of his way to get the best quote possible, which had earned him a ride in the Ferrari, plus some extras. The end result was a sad, disillusioned Belinda and a sympathetic, understanding George. They'd commiserated with each other for the entire eight days of the trip, discussing the sad lack of commitment of their respective partners and the general promiscuity taking place all around them. They were perfect soulmates and were married within the year, baby Emily appearing precisely nine months later. George was ecstatic.

Eve felt a mixture of relief and sadness. She was happy for George because he'd got exactly what he'd always wanted, and what she wasn't prepared to give him. Nevertheless, she did miss him and had to admit that, just sometimes, she felt a teeny bit lonely.

CHAPTER THIRTY

Eve

Molly was about to pay a visit to London. She was coming, alone, for three whole days, to attend the christening of her brother Liam's newest baby. Mario was on a business trip to Scandinavia which couldn't be cancelled, and so the children were going to be looked after by Graziana.

'I'm so looking forward to seeing you and Vanessa again,' she said on the phone to Eve, 'and catching up on all the gossip, not to mention getting a few days away from this crazy lot.'

Over the years, Eve had visited her several times in Frascati. Molly, Mario and the three boys lived in a three-bedroomed apartment with glorious wrought-iron balconies outside every room and far-reaching views. The children were adorable but very noisy, and Eve swore that she could still hear their little voices reverberating inside her head for days after she got home. It would be good to talk without kids in the background. Furthermore, Vanessa had asked them to lunch, and *that* was a first.

Molly

Molly double-checked everything in the apartment before she left. She'd taken the boys to Graziana's in the morning, along with countless changes of clothing, toys, schoolbags, lunch boxes and other sundry items. It would have been so much easier if only Graziana had agreed to move into *their* apartment for a few days. But no, the old bat would not. Donatella, on a visit home from Milan with her husband and one-year-old twins, had kindly offered to share the childcare, so goodness knows how they'd all cram in together.

Now, the apartment felt strangely empty. No noisy Stefano crashing around on his roller skates, no mischievous Marcello kicking a ball against the new furniture, or chubby little Carlo trying to keep up with his brothers.

Her friend, Elena, was coming within the hour to drive her to Fiumicino to catch the evening flight to London. She'd stay one night with Liam, then move on to Eve for three nights. Vanessa was keen for the three of them to have a wander down Bellingham Road, for old times' sake, and was doing them a lunch the following day. Molly was so looking forward to it.

'I can't believe it!' Molly exclaimed as they sipped glasses of wine in the Mucky Duck, at the end of Bellingham Road. 'That ugly office block where our flat used to be!'

'We should have expected this, I suppose,' Eve said morosely. 'It's happening everywhere.'

Vanessa gave a deep sigh. 'I'd come to love that little flat, and we made it really nice.'

'Our little sunshine club,' Molly added. 'I wonder when they knocked down the old houses?'

'Probably quite recently because that office block looks very new and very empty,' Vanessa said.

Molly looked round at the interior of the Victorian pub, which had changed little over the years. 'My brothers stayed here when they came to our New Year party.'

'It's still pretty naff,' Vanessa observed, 'but at least they've got rid of the flock wallpaper.'

'And the jukebox,' Eve added. 'Perhaps we shouldn't have come, because it would be better to remember everything the way it was.'

'Not that we came in *here* all that often,' said Molly.

'And I certainly shan't be coming again,' Vanessa said decisively, draining her wine glass. 'Let's go.'

Vanessa

Vanessa had prepared a three-course lunch. There was champagne and Chablis chilling in the fridge, and a line-up of bottles of Nuits-Saint-Georges on the sideboard. Hopefully, the meal would continue for most of the afternoon and well into the evening, because there was so much to talk about! She did see Eve at the airport occasionally, and they did try to get together about once a month for lunch, and to catch up on the gossip. But Vanessa still missed them both, particularly Molly's cheerful chatter.

Now, in view of her recent doctor's appointment, she felt the need to talk to them more than ever. They'd had that brief visit to the pub in Bellingham Road shortly after Molly's arrival yesterday, but they'd saved all their news for today.

She had to stop herself from rushing to the door at the first peal of the doorbell!

Vanessa hugged them both and went to fetch some champagne from the fridge. Then, the three of them comfortably seated with full glasses, Vanessa said, 'Wow, this is almost like old times! Now, I want to hear what's been going on. You first, Molly.'

Molly sipped her champagne. 'Well, Mario and I are looking for a bigger apartment or house now we have the three boys. Mind you, after the couple of years we had to spend with Graziana, the place we have now is heaven, but it's just getting a little cramped.'

'And the boys?'

'Well, Stefano's eight and is doing well at school, and of course he's completely bilingual now. Marcello just had his sixth birthday and wants to be a famous footballer and Carlo's only four but already says he'd like to be on the telly! He watches far too much TV!'

'And how's the fearsome *mamma*-in-law?'

'Graziana is the same as ever, but fortunately she's now half a mile away.'

'And the lovely Mario?' Eve asked.

'The lovely Mario's in Sweden right now. The business is doing well fortunately, but it means he's away a lot. What else? Ah yes, I am nearly fluent in Italian!'

'That's great,' Vanessa said, standing up. 'Come to the table now and let's have all your news, Eve. You must hear all the Skyline scandal now that you're in the office so much.'

As they ate their avocado starter, Eve regaled them with all the gossip: who'd left, who'd got married and who was having affairs with whom.

'Oh, I do miss it all sometimes,' Molly confessed. 'Much as I love Mario and the boys, there are days when I dream of being down the routes again.'

The Skyline gossip continued for most of the meal, and it wasn't until Vanessa was clearing away the plates and brewing coffee that Eve asked, 'And what about you, Nessa? We haven't heard yet what you've been up to, although I keep seeing your picture in the papers, you glamorous thing!'

Vanessa was concentrating hard on pouring the coffee. 'Well, yes, I do have some news, which will doubtless shake you both rigid... I'm pregnant.'

There was a moment's astounded silence.

Molly found her voice first. 'Nessa, *wow*! *Unbelievable*! My God, you're nearly forty!'

'Yes, I'm aware of that, but the doctor says I'm fine and everything is proceeding normally.'

Eve remained silent.

'I hardly dare ask this,' Molly said, 'but I assume it's Johnny's?'

'*Of course* it's Johnny's! And now I've got used to the idea, I'm thrilled to bits!'

'Did you forget to take your pill or something?' Molly asked.

'Not sure. I did another round-the-world, east to west, so I get all confused with that bloody dateline.'

'And have you told Johnny yet?' Molly asked, casting an eye at the silent Eve.

'Not yet. I'm gathering my courage to tell him next time I see him.'

Eve cleared her throat. 'And what exactly are you planning to do about it?'

'*Do* about it?' Vanessa echoed. 'What do you mean? I'm not going to *do* anything about it except plod through the next six months and then, presumably, give birth.'

Eve was studying her intently. 'And then what?'

'And then I'll have a baby.'

'You mean you're planning to *keep* it?'

'Of course I will! What do you expect me to do with it – raffle it off?'

Eve pulled back her chair and stood up. 'I think that is the most selfish thing I've ever heard! How can you possibly bring up a baby on your own?'

Vanessa was quite taken aback. 'Eve, I didn't plan this, but now it's happened, I've discovered that I want this baby very badly. It's Johnny's, and it means I'll have a little bit of him, come what may. I'm sure I'll manage, and I'm hoping Johnny might help out too. I'll probably go back flying part-time and hire a nanny or something.'

'I think that's great,' said Molly.

Eve was still standing and glaring at Vanessa. 'And what about the stigma? How are you going to explain the lack of a father to him or her when it's older? How are you—'

'Whoa! Whoa!' Molly interrupted. 'Calm down, Eve! This is a happy event! It's 1982, so stop going on like some old fuddy-duddy!'

'*Fuddy-duddy!*' Eve was pink with fury. 'Neither of you have the faintest idea what you're talking about! You're coming up to forty, Nessa, and you're single. The father of your child is a married man, who shows no inclination to be otherwise. The only thing you should do is have the baby adopted.'

Adopted!' Vanessa and Molly chorused.

'Calm down, Eve,' Vanessa went on. 'I don't know why you feel so strongly about this, but I'm betting that, if this ever happened to you, *you'd* choose to keep it too!'

Eve's face had gone white. 'It *did* happen to me. I had a baby, nineteen years ago. And he was adopted. My mother told me it was the only decent thing to do. I never intended to tell you, but I did what was best for my son and, if you have any sense at all, you'll do exactly the same.'

There was a further shocked silence as Eve walked over to where she'd left her coat and bag on a chair, picked both up and turned to leave.

'Eve, *please* don't go!' Vanessa was in tears. 'Please! Can we talk about this?'

As she reached the door, Eve turned round and gave Vanessa an icy stare. 'You have alternatives that I didn't have.'

Vanessa wiped her eyes. 'I *want* this baby!'

Molly was standing up now. 'You must do what you feel is right for you, Nessa.'

Eve pulled on her coat and headed out into the hallway. A few seconds later, they heard the outer door slamming.

Molly put her arm round a sobbing Vanessa. 'Please don't cry. But I cannot *believe* what she just said!'

'It explains a lot though,' Vanessa said, wiping her eyes. 'I always knew there was *something* about Eve, something she wasn't telling us. And she's never got over it, has she? So why the hell would she expect me to do the same?'

Molly's eyes were welling up too. 'We were having such a lovely lunch. And I really was happy for you – and still am. But what are we going to do about Eve?'

'She'll calm down, but you'd better stay here tonight, Molly.'

'No, no, I won't, but thanks anyway. I'll go back to Chiswick and talk this through with her.'

'But, Molly, why has she never told us before? Why has she kept something so life-changing to herself? We're her friends, for goodness' sake.'

'Nessa, don't let her spoil things for you. And that was around twenty years ago; things have changed a lot since then.'

Molly

'But why did you never tell us?'

Molly had come back in a taxi. She found Eve heavy-eyed and exhausted from weeping.

'I don't know, Molly. I suppose I was ashamed. Believe me,

back in 1962, when I got pregnant, you were *made* to feel ashamed. Even my own mother turned her back on me. And the baby's father didn't want to know of course. Since then, I've just tried to put it behind me, not to think about it. And then, to hear Nessa going on about how thrilled she was... it just broke me.'

Molly hugged her friend. 'It must have been absolute agony. I can't even begin to imagine what you went through, handing over your little baby... I know that if I'd had to part with any of my three, I'd just die.' She sat back for a moment and regarded Eve. 'But don't you ever think you might want more children?'

Eve shook her head. 'Not really. I suppose I wanted to punish myself, and to avoid getting involved again, which is probably laughable these days, with people being so much more open-minded. But I can't help feeling resentful of Vanessa!'

The afternoon Molly was returning to Rome, she and Vanessa met up for a coffee in Terminal 2.

'It was a lovely lunch, Nessa, even if everything did go pear-shaped.'

'It was a pleasure, Molly, or it should have been. What's Eve been saying?'

'We spoke about it well into the night. That incident has ruined her life, but I've tried very hard to get her to see things from your point of view. However, she's not having any of it. I never thought Eve could be so stubborn. But I'm thrilled for you, I really am! You do know, don't you, that life will never be the same again? That you will love this little person more than you ever thought possible? And that you'll worry about him, or her, every day for the rest of your life?'

Vanessa nodded mutely then hugged her friend closely before Molly headed towards passport control.

CHAPTER THIRTY-ONE

Vanessa

Vanessa surveyed her reflection in the mirror. She'd taken particular care with her appearance as Johnny was about to arrive for three days' standby, and she hoped and prayed he wouldn't be called out. Of course, once he heard her earth-shattering news, she might feel differently – and so might he. She felt sick with apprehension.

'You look even lovelier than usual,' he said when he'd released her from his arms. 'Radiant in fact.'

She helped him hang up his things in the bedroom. 'I'm going to make some tea, so come through when you're ready. I've lots to tell you.' Vanessa realised she was actually shaking.

Five minutes later, Johnny settled himself in an armchair. He was still a good-looking man; age had certainly not withered him.

Vanessa placed the mug of tea on the table beside him.

'So,' he said, 'what have you been up to?' He picked up the mug and took a sip.

'Put the mug down first, Johnny, because you're liable to drop it.'

'Why? What's been happening?'

She took a deep breath. 'I'm pregnant.'

'*What*?'

'I'm pregnant – four months gone. And before you ask, I can assure you I have *not* been with anyone else.'

Johnny appeared stunned. Finally, he said, 'But I thought you were on the pill?'

'Of course I'm on the pill, and that's all fine until you cross the bloody dateline and lose track of what day you're supposed to be on. I cannot believe that, even if I missed one damned pill, this could happen.'

He rubbed his forehead. 'My darling, I hardly know what to say!'

'How about "congratulations" maybe?'

'Nessa, what are you planning to do?'

'What do you mean? What I'm planning to do is have a baby.'

'Just give me a minute to recover,' he said, picking up his mug of tea, but his hand was shaking so much he had to put it down again.

'Do you need some Scotch?'

'Maybe later. Don't forget I'm on standby.' He stared out of the window. 'Nessa, you *know* how much I love you. And you've always known that I was married, and that that's non-negotiable.' He hesitated for a moment. 'I assume you don't want to have it adopted?'

'No, Johnny, I do not want this baby aborted or adopted. I plan to bring him or her up on my own.'

'Come here,' he said, patting his knee. 'Let me hold you.'

As she positioned herself on his knee, he held her tight and kissed her gently. 'You must realise that this has come as a hell of a shock, darling, and I'm trying to work out what I can do; perhaps send you a monthly allowance? Would that help?'

'Well, yes, it would. But what about Bryony?'

'She needn't know. I'll have a word with my solicitor, and hopefully we can arrange for a set sum of money to be transferred from my account to yours every month as some sort of miscellaneous payment. Not that Bryony bothers to check bank statements.' He'd relaxed a little and managed to sip his tea.

Vanessa was also beginning to relax a little. 'I shall probably carry on flying part-time and engage a nanny or something,' she said.

'Have you told your friends yet? Or your mother?'

She laughed bitterly. 'I've had mixed reactions from my friends, but I haven't told my mother yet, no, and there's no telling how she'll react.'

Johnny grinned. 'So there's life in this old boy yet,' he said proudly, 'and to think that my eldest is in her thirties!'

'Johnny, I—'

He held up his hand. 'You *know* I love you, and I want you to be OK. And I promise to do whatever I can for you and our baby.'

Hermione had acquired a flat in Richmond and a toy boy, called Desmond, who sold cars.

'Surely not a second-hand-car dealer, Mother!' Vanessa had exclaimed when he'd first appeared on the scene. She'd been more shocked than she would have believed possible after all the well-bred, upper-crust men her mother had amassed over the years. Was Hermione *really* that desperate?

'Not just *any* old second-hand-car salesman, Nessa. He only sells Porsches, Lamborghinis, Ferraris, things like that. He makes an awful lot of money, you know.'

'I daresay he does. But, Mother, you're *sixty-three*! And how old did you say he was?'

'I didn't. But since you ask, he's forty-five. You'll like him, Nessa – he's awfully nice.'

Vanessa had been in no hurry to meet Desmond. He was the last person she wanted to have around as she positioned herself on one of Hermione's uncomfortable antique chairs a few days after Johnny had departed.

'Why on earth don't you get some comfortable chairs, Mother?' she asked as she wriggled her bottom around.

'Nothing wrong with my chairs! The problem is, Nessa, that you're putting on weight. High time you thought about dieting.'

Vanessa laughed. 'Dieting won't help. How do you fancy becoming a granny?'

Hermione gasped. 'You never *are*!'

'Oh yes I am.'

'Tell me you're joking! You're nearly forty!'

'Yes, I have been keeping count.'

'And you're not *married*!'

'Yes, I'm aware of that too.'

Hermione fanned her brow theatrically. 'My God! I cannot believe what I'm hearing! And who, may I ask, is the father?'

'My lover.'

'Well obviously – I didn't think you'd be having a virgin birth. But who is he? And how long has this been going on? Do you plan to get married?' She frowned and narrowed her eyes. 'Or is he *already* married?'

Vanessa felt strangely calm.

'I need a large Scotch,' Hermione retorted, getting up from her chair. A few minutes later, she returned with drinks for them both. 'So who is he?'

'He's a captain, with Skyline.'

'And married?'

'Yes.'

'How long has this been going on?'

'Just over seventeen years.'

'*Seventeen years*! Are you *mad*? And is he still with his wife?'

'Yes.' Vanessa took a large gulp of her wine.

'And it's never once entered your head that this relationship is going nowhere? Achieving nothing? Perhaps jeopardising his family? Buggering up your hopes of ever finding anyone eligible?'

'Yes, Mother, I've thought of all these things.'

'And still you continue to see him! So what happens now?'

'I want my lover's baby because, if I can't have him, at least I can have part of him. And I'm willing to settle for that.'

Hermione shook her head sadly. 'I used to think you had your head screwed on right, but now I'm beginning to wonder. I hope you're not expecting *me* to look after it?'

'No, I don't expect you to do a damned thing, but I just thought you might be pleased to be having a grandchild and that you might even be pleased for me.' Vanessa stood up. 'I'm going, and I shan't bother you again.'

Her mother sighed and rolled her eyes. 'Don't try to make out you're some sort of martyr, Nessa. But you've always been strong-willed, and so I know there's little point in trying to persuade you to do something you don't want to do. I'm just incredibly sad that you've wasted your youth, and your beauty, on some married man. *That's* what breaks my heart.'

Vanessa's next port of call was to Barty.

After he'd recovered his composure, he said, 'I suppose I can always get you some modelling with Mothercare or someone, darling.'

Vanessa gave him a weak smile. 'I shan't be pregnant

forever, Barty. I'll slim down as quickly as I can afterwards. But are you pleased, honestly? Pleased for me?'

'Of course I'm pleased; it'll be the making of you. Just so long as I can be godfather? I'm sure it'll be a beautiful babe, so perhaps we can get you lots of mother and baby work. How's old lover boy taking it? I gather you've told him?'

'Yes, I have told him, and he's OK about it now that he's got over the shock.'

'I'm amazed he didn't have a heart attack on the spot at his late age. And I do hope he's going to pay up?'

'He's not *that* old, Barty, and of course he's going to pay up.'

Vanessa was quite sure he would, because, regardless of what Barty and everyone else might think, she *knew* that Johnny really loved her.

CHAPTER THIRTY-TWO

Molly

'Mamma, why you speak English so much with Stefano?' Marcello asked as he climbed onto his mother's knee.

'Because it's good for him to practise. And your English is very good too.' She kissed the top of his head. 'You know I've just come back from England, where I was speaking English all the time, and sometimes it's nice to speak in my own language.'

Marcello was the son who most resembled his mother, and who was closest to her. Stefano, on the other hand, was quite an independent character, and little Carlo was a dreamer and very much a daddy's boy. Molly loved them all so much sometimes that it hurt, and whenever she thought of Eve handing her baby over to strangers, she could feel her eyes fill with tears. She felt such concern for Eve that she was beginning to wish she could have stayed on in London for an extra day or two to smooth things out between her two friends. She couldn't even talk it over with Mario because he was now coming home via Berlin and Vienna and wouldn't be back for a further two days.

Molly found herself at a loose end when the children went

to school the day after her return, and it seemed almost fortu-
itous when she received the phone call.

'*Who? What* did you say? Patrick? *Patrick*! I can't believe it!
Of course I remember you! How on earth did you find me here?'

'I don't know if you remember, but you gave me your
parents' telephone number in Bristol, just in case I ever wanted
to contact you? It's been such a long time, Molly, but I finally
have business here in Rome.'

'How marvellous! Where are you? I can be in the city in
thirty or forty minutes.'

A little later, as she sat on the train heading for the Termini in
Rome, Molly had mixed feelings. Was she being a little hasty?
Or naughty, now that she was an old married woman? But she
was so looking forward to seeing Patrick again. They'd arranged
to meet at the Basilica di Santa Maria Maggiore, on Via Cavour,
which was close to his hotel.

She stood uncertainly on the steps of the Basilica for a few
minutes before she heard an American voice behind her. 'Well,
if it isn't that high-flying Irish colleen!'

Molly whirled round. 'Patrick!'

He gave her a bear hug, a peck on both cheeks, then studied
her at arm's-length. 'You look *just* the same!'

She roared with laughter. 'And you're still full of blarney!
Apart from a few grey hairs, Patrick, you look much the same
yourself!'

He took her by the arm. 'Are you free for some lunch?
We've got a lot of catching up to do.'

'Yes, I'm free until the boys come home from school, so I
need to leave by two thirty latest. But we have nearly four
hours, so why don't we have a coffee here?' She indicated the
half-empty pavement café.

'What about the fiery Italian husband?'

'The fiery Italian husband's in Vienna, as we speak, and not due home for a couple of days.' She signalled the waiter. 'Cappuccino?'

'Yeah, that's fine.' After she'd given the waiter the order, he said, 'I'm impressed by your Italian.'

'Well, I've been here ten years now, but I'm always so relieved to be able to have a conversation in English. Tell me about yourself – has some lucky lady snaffled you up?'

'Not so sure she's lucky, Molly! But yes, I've been married for seven years now. I finally had to accept the fact that you were here for keeps! My wife is from Seattle too, and we have two little girls.' He dug some photographs out of his pocket.

'They're lovely, Patrick,' Molly said as she studied them. 'And I have three boys, so perhaps one day we can marry some of them off to each other!'

They chatted animatedly, exchanging news of the past decade.

'Do you miss Skyline?' he asked.

Molly considered for a moment. 'Only sometimes. I don't think I really appreciated the freedom. Don't get me wrong – I love it here, I love Mario and I love the boys, but, sometimes, I just feel a teeny bit stifled. Does that sound awful?'

'Not at all – perfectly natural. This is a completely different life in a different country, with a different language. But you're looking mighty good on it, Molly!'

She grimaced. 'At first, there were times when I thought I'd made a terrible mistake.'

'How come?'

Molly thought for a minute. 'I was actually just pregnant when we got married, and so we never had much time for just the two of us. To make matters worse, we had to live with his mother for a year and a half.'

He grinned. 'Not ideal!'

'You have no idea! Graziana, that's my mother-in-law, is an old-fashioned Sicilian, and she doesn't much trust the Romans, never mind the British! Right from the start, Mario had to travel a lot for business, and when he was away overnight, would you believe, she would *lock me in my room!*'

'You are kidding!'

'No, I'm not. She plainly thought I might go out on the town! She said that it wasn't that she didn't trust *me*, but that she didn't trust the men round here, particularly with a foreign girl!'

'What a crazy woman!'

'Don't forget I was pregnant as well, so God only knows what she thought I was planning to get up to. The furthest I was allowed to go was to take a short stroll – with her – or have a coffee with Elena, who's the wife of one of Mario's cousins and who's become a friend. There were endless rows, and Mario always seemed to come off worst in arguments with his mother. He's not a wimp, far from it, but these Italian women have such influence over their precious sons. I think someone forgets to cut the umbilical cord!'

'That's unbelievable in this day and age,' Patrick said. 'I bet you were mighty relieved to get your own place.'

'Yes, we both were. I was pregnant with Marcello just months after I had Stefano, so we needed more space. Now we have Carlo as well, we should really be looking to move on again.'

'Do you work at all, apart from looking after the children?'

'I teach English to adults two evenings a week. It doesn't pay much, but I enjoy it. How's the aeroplane business?'

'That's booming, fortunately for me. I'm here for a couple of meetings with Alitalia, and then I move on to Tel Aviv. But I'll be back.'

'Is this your first visit to Rome?'

'I was here on a student trip many years ago. But do you know what? I can't remember ever seeing the Trevi Fountain.'

'Well, we'd better get a move on then,' Molly said, standing up.

They could hear the sound of gushing water well before they got to the Piazza di Trevi. As always, there were crowds surrounding the fountain on all sides, and they had some difficulty weaving their way through.

The rococo extravaganza of rearing seahorses and conch-blowing tritons, cavorting beneath the wall of the Palazzo Poli, took Patrick's breath away.

'But this piazza is far too small for such a magnificent fountain!' he kept saying.

Molly laughed. 'I don't think Salvi considered that when he designed it back in the eighteenth century!'

'You are such a font of knowledge!'

'I have to be, because we get so many visitors. There's all my family, just for a start. Now, chuck in a coin, to make sure you'll return to the Eternal City!'

As he dug into his pocket, he said, 'As long as you're here, I will return!' But, nevertheless, he threw in a couple of coins.

It was a beautiful, cloudless day in Rome. They wandered across to the Piazza del Quirinale and admired the palazzo, which had begun its existence as a papal residence, and was now the home of the Italian president. It also boasted a very charming *ristorante*, where they lunched outside and talked non-stop.

Finally, Molly checked her watch. 'Patrick, I must go. The boys will soon be home from school.' She laid her hand on his arm. 'It's been *so* good to see you again!'

He covered her hand with his. 'I'll be back in Rome from time to time, Molly, and we *will* do this again!'

They took a cab to Via Cavour and parted company close to where they'd met at the Basilica. Molly had very much enjoyed his company and was aware that he'd held her just a little longer than was necessary when he'd kissed her goodbye.

CHAPTER THIRTY-THREE

Eve

Eve had just set off on a ten-day trip when a young man came knocking at her big red door. He knocked and he knocked. He checked a slip of paper, and then he knocked again. He looked at the shop next door and wondered if there might be any connection, but it was closed. Hours 10 a.m. to 5 p.m., the notice on the door said, and he had to be at a lecture in less than an hour's time.

With a sigh, he turned and walked away.

———

The Skyline jumbo was heading towards Singapore. Eve was patrolling the economy cabin, to all intents and purposes as an extra crew member, but, in reality, making reports on two of the newer stewardesses. One was having her three-month standard appraisal; the other presented more of a problem as several complaints had been lodged against her. Tracy allegedly spent most of her time chatting up male passengers and completely ignoring the women, particularly those who needed help with children. She'd already been called into the office to answer some of the complaints against her and had been told in no uncertain terms that, if her attitude didn't improve, she would be dismissed. Eve had the unenviable task of being one of the key personnel to decide on the girl's future.

'I expect they've sent you to check on me,' Tracy said sourly, pulling a face as she set off with a trolley down one of the aisles. Eve didn't find her likeable and could only wonder why she'd been selected in the first place.

The flight was full, and the crew were working flat out. After helping with, and making notes on, a very long meal service, Eve was finally able to escape through business class towards first class to try to find a quiet corner in which to write up her reports.

As she walked through business class, a woman stopped her to ask for a glass of water. When Eve returned and placed the glass in front of the woman, she met the eyes of the man sitting in the seat immediately behind.

Eve's heart lurched. No, no, surely it wasn't *him*! The man in question, obviously thinking along the same lines, was staring back in astonishment. Eve, shaken to the core, rushed forward to the front galley, which fortunately was empty, leaned against the work surface and wiped her brow.

No, it wasn't possible; it *couldn't* have been. But if not, why had he been staring at her like that?

She was aware of someone approaching, and hadn't enough time to pull the curtain across before he stopped and looked her straight in the eye.

'It's Eve, isn't it?'

'Yes,' she replied shortly, 'and you're Costa.'

He nodded. They looked at each other silently for a minute. Costa was still an attractive man, greying at the temples and with a slight paunch.

Finally, he cleared his throat. 'How are you? You haven't changed.'

'Oh, I've changed all right,' Eve retorted. 'You have absolutely no idea how much!'

He had the grace to look uncomfortable. 'I'm sorry about what happened. But we were very young, weren't we?'

'I can assure you that I matured considerably after that.' Eve found it hard to believe they were having this conversation after all these years.

'Did you, er, you know...?' He paused. 'What did you do, Eve?'

'I gave birth to your son, and I had him adopted. There was nothing else to do. You'd done a runner; I had no money or support.'

He swallowed hard. 'I was an irresponsible student, and I took the easy way out. I can see that now, and I'm sorry. You must have gone through hell. Did you marry, have more children...?'

'Neither. This is my life now, and it suits me perfectly. I'm not going to chance falling for someone again. I expect you've married someone suitable and had more children?'

He avoided her eyes for a moment. 'Well, yes, I did. Can you bear to tell me about the baby? Did you say "son"?'

'Yes, I had a beautiful little boy, and I had to give him away. I thought Nadia might have told you?'

'No, Nadia refused to speak to me after that.' He had the grace to look ashamed. 'A *son*. I've got two daughters now, but a *son*...' He looked wistful. 'Look, I'm in Singapore for two days on business. Won't you have dinner with me?'

'No, thank you, I won't. I've nothing to say to you, and I'd be glad if you returned to your seat now.'

Eve could feel tears pricking the back of her eyes but was determined not to cry in his presence. Soundlessly, he turned and went back through the cabin. Eve pulled the curtain across and gave way to tears.

Andy Mason, the chief steward, came along at just that moment.

'What's up, Eve?' He looked shocked. 'This isn't like you. Has a passenger upset you?'

She shook her head dumbly, and he put an arm round her shoulders.

'Care to bare your soul to an old sod like me?'

'I'm fine, really, Andy. And there's work to do.' She waved in the direction of the cabins.

Andy sat immediately behind Eve on the bus from the airport into the city. He tapped her lightly on the shoulder. 'Fancy a quiet drink together later?'

Eve turned her head. 'Do you know what, Andy? That would be great. I don't really want to get together with all the crews this evening.'

There were fifteen cabin-crew members on her 747 alone, plus the four flight-deck crew, and probably at least two other crews in the Orchard Hotel. Since she'd become a training stewardess, she didn't always feel comfortable mixing socially with some of the cabin crew on whom she'd been reporting, as they were inclined to keep her at arm's-length. Understandable; she could remember how it felt when she was being checked on herself.

'I'll knock on your door about seven,' Andy said quietly.

'There's a great Malaysian pub and restaurant further down Orchard Road,' Andy said as they strolled out of the hotel. 'I discovered it last time I was here and, luckily, no one else has. Yet anyway.'

The sticky Singapore heat engulfed them as they passed the CK Tang department store and turned into a little side alley, and found Andy's chosen spot. Within minutes, they were sitting opposite each other over ice-cold lagers.

'Now,' said Andy, 'I'm not being nosy, but I'm a bloody good listener, so, if you need to cry on my shoulder, I'm loaded with tissues.'

Eve laughed. 'I feel so much better already, Andy. It was just...' She hesitated for a moment. 'It was just that I saw a ghost from my past sitting in business class, and it really threw me.'

'I take it it's a male? And he was important to you?'

'Twenty years ago he was, but I haven't seen him since. In fact, I'd almost forgotten he existed.'

'He managed to upset you though? Even after all this time?'

Eve sighed. 'Let's just say that he changed my life.'

'And not for the better?' Andy was studying her over the rim of his glass.

She shrugged. 'I'm not altogether sure about that because I have a great life now, and who knows what the alternative might have been.'

'Well, you're a very lovely and successful lady, and I've been admiring you and your glorious red hair for years. But you were all tied up with that first officer.' He obviously noted some alarm on Eve's face because he quickly added, 'Don't panic! I'm not trying to chat you up! But he was a fool to let you go.'

'Actually, I let *him* go. Anyway, we – the guy on the plane and I – were very young at the time. I'd just arrived from the wilds of Scotland, wet behind the ears, believing everything everyone said to me.'

'And he said all the right things?'

'I thought so, at the time.' Eve gulped her beer.

'Dare I ask – how did it end?'

'I'm not sure you'll want to hear this.'

'Eve, I really do, but only if you want to tell me.'

She hardly knew this man, but there was something very kind and caring about him, and she was sure he'd be discreet. For the first time in years, Eve felt the need to talk, really talk, about what had happened. What with the Vanessa business, and then the chance meeting with Costa, the whole episode had resurfaced in her mind, and she felt a desperate need to unload to someone.

'Hardly anyone knows this, and I've no idea why I want to tell you, but I do. The fact is, he got me pregnant.'

Andy didn't look either shocked or horrified. He sipped his beer. 'That was tough luck, Eve.'

'Yes, and then he disappeared as fast as he could and left me to it. My mother, up in Scotland, was horrified – and mortified by the thought that anyone in our town might find out. What other people think is very important to her. And so I was on my own.'

Andy appeared thunderstruck. 'The bastard! I wish you'd pointed him out to me because I'd probably have tracked him down and punched him one!'

In spite of herself, Eve giggled. 'That's how it was then of course. I worked, making out I was a widow, for as long as I could, ended up in a home for unmarried mothers, gave birth to a baby boy and had him adopted.'

She was astonished to see his eyes looking distinctly moist.

'Oh God, that must have been bloody awful!'

'It broke my heart.' Eve fished out her locket and opened it. 'That was him, and there's a lock of his hair. That's all I have of him. I don't know who his adopted parents are, or where they live, or anything about him. I just did the only thing I could do at the time.'

Andy looked sad. 'My story is a little different, but I, too, had a life-changing experience.' He took a large gulp of his drink. 'I lost my little boy when he was just five years old.

Leukaemia. There's no pain on this earth that compares to losing a child. He was our only one.'

'Oh, Andy, how dreadful! I'm so very, very sorry.' Eve was beginning to feel her eyes mist up as well.

'So,' he continued, 'I can understand your pain. And I think we need another drink – something stronger?'

'Gin and tonic please.'

Eve watched him as he went up to the bar. He was a chunkily built man with close-cropped greying hair, and kind, hazel eyes. She'd liked him enormously before she knew about his loss, and now she felt they were kindred spirits.

As he returned with two large gins, Eve asked, 'What about your wife? I hope it brought you closer together?'

Andy grimaced. 'On the contrary, it had the opposite effect. For a start, having a sick child puts a hell of a strain on a marriage, particularly as I was away such a lot and she had to handle so much on her own. No, after Ben died she had a sort of breakdown. I got time off and did everything I could, but, when she recovered sufficiently, she wanted out. No reminders of her past life. She went to Australia shortly afterwards.'

'So you had a double loss. I can't begin to imagine how you coped.'

'It's quite a long time ago now. We got divorced, but neither of us has remarried. At least she hadn't, last time I heard of her.'

Eve was silent.

'Death is so final, Eve. You have to grieve and then get on with life, but you never get over it. There isn't a day when I don't think of our little guy, and I'm sure the same applies to you.'

Eve nodded.

'Just remember,' he went on, 'when you need cheering up, that your boy is alive and well, and almost certainly very much loved, somewhere in the UK. It's just a great shame that he has no idea what a very nice and very lovely birth mother he's got.'

Eve, her eyes full of tears, nodded. 'Hopefully he hasn't inherited my red hair and freckles.'

'I happen to think red hair and freckles are delightful! Now, all this baring of souls has made me feel quite peckish. What do you say we go through the menu?'

'Great idea – I'm starving!' As she spoke, Eve realised that she felt hungrier and more relaxed than she had in years.

One and a half hours later, having sampled almost everything on the menu, Eve sat back, dabbed her mouth with her napkin and stifled a yawn.

'You and me both,' said Andy, doing the same.

'I think I'm going to crash out for twelve hours,' Eve said.

'Me too. But perhaps we could meet up tomorrow, if you haven't made any other arrangements?'

'All I have to do tomorrow,' Eve replied, 'is collect two dozen silk cushion covers from a little lady who used to have a stall down Change Alley, but she works from home now and produces the most beautiful stuff.'

'*Two dozen*? How many chairs do you have in your house?'

Eve laughed. 'No, not for me. I'm the part owner of an interior design business.'

'Is there no end to your talents? I'd love to hear how you got into that!'

'I'll tell you all about it tomorrow.'

'I'll look forward to that. And, later, perhaps we can wander down to Bugis Street and watch the world go by?'

'Why not? I haven't been there for ages.'

As they walked back to the hotel, she recalled her very first visit to Singapore, when the crew had said, 'You haven't *lived* until you've been down Bugis Street!'

Keen to do as much living as possible, Eve, along with her crew, had made their way through the throngs of people heading for the Singaporean night-time haunts, eating at street-side stalls on the way. She'd been fascinated; fantastic food put together by usually only one person, chopping, slicing and stir-frying on woks which sizzled on gas burners. And, incredibly, washing hands in between, everything spotlessly clean; lanterns swaying on wires overhead. Then, later, sitting with drinks at a table on the notorious Bugis Street, watching the world go by. And what a world!

CHAPTER THIRTY-FOUR

Vanessa

The Skyline personnel officer had looked astonished but then quickly composed himself.

He studied Vanessa intently for a moment. 'Yes, I'm sure it can be arranged for you to have three months' unpaid leave before the birth. I had no idea you were pregnant, Vanessa; it certainly doesn't show.'

Dr Kyle hadn't informed Skyline of her condition. Vanessa wanted to fly for as long as possible, but, by November, her condition was becoming noticeable and she was fed up with comments about putting on weight. She wasn't at all sure how many single stewardesses had approached the company with this problem, but, judging by the look on the personnel officer's face, she guessed there weren't that many. She then informed him she would take the full amount of maternity leave she was entitled to after the birth.

He cleared his throat. 'You're a well-known face now, and a great asset to the airline, so we'll look forward to welcoming you back.'

Vanessa thanked him and left, en route to her bank manager.

The bank manager was due for retirement, and this wasn't the type of situation he enjoyed dealing with. He looked embarrassed, and Vanessa reckoned he couldn't decide if he should be congratulating her or not.

He wiped his brow. 'If there's anything we can do to assist you through this... er, *difficult* period, please do let us know. A temporary loan perhaps?'

'No, thank you,' Vanessa said, standing up. 'I'm hoping to be able to manage.'

Her next stop was her mother's flat in Richmond, where the uncomfortable chairs were still in pride of place. Vanessa plonked herself down on the marginally more comfortable settee.

'Mother, I've come to ask you a favour.'

'Well, well, and here was I thinking you just wanted to see your dear old mother!'

'It's about money.'

'*Surprise! Surprise!*' Hermione rolled her eyes.

'I'm going to need a bigger place,' Vanessa continued. 'I'll need a room for the baby and a room for the nanny, and a bit more space generally. And a proper garden of course.'

'You expect me to buy you a *house*?'

'I don't *expect* anything, but I am your only daughter and *this*, I can assure you' – Vanessa patted her bump – 'is the only grandchild you're going to have. And one day I will probably inherit some of that money you have stashed away in stocks, shares and God knows what, so all I'm suggesting is that I have some of it *now*, when I really need it.' She hesitated. 'Would you at least consider it?'

There was a long silence.

'But those investments provide me with an income,' Hermione said eventually.

'But James pays you an allowance, doesn't he? And you have a rich boyfriend as well. So couldn't you spare me just *some* of it? I can't promise to pay it all back, but I could try.' She paused for a moment. 'I couldn't very well ask the bank manager to increase my mortgage when I won't have any income.'

Hermione sniffed. 'What about the feckless father? What's he doing about all this?'

'He's arranged a monthly allowance, but that's mainly to buy what's needed for myself and the baby. He can hardly afford to buy me a *house*.'

'On a captain's salary, he probably could. What you're saying is that none of this little inconvenience must encroach on his cosy home life, but you should have thought of all that before you got yourself pregnant.'

I'm not going to rise to the bait, Vanessa thought. *I have to play it cool, perhaps go for the sympathy vote. I need the money.*

She hung her head. 'You're right of course, but this certainly wasn't planned, Mother. I only want what's best for him. After all, none of this is *his* fault.'

'How do you know it's a boy?'

'Because of my great age, I was offered an amniocentesis and they asked me if I wanted to know the sex of the baby, which I did. He's a real little person already, and he's kicking the hell out of me!'

There was a further silence.

She had to go in for the kill. 'He's all I've got, Mother. After you've gone, and my lover has gone, I'll probably be heading for a lonely old age.'

'Cut the sob story, Nessa, because it doesn't suit you. OK, so let's get down to it – how much were you thinking?'

An hour later, Vanessa got back into her Triumph Stag and roared across the river to Twickenham. Her next move would need to be to contact all the estate agents in the area. Then she was going to do something she'd been thinking about for a while. She was going to phone Eve.

She missed Eve; their leisurely lunches and long chats; the familiarity of a friend known for nearly twenty years. Now that Molly was in Italy, there really wasn't anyone else to whom she could bare her soul. Barty, of course, was a dear, and very supportive, but it wasn't quite the same. And she'd had several close friends from school, but those contacts had waned over the years since she'd been flying. Normal women, in normal jobs, had routines, got married, had babies. And any career woman, but especially an air stewardess and one as attractive as Vanessa, could pose a potential threat to all of that, particularly to the husbands.

Unsurprisingly, when she tried to phone Eve, after her tour of estate agents, there was no reply. Vanessa wondered if she should write a letter. The wording in a letter could be carefully planned and edited, whereas one wrong word on the telephone could ruin everything. She badly wanted to get it right. Surely Eve would have mellowed by now? Vanessa tried to imagine herself in Eve's position twenty years ago and how she might have felt at the time. Then she tried to imagine how it might feel when someone, years later, virtually gloated about being in the same situation.

All this Vanessa wrote, with apologies, and begged Eve to forgive her for being so insensitive. Please, please, could they be friends again? She wrote and rewrote it several times until she

was completely satisfied, then popped the letter into an envelope, addressed and stamped it, and went straight out to the
postbox.

Then she decided to visit Molly in Italy.

CHAPTER THIRTY-FIVE

Molly

Molly was amazed, and delighted, that Vanessa was finally coming to visit. At eight months pregnant it could be a little risky, but Vanessa was clearly bored at home because never in ten years had she come to stay.

'You still manage to look amazing!' Molly exclaimed as she hugged her friend at Fiumicino Airport. 'Why aren't you bloated, with puffy ankles, like the rest of us in the final stages of pregnancy?'

Vanessa laughed. 'I've been so lucky; no problems at all, although my doctor was so concerned about a woman of forty giving birth for the first time that he's booked me into Queen Charlotte's for the birth.'

Molly unlocked the Alfa Romeo. 'Just make sure you get back there in time!'

'I'll try to. Nice car.'

'Mario had a brand new one, so this is mine now.' As they sped away, Molly cleared her throat and asked, 'Any word from Eve?'

Vanessa sighed. 'No. And I carefully composed a letter, full of apologies, and sent it to her weeks ago. It was a good letter, if I say so myself. But I've had no reply. Has she said anything to you?'

Molly shook her head. 'No, she hasn't mentioned you at all, but she has said that she has a new man in her life. He's a chief on 747s, Andy Something-or-Other – Mason, I think she said. Know anyone of that name?'

Vanessa thought for a moment. 'I seem to have heard the name, but I can't put a face to him. A *steward* though?' She sniffed.

'Don't be such a snob, Nessa! I've always got on well with stewards. Anyway, this Andy sounds nice. Apparently, he lost his little boy to cancer, and then his marriage broke up, so I think Eve considers him a kindred spirit.'

'Well, I'm pleased for her of course. But I do wish she'd get over this baby business, because I really miss her.'

It was getting dark when they arrived in Frascati, and there were flakes of snow on the windscreen.

'I didn't think you went in for snow in Italy,' Vanessa remarked, peering out from her fur.

'Oh, we get lots of it up here, because we're high up, and it's quite usual for us to get blocked in sometimes. Nobody here believes that we don't get much snow in Bristol, because they have this pre-set idea about the terrible English weather. But it's so lovely up here in the summer when everyone is sweltering down in the city. That's why the Pope comes here to his summer palace at Castel Gandolfo in the hot weather.'

Molly parked and opened the boot, just as Mario appeared at the main door.

'*Ciao*, Vanessa, how are you? Let me carry your bags.'

'I'm much better for seeing you, gorgeous man!' Vanessa

laughed as she stooped to receive a kiss from Mario, who was a good three inches shorter than she was.

The apartment on the first floor was high-ceilinged, spacious and warm. When they entered, three boys appeared in the hallway.

'Hey, boys – I can't believe how much you've grown!' Vanessa exclaimed as she hugged them. 'Now, where is Carlo?'

Carlo had taken refuge behind his brothers.

'His English isn't too good,' Molly explained, 'but we're working on that, aren't we, Carlo?'

Eventually, he was persuaded to emerge from Marcello's shadow and submitted himself to Vanessa's embrace.

'I speak English good,' he said when she released him. 'And you got my *room*.'

Vanessa had indeed been given Carlo's room, and he had to share, unwillingly, with his two older brothers.

'We really need a bigger place,' Molly sighed as she helped Vanessa hang up her things, 'and I'd quite like another *bambino*. Correction: *bambina!*'

'*What*? You're *not*, are you?'

'No, but I'm thinking about it.'

'But, Molly, *four*! Isn't three enough?'

'But I *do* want a little girl.'

'No guarantee that's what you'll get of course. Strange that we all have boys,' Vanessa remarked. 'I'm having one, you've got three, and even Eve's was a boy. It's certainly time someone produced a girl!'

They ate supper round the big table in the kitchen. Vanessa ate heartily and permitted herself a small glass of Mario's famous wine. The boys were well behaved, if a little noisy, and Carlo, fully recovered from his shyness, chatted non-stop in a mixture of Italian and English. Molly hoped he wouldn't irritate

Vanessa, who wasn't at all used to children, but she seemed to be coping well. She might as well get used to it, Molly thought, because she'd soon have one of her own, and it would be a shock to her system.

The following day, Molly took Vanessa up to see the Pope's summer palace, and they found a little *ristorante* in Castel Gandolfo where they had lunch and watched snow falling from the window.

'You are lucky, Molly,' Vanessa said, nibbling an olive as she awaited her pasta. 'This is such a lovely place to live.'

'Yes, I am. I have a good husband and three lovely sons. But, believe it or not, sometimes I get bored. Mario works long days and is often away on business, the boys all go to school, and we have Mina, who comes in to do the laundry and the housework. Mario doesn't want me to have a job, other than the English tuition I do a couple of nights a week.'

'I can think of worse places to be bored in!'

'Yes, you're right, and I'm not complaining. By the way, have I ever told you that Patrick contacted me? Do you remember Patrick? The American I went out with a couple of times before I married Mario?'

'Yes, vaguely. How on earth did you manage to come across him?'

Molly explained. 'I've seen him a couple of times and, do you know, I really enjoy it! I can *see* the look on your face! No, I do not fancy him, never did. But he's very likeable – and good company.'

'I'm sure he is, Molly, but bear in mind – just because you don't fancy him, that doesn't mean that he doesn't fancy you! Why else would he look you up after all this time?'

'Oh, no danger there. He's married now too, with kids.'

Vanessa sighed. 'When did that ever stop them?'

. . .

Vanessa was summoned to visit the fearsome Graziana. They'd only met briefly at Molly's wedding, and it was plain she didn't approve of a single forty-year-old giving birth at all, far less gadding around in a foreign country when she should be at home, bag packed. With a husband. She wasn't fluent enough in English to impart this information to Vanessa, but she muttered much of it under her breath as she set out the coffee cups.

'Eight months!' she said in English as she poured the coffee. 'And you fly on *plane*!' She narrowed her eyes as she studied Vanessa. 'You no have baby on *my* floor, thank you very much!'

Vanessa

Sitting in her business-class seat, to which she'd been upgraded by a friendly chief, Vanessa felt some relief at escaping the noise and chaos of three boys. It had been overpowering at times, probably because it was too cold for them to go outside and play. Molly didn't seem to notice it, because she was so used to it, but Vanessa most certainly was not. She would bring up her boy to be well mannered and quiet.

She would be relieved to get home, and to see Johnny again in a few days' time. She'd already decided on a name for the baby. She'd have liked to just call him John, but Johnny already had a son called John, so she'd call him Jonathon. And, as Barty wanted to be godfather, he would be Jonathon Bartholomew. Jonathon Bartholomew Carter-Flint. A good name. He should go far.

CHAPTER THIRTY-SIX

Eve

Eve lay curled up against Andy's back. He was a cuddly person to sleep with, and he made her feel contented and relaxed. Although he had a flat in Windsor, he frequently stayed over in Chiswick, where he was an absolute godsend as far as Eve was concerned. Not only did he help put up displays in the shop, but he'd doctored two dripping taps, sorted out a leaking radiator, built shelves in the alcove by the fireplace in Eve's living room and was an accomplished chef to boot.

There was only one blot on Eve's carefully organised horizon, and that was Vanessa. Eve calculated that the baby was due any day and she felt very guilty. Furthermore, she'd received a very nice letter from Vanessa a couple of months back but had never got round to replying. Then she'd had a call from Molly, telling her all about Vanessa's visit.

Perhaps she *had* overreacted to Vanessa's news, even if she did think Vanessa was a fool, and a spoiled one at that. According to Molly, Vanessa was about to buy a smart four-bedroomed house and was looking for a nanny. Eve sighed. How many women in her condition could do that? Mother to the rescue, she supposed, so that Vanessa could land on her elegant feet, as usual.

Eve decided to wait until she knew Vanessa had given birth, and then she would send a card and a gift for the baby. Then that would be that, because the last thing Eve wanted to see was Vanessa cooing over a new baby.

Would these feelings never go away?

In early February Aileen, Eve's mother, had had a minor heart attack but was released from hospital after a few days.

'Oh, I'm fine,' Aileen said on the phone. 'It was just a wee warning. And I have a mountain of pills to take.'

Nevertheless, Eve did worry about her. She hadn't been up to Strathcannon for some months as she'd been so busy with her two jobs – and with Andy as well.

'No point in worrying,' Andy said. 'I can drive you up there, no problem. You'll feel better if you can see her for yourself.'

The more Eve thought about it, the more she liked the idea. She had leave owing and she'd enjoy going with Andy, who was easy company and made her laugh.

'I'm coming up with a *man*, Mum,' she said.

'A man at last!' said Aileen, who'd never set eyes on George. 'I'll put out the flags!'

Much to Eve's relief, Andy got on famously with her mother.

'I've always loved Scotland,' Andy said, having demolished four of Aileen's home-baked scones. He looked fondly at Eve. 'And I've always liked these Scottish lassies with the red hair. I bet you were a red-haired beauty too, Aileen?'

Aileen simpered. 'Och, away with you! Now, why don't you try the chocolate sponge?'

'Just a wee bit then,' said Andy.

Dear lord, thought Eve, *I know she'd like to see me married, but this is ridiculous.* In spite of herself, she grinned – there was something so humorous and endearing about Andy's approach to her mother. She had, of course, forewarned Aileen about Andy losing his little boy, and Aileen was plainly pulling out all the stops to be amenable.

Towards the end of the visit, Aileen took them both on a guided tour of what would become her vegetable garden 'after the frost', pointing out the few things bravely surviving the Highland winter.

As they walked back towards the house, Aileen stopped and faced Andy. 'Eve's told me about your awful tragedy, and I just wanted to say how very sorry I am. There can't be anything worse.'

What a strange time for her mother to say this, Eve thought, standing stock-still on the path.

Andy laid his hand on her mother's arm. 'You're right, there isn't. But that's probably one of the reasons Eve and I get on so well. She can understand what it's like because she's been through something similar.'

Aileen didn't speak for a moment. Then she nodded and began to tell him where she planned to plant this and that.

When she'd finished, Andy said, 'Did you know that one of Eve's best friends is about to have a baby? She's single, and proud of the fact. She's able to keep her baby, even though there's no way she could marry the father.'

'May I ask who it is?' Aileen asked.

'It's Vanessa,' Eve chimed in. 'She's due any day now.'

Andy wasn't finished yet. 'Twenty years ago, attitudes were very different, and of course Eve didn't have money. I think she's coped fantastically well.'

Aileen resumed walking towards the house. 'Eve's made a

successful career for herself, Andy, so life hasn't treated her too badly.'

'She's worked hard for it, almost to the exclusion of everything else.'

Aileen sighed. 'Yes, I know. But I always hoped she'd meet someone and get married, have more children. That would have helped, I think.'

'I'm still *here!*' Eve shouted. 'When you've finished discussing me, can we have some tea?'

Aileen stood still. 'I'm sorry I wasn't more understanding, Eve. I just didn't know how to handle it.'

Eve turned, surprised, then walked forward and embraced her mother. 'I know, Mum, I know.'

Eve flicked through the pile of mail awaiting her on their return and withdrew a handwritten envelope in familiar writing. 'Jonathon Bartholomew Carter-Flint – born 28 February 1983, at Queen Charlotte's Maternity Hospital, Hammersmith. Seven pounds, six ounces. Mother and baby doing well.'

'What a moniker she's given him!' Eve remarked, handing the card to Andy. 'Trust Vanessa to make him sound like some kind of aristocrat!'

Andy put his arm round her shoulders. 'I'm sure he'll do well for all that. Babies have been born on the wrong side of the blanket for centuries, particularly amongst aristocracy and royalty. Try to be pleased about it, and perhaps write her a little note?'

Andy was right of course, but as Eve stared at the blank piece of notepaper in front of her, she couldn't think of a single word to write. She wished now that she'd responded to Vanessa's letter. She'd meant to but kept putting it off until it just seemed to be too late.

Now it would probably be easier to send a card and just say

something like 'with love from Eve'. Or would something like 'Wishing Jonathon a long and happy life' be better? Some message would have to be included with the beautiful white crocheted shawl she'd picked up on her travels in the Far East. Her own poor little baby had never had such a shawl; he'd just been wrapped in a much-washed old blanket.

She'd go out tomorrow and buy a nice card.

CHAPTER THIRTY-SEVEN

Vanessa

Vanessa spent five days in Queen Charlotte's. There were three other mothers in the ward, all nearly young enough to be her daughters. She would have liked to have a private room, but she did have to keep an eye on the purse strings these days.

Despite the age differences, Vanessa discovered what every mother knew – that giving birth was a great leveller. She couldn't believe she was comparing her sore teats and the stitches in her fanny with women she hardly knew! Jonathon, although without doubt the most beautiful infant in the world, also turned out to be the noisiest and the messiest. She longed to be at home and with Johnny.

Luckily, Johnny had been with her when the pains had started. In the circumstances, he'd decided he'd better extend his stay and had gone into the spare bedroom, where Vanessa, listening at the door, had heard him give Bryony some long-winded story about having to do extra simulator checks. What Bryony said was anyone's guess, but Johnny had seemed relaxed when he'd reappeared.

'How far apart are these contractions now, darling?'

Vanessa had had to remind herself that this was his fourth child, and he knew more about the process than she did. He'd carefully monitored each contraction and knew when it was time to load Vanessa and her suitcase into his Jaguar, and head for Hammersmith.

'I still can't quite believe this is happening,' he'd mused as he'd navigated his way round the Chiswick roundabout.

Vanessa had gritted her teeth at another strong contraction. 'Well, I can bloody well believe it all right!'

A few minutes later, there had been another one, causing her to scream and writhe on the front seat.

'We're almost there, Nessa,' Johnny had said consolingly as he'd entered the hospital car park, which seemed unusually full. Finally, he'd found a space some distance from the hospital entrance. 'Stay there!' he'd ordered as he'd got out of the car. 'I'm going to find a wheelchair.'

'Don't *leave me!*' Vanessa had screeched. ''Cos I'm going to have this baby in *your car!*'

'No, you're not,' he'd said firmly. 'You've got a while to go yet. Just hang in there!'

Damn the man for being such a bloody know-all, she'd thought. It wasn't *his* body that was going through this hell every few minutes! *Serve him right if I have the baby here and now, all over the cream leather seat. The stains may never come out!* And what would Bryony think when next she positioned her respectably married arse on the seat beside her two-timing husband! She had screamed again.

Johnny had reappeared, pushing a chair, just as she was about to get out and stagger towards the hospital door, even though she was sure she'd probably have collapsed and given birth in the middle of the car park. For the first time ever, she'd started to hate her lover for putting her through this torture.

Jonathon Bartholomew Carter-Flint had taken his time, in

no hurry to emerge into the big, wide world. Vanessa had been measured and monitored and then left on her own, in *agony*, she'd told everyone later, for what seemed like hours. Johnny had been told there was quite some time to go, so he'd gone off in search of coffee.

Coffee! Vanessa had been furious. Why would he need coffee at a time like this?

'He should be *here*! He's going to miss the birth!' she'd yelled at the midwife.

The midwife had been infuriatingly calm. 'No he won't, dear,' she'd soothed. 'You've got some time to go yet. Would you like some gas and air?'

'No, I want one of those new epidural things, *now!*'

She'd had to wait for that too, but eventually it had been administered and Vanessa had finally given birth.

Later, when she'd lain back exhausted, the baby had been placed in her arms. Johnny had kissed her and said that he'd never seen such a beautiful infant. Vanessa had been pleased, although she hadn't altogether believed him. He'd probably said that each time. Jonathon *was* truly beautiful though.

But *never* again! How could women go through this torture year after year? And what had they done before there were epidurals or much in the way of pain relief? And no birth control then either! And there was Molly, about to have a fourth!

None of these people were obviously as sensitive to pain as she was. That was it, and she most certainly wouldn't be doing it again.

Johnny headed home to Dorset after a couple of days, leaving Vanessa and his new son at the mercy of Hermione. Vanessa wished fervently that Eve would come to visit her. Poor, poor

Eve! To go through all that hell and then have to hand the baby over. It didn't bear thinking about.

At least Johnny had been there for the actual birth, which was more than he was for Bryony's three, or so he'd said. Men didn't get so involved then, he'd told her. He'd been quite emotional, if a little queasy, when he'd been asked if he'd like to cut the umbilical cord, and he obviously hadn't enjoyed the experience quite as much as Vanessa would have wished.

She wasn't keen on breastfeeding or nappy changing. All very messy, and her nipples felt raw. She'd persevered while in the hospital, because it was expected of her, but she'd previously instructed her mother to organise a steriliser and all the necessary trappings, so that she could begin to bottle-feed the second she got home.

In the meantime, Hermione had settled herself in Vanessa's spare bedroom, where she intended to stay for only as long as it took for the baby to get into some sort of manageable routine. The crib had been placed next to Vanessa's bed, as there was nowhere else for it to go until such time as she moved into the new house, where there would be a smart nursery.

Hermione was none too happy with the situation. She didn't care all that much for babies, and she was missing Desmond. She refused to see him until she got back to Richmond, mainly because she didn't particularly want him to see her doing grandmother-type things. After all, he was a lot younger than her.

Vanessa certainly didn't want her around either but had to admit she couldn't yet cope on her own.

CHAPTER THIRTY-EIGHT

Molly

Molly strolled along Via del Plebiscito, having bought herself a red sweater in Upim's sale. It was May, and warm, but she had to think about next winter and, besides, she had half an hour to kill before she was due to meet Patrick again at the Piazza Navona. Mario wasn't due back from Paris until the end of the week, the boys were in school and Mina was in the apartment until 5 p.m., so there was no need for her to rush back.

She was looking forward to what her father would call 'a good craic', because Patrick was always so humorous and entertaining. It was such a joy to joke and converse in English because, although she was now largely fluent in Italian, she still found it difficult at times to understand the Italian colloquialisms and play on words, which formed the basis of much comedy on TV.

Molly wondered, and not for the first time, why she hadn't yet told Mario about meeting up with Patrick on his very first visit to Rome. He'd been away on that occasion too and, by the time he'd got back and gone on at length about his experiences in Scandinavia, and she'd told him all about the children's doings, somehow or other she hadn't got round to mentioning it. Now Mario was away again and Patrick had once more appeared out of the blue. This time, she thought, she would definitely tell him as soon as he returned. After all, Patrick was a friend from her Skyline days, much like Eve and Vanessa really. They were both happily married and, despite Vanessa's cynical remarks, she was perfectly sure Patrick didn't fancy her any more than she fancied him.

'Sure and begorra, if it's not Molly Malone!' Patrick greeted her then hugged her before they set off towards one of the busy restaurants in the Piazza to order some *aperitivi*.

Molly laughed. 'And you're still full of blarney!'

'I love people-watching,' Patrick admitted as they sipped their Camparis and watched the world go by. 'Particularly Italian people. Is there anywhere else in the world where you see such elegant, well-dressed men? I feel like a bundle of rags when I come here!'

'They have this innate sense of style,' Molly said, 'and it starts when they're little. Mario won't let the boys out of the door unless they're dressed just so. And he's very hot on grooming – nails, hair and all that. I fear he may have given up on me!'

A couple of hours later, having laughed their way through lunch and imbibed a bottle of Lambrusco, Molly accompanied Patrick to the Pantheon. He was, like everyone, mesmerised by the symmetry of the design in this ancient monument to the glory of concrete, and how it had withstood the centuries. As they emerged back into the sunlight, Molly pointed opposite. 'That's where I first met Mario!'

'Let's have coffee there then, to celebrate your union!'

As they sipped their coffee, Molly asked, 'When do you

think you might be back in Rome? If Mario's at home, you must come to dinner with us, but I hesitate to ask you when I'm on my own, as somebody is bound to get the wrong idea. My neighbours are nosy enough, but Graziana – that's the Sicilian mother-in-law – likes to make random visits. Even after all these years, I'm not at all sure that she trusts me! I mean, here I am, forty years old, expecting my fourth child, so what the hell does she think I'm likely to get up to?'

'You're pregnant? *Again*? Well, congratulations!'

'Again. Maybe it'll be a girl this time!' She checked her watch. 'Patrick, we should get moving. Let's get a taxi. Are you still in that hotel on Via Cavour? Good – he can take us to the Termini.'

They found a taxi, which duly deposited them both at the Termini. From there, it was a short walk to Patrick's hotel.

'It's been so good to see you again, Molly,' he said, placing his hands on her shoulders. 'I hope to be back again sometime in the coming months.'

'I'll look forward to that,' Molly said. She glanced at the departures board. 'Now, there's a train for Frascati in about six minutes' time, so I'm going to have to run for it.'

Patrick put his arms round her. 'You look after yourself and that new little baby! And I'd very much like to meet Mario next time I'm here. But, if he's not, promise me that we can meet up again?'

'Of course we can! And thank you for a lovely lunch!'

They hugged and Patrick kissed her tenderly on the cheek. '*Arrivederci*, Molly!'

As Molly ran towards the platform for her train, she didn't see Graziana and her friend, Silvana, who went shopping in Rome once a month. The two elderly ladies had just alighted from the Frascati train – and, at the exact moment of her parting with Patrick, had been heading towards the exit.

CHAPTER THIRTY-NINE

Eve

Eve replaced the telephone receiver.

Andy was emulsioning the kitchen wall. 'I gather that was Molly?'

'It was. And would you believe she's pregnant *again*? I mean, Carlo's five and she wasn't planning to have any more as far as I knew.'

He looked at her. 'Does it upset you?'

'No, it doesn't upset me. It's just that I can't believe that the two women who were my close friends are both having babies now!

Andy laid down his paintbrush. 'Apart from the baby thing, have you got a bee in your bonnet about marriage generally?'

'Why do you say that?'

'I just wondered if you were anti-marriage? Probably because you're so independent.'

'Of course I'm not anti-marriage! Molly's got a good marriage, and so have lots of my friends.'

Andy wiped his hands on a damp rag and took a deep breath. 'I just wondered if you'd ever consider marrying *me*?'

'Marry *you*?'

'Don't sound so horrified! I'm not that bad, am I? Just an idea!' There was laughter in his voice. 'You don't expect me to get down on one knee at my age, do you? Apart from anything else, I'm covered in paint!'

'Andy!'

'Well, could you give it some thought? I'm not the kind of bloke who says flowery things, but I do love you.'

Eve was speechless. She looked at Andy, who had resumed painting and was whistling softly to himself. Had she heard correctly? Marry Andy?

She'd long ago decided not to marry anyone. What would be the point? Life was quite satisfactory. Then again, she'd become very fond of Andy and, if she refused, he might go looking for someone else, just like George had done. It suddenly dawned on her that she couldn't bear the thought of that, particularly as there were hordes of stewardesses out there who would be only too happy to snap him up.

'Can I think about it, Andy?'

'Of course. The offer is valid until I get a definite response!'

Andy went home to Windsor to get ready for a two-week Sydney trip.

'If you come up with an affirmative reply while I'm away, you know my roster and all the hotel numbers. Just bear in mind the time differences, and don't call in the middle of the night. If you can't decide, or the answer is a "no", then I don't want to know until I get back. OK?'

'OK,' Eve said, hugging him. 'I'm only doing a Toronto trip while you're away so I'll have plenty time to think!'

'It would be quite nice to get old and crotchety together,' he said as he was leaving.

'I do miss you when you're away,' Eve admitted as she kissed him goodbye.

'Not just my painting then?'

Eve could hardly sleep that night. Surely he didn't really think that she only valued him for his do-it-yourself and painting skills? After all, they had good sex, and she always felt happy when she was with him. She'd never felt this way about George, or any of the other men she'd gone out with over the years.

It suddenly struck her, at about 1.30 a.m., that she'd been taking Andy for granted. He'd become a comfortable, easy part of her life and she'd assumed he'd always be around, just like she had with George. She should probably assume no such thing. But, in this day and age, was it really necessary to tie the knot legally? Weren't they just fine the way they were? Why rock the boat? But...

Andy

Andy Mason awoke to the sound of the surf on Bondi Beach. It was 8 a.m., and he wondered if he'd have that early-morning swim he'd promised himself. It had seemed like a good idea when he was drinking with the crew last night, but not so good now. Perhaps he should settle for an extra hour's sleep instead because, later in the day, they'd be leaving for Singapore.

Just as he was trying to decide, the phone rang. Probably one of the crew wanting to know why he wasn't down in the lobby with a towel under his arm.

He picked up the receiver.

'Hi, Andy. It's Eve.'

'Eve! Is everything all right?'

'I'm fine. Just wondered does your offer still hold?'

'My offer?' He shook his head to ensure he was fully awake. 'Do you mean the marriage bit?'

'That's it, the marriage bit.'

'Of course it still holds!'

'Well, I've decided to take you on. That's if you still want me?'

'Of course I do! Oh, that's fantastic! Eve, I love you!'

'I love you too. Besides, you haven't finished painting the kitchen.'

'I suspected there might be an ulterior motive! That'll cost you a pile of uniform shirts to launder when I get back!'

'It'll cost you an engagement ring!'

'Bloody hell, woman, whatever next?'

As he hung up, Andy was grinning from ear to ear.

CHAPTER FORTY

Vanessa

Vanessa couldn't believe how much her life had changed. She rarely got out of her nightie before lunchtime, and some days she didn't get dressed at all. Jonathon suffered from colic and screamed half the night, leaving her sleepless and exhausted.

Hermione, who had only intended to stay for a few days, was still spending most of her time at Vanessa's weeks later, and, in the middle of all the chaos, Pickfords arrived to pack everything up in preparation for the move to the new house in Teddington.

'Why the hell did I ever contemplate moving with a new baby?' Vanessa wailed.

'Well, you wouldn't be told. *You* knew best,' Hermione snapped. 'And it's not as if you have to pack as much as a teaspoon because Pickfords are doing everything, and I'm here to help with the baby. So stop complaining.'

Deep down, Vanessa knew she was right, and it wasn't as if she didn't adore baby Jonathon, because she did. It wasn't his fault he was colicky, but, at times, she dreamed of freedom. She was just so *tired*.

'He looks just like my youngest did when she was born,' Johnny mused.

Vanessa really didn't need to know that. And she didn't fancy sex either. She'd had lots of stitches and the area down there, in spite of countless salt baths, was still very tender. Not only that, but every time she assumed a horizontal position, she was asleep in seconds.

And Hermione kept harping on about how it was high time she got a nanny. 'I can't keep coming here every five minutes,' she said, 'and I'm missing Desmond.'

'Why doesn't he come here then?' Vanessa demanded. 'It's time I met him. Or are you afraid I might fancy him, or he might fancy me? Nothing to worry about as far as I'm concerned, because I couldn't even fancy Paul Newman right now.'

'Don't be ridiculous. Anyway, we're planning a holiday to Kenya, Desmond and I. I'd so like to see the old place again.'

'You could exchange him for something better at the Muthaiga Club or one of your other old haunts,' Vanessa said, 'like you used to do!'

'Don't be so horrid! Do you suppose the old place has changed much?'

'I don't need to suppose; I go there regularly. Of course it's changed, and so have you! You're over sixty! You don't expect all these old expats you once knew are going to be rushing to bed you again, do you? They'll be tottering around on their Zimmer frames by now.'

'Being sixty-four isn't old these days, Vanessa. And I do still keep in touch with some of the crowd down there. I sometimes think I should have stayed in Kenya instead of marrying James.'

Vanessa had heard it all before. She was scouring the situations-wanted columns in the newspapers in the hope of finding a nanny. 'There are plenty of au pairs around looking for jobs –

or husbands more likely,' she told her mother. 'But *where* are the nannies?'

'Try an agency in town – the one in South Kensington,' Hermione replied. She hesitated for a moment. 'Can you get me a cheap ticket to Nairobi?'

'I can get one for you but not Desmond. Unless, of course, he decides to become my third stepfather in the meantime.'

'Not likely,' Hermione retorted as she headed out of the door.

Vanessa sighed. She just wanted this move to be over, with a nanny installed, and her mother back where she belonged, in Richmond, or Nairobi if necessary. She also wanted normal sexual relations with Johnny to be resumed as soon as possible.

CHAPTER FORTY-ONE

Molly

'*Who* is he, this man?'

Molly had never seen Mario so angry. She was going to tell him about Patrick, the moment he got home from Paris, but unfortunately he'd stopped off at his mother's on the way, to be told that his wife had been seen at the Termini with a lover. Furthermore, they were kissing passionately.

Molly scoffed. 'It was only Patrick!'

'*Only* Patrick? There are *others*?'

'Of course not! I mean "only" in the sense that he's just a friend from my flying days, much like Eve and Vanessa. Nothing more!'

'So he is crew?'

'No, he's not crew. He was an American passenger—'

Mario exploded. 'A *passenger*! So an *admirer*, no? And how did he know where to find you after so many years? Tell me that!'

'He got my number from my parents.'

'How many times you meet this man in Rome? Once only?'

'Well, no, and I was going to tell you—'

'You were going to tell me that you had an American lover who has come many times to Rome?'

'He is *not* a lover! He has *never* been a lover!'

'You expect me to believe this? Mamma tells me what she sees with her own eyes – that he kisses you *appassionatamente*! While I am out of the way! Do you let this man know when I am going to be away?'

'Of course not, Mario! He means nothing to me. I swear to you that he is just a friend. He's *married*, with children!'

'So are you! And you leave your children with the maid so that you can go to meet him in the city!'

'They were at school, for goodness' sake, and I was home before they got back. If you'd been at home, I was going to invite him to dinner but—'

'But I am in Paris!' Mario interrupted. 'So does he come every time I am away?'

Molly was becoming exasperated. 'He was here only once before, when you were in Scandinavia. He just phoned out of the blue.'

'Out of the blue what?' Mario appeared puzzled.

Damn and blast, Graziana, Molly thought. Why oh why did the wretched woman have to witness what was no more than a brief affectionate moment? Why, among all the thousands of people thronging around the Termini that day, did Graziana have to come along right then? Nevertheless, she should have told Mario after that first meeting, and it wasn't going to be easy to convince him that it was pure coincidence that Patrick should appear each time he was away.

Mario was seething. 'I have a wife who is still meeting with an Americano ten years after she is married to me! How many times, Molly?'

'We've only met twice. In the middle of the city.'

'So where do you go?'

'We had lunch at the Piazza Navona, and then we shared a cab to the Termini, so I could get my train and he could walk to his hotel nearby.'

'You go to his *hotel*?'

'Of course not! Look, you can ask Eve or Vanessa – he is only a *friend*.'

'But he kisses you passionately?'

Molly was now beginning to get angry. 'He did *not* kiss me passionately! Why don't you believe me? I have never lied to you. Why do you believe your mother and not me? What is it with you and your damned mother?'

'You do *not* refer to my mother in this way! She would *never* lie to me!'

'But *I* would? That's what you're saying? Thanks for that, Mario. In which case, I suggest you go back to live with your saintly mother!'

'This I will do!' Mario shouted. 'And then your *Americano* can come here, to *my* apartment! No, I don't *think* so! And this *bambino*, is it mine or his?'

'How *dare* you suggest such a thing!' Molly looked around in fury until she spotted a particularly hideous vase that his mother had brought back from Sicily. She picked it up and hurled it at her husband. It missed, hit the wall and shattered into hundreds of tiny pieces. She'd always hated that vase, and right now she hated Mario even more.

Mario fled.

Molly sat down and wept with frustration and anger. How *dare* he suggest that the baby was Patrick's?

When she recovered, she made herself a strong coffee. *Tomorrow,* she thought, *all will be well. Once he's slept on it, his anger will diminish, and he'll be able to see it for what it is: a complete misunderstanding.*

Mario's nature was fiery, and he was inclined to go off the deep end at even minor irritations. That was what came of being married to an Italian, but she wouldn't have it any other way.

The following morning, after a sleepless night, Molly waited until she knew Mario would have gone to the office before she walked round to Graziana's. Although she hadn't slept, she felt surprisingly calm.

'What do you want?' Graziana asked as she peered round the door.

'I want to talk to you. I want to know why you lied to Mario.'

'I not lie. I see with my two eyes.' She pointed at them for clarification. Then she looked around anxiously. 'I'm not having a row on my doorstep for the neighbours to hear, so you'd better come in.'

Molly marched into the kitchen, where she knew Graziana would be making her daily supply of pasta.

'You saw an old friend giving me a goodbye kiss and, as we say in England, two and two made five, as far as you were concerned. I never have been, and never would be, unfaithful to Mario. Why do you think the worst of me?'

Graziana rolled her eyes. 'I am only concerned for my son. If this man is such a good friend, then why has Mario not met him before now? Or even know of his existence? What am I to think? I am very perceptive, you know.'

'No, Graziana, you are nosy and suspicious! And if this has damaged my marriage in any way, it will be entirely your fault, and I will never, ever forgive you!'

Graziana's eyes blazed. 'You do not hurt my son!'

'If you hadn't interfered, I would have told him all about it anyway. You've made an innocent friendship into a big deal. I sincerely hope that I will never think as badly of my sons' wives as you do of me.'

With that, Molly turned and marched out of the apartment, slamming the door behind her. Her eyes blurred with tears, she rushed down the marble staircase while desperately searching in her shoulder bag for a tissue. Halfway down the final flight of steps, she missed her footing and fell head-first onto the floor.

Shocked and dazed, she made an unsuccessful attempt at getting to her feet, aware of a searing pain in her left leg and a trickle of blood slowly emerging from underneath her skirt. Then Molly passed out.

CHAPTER FORTY-TWO

Eve

'I'd like to go to Rome for a couple of days to see Molly,' Eve said as she and Andy walked back to her flat after dinner at the local Chinese. 'Would you mind?'

'No, of course not,' Andy replied. 'I should think she'd be delighted to see you. Not much fun having your leg in plaster.'

'And she's lost the baby too. She's been having a rough time, and I gather things aren't too good between Mario and herself either.'

'Poor Molly,' Andy agreed. 'And, of course, you'll want to show off that ring of yours!'

'Oh, Eve, you've no idea how pleased I am to see you!'

The two friends embraced with difficulty as Molly wobbled about on her crutches.

'I was going to phone you,' Eve said, 'but when I got your call, I thought my news could wait until I could get here to see you.'

Molly's eyes filled with tears. 'Mina will take your bag to the bedroom. She's been an absolute gem, staying here all day to help with the boys, as well as everything else. And she'll bring us some coffee in a moment, and perhaps something a little stronger!'

'I'm so sorry about the baby, Molly.'

'Oh, it's been awful. Just *awful*!'

At this point, Mina arrived with a laden tray.

An hour later, fortified by coffee and half a bottle of grappa, Eve had been given a detailed account of Molly's meeting with Patrick, the interfering Graziana, the row with Mario and then the accident. Mario, apparently, had been 'full of love and forgiveness'.

'Forgiveness!' spluttered Molly. 'I'd done nothing wrong, but I'm not sure he's ever going to believe it. And his damned mother had hinted that the baby might not be Mario's!' She burst into tears. 'I wanted that baby very badly. I wanted a little girl to complete my family, but they said at the hospital that it was unlikely I'd be able to have another one now. If it had only been a month or two later, the baby might have survived...'

Eve squeezed her hand. 'I know how emotional you must feel, Molly, but you do have three lovely boys. And a jealous husband! But surely that's better than an indifferent one? It's only because he loves you so much. He's a passionate man, Molly; he's *Italian* for goodness' sake!'

Molly dried her eyes. 'You're always so sensible, Eve. You lead such an orderly life. Tell me what you've been up to.'

'I've just married Andy.'

'*What*?'

'We got married ten days ago. Quick trip to the registry office, grabbed two witnesses off the street; job done!'

Eve had rarely seen Molly speechless.

'We didn't want any fuss, or presents or anything,' she

continued. 'We just wanted to make it legal and get on with our lives.'

'Oh, Eve!' Molly had finally found her voice. 'I am *so* pleased for you but only wish I could have been there.'

'There was nothing to see. We had a pub lunch afterwards, and then I phoned my mother. She was a bit shaken, as you can imagine, but very pleased because she liked Andy and was desperate for me to get married. I know you'll like Andy, but this didn't seem an appropriate time to bring him along.'

Molly was struggling to stand up again. 'I must congratulate you!'

'Stay put!' Eve bent down and let Molly hug her.

'So what's your new name? Did you say his name was Mason?'

'I suppose I am Mrs Mason, but I'm keeping my maiden name. Don't see the point in changing it and having to inform all and sundry. I'm certainly not telling Skyline, although no doubt word will get around.'

'That's like here in Italy; women don't change their names. I'm still O'Hara, but the boys are Bellinis of course. Have you told Vanessa?'

'Good Lord no! I haven't spoken to Vanessa in months.'

'She really misses you, Eve. She'd love to hear from you.'

'I miss her too, particularly recently. But I've left it so long now that I don't quite know how to resume the friendship. Anyway, I imagine she's busy with the baby.'

'You know Nessa! She's got herself a four-bedroomed house, a live-in nanny and some modelling work to boot! And she's planning to go back flying part-time, next month. She certainly doesn't let the grass grow under her feet!'

Eve snorted. 'She doesn't change. And I guess that old lover of hers still visits whenever it suits him? He must be near retiring age, surely?'

'Yes, apparently he retires later this year.'

Eve rolled her eyes. 'I still find it hard to believe that she's wasted nearly twenty years of her life – the best years at that – on somebody else's husband. I mean, she was so stunning that she could have had anybody.'

'I know, I know.' Molly sighed. 'But she says she's still in love with him and is still excited at seeing him even for just a few hours at a time. I do think it's a real love affair, you know.'

'You're such an old romantic, and I'm an old sceptic! But that Johnny Martell has had the best of both worlds for years and years. Who knows if he hasn't had a few other dalliances as well? And if he's as keen on her as she is on him, then why hasn't he left his wife? After all, the children must have flown the nest by now.'

'She says she admires him for not leaving his wife. She reckons that, if he could walk out on one wife, he could walk out on another.'

'True enough. You know the old adage: when a man marries his mistress, he creates a vacancy.'

Mario had been relieved to see Eve. She had cheered Molly up and she had also taken him to one side to assure him that his wife had no feelings whatsoever for this Patrick, and that her only fault had been in not telling him when Patrick first appeared on the scene.

He, in turn, had confessed to her that perhaps he had over-reacted, '*un poco*', and he realised that his mother was inclined towards exaggeration at times, and that she should perhaps have given Molly the benefit of the doubt. Yes, he too would have liked another baby, but three children were really enough in this day and age. Even Italian families were much smaller than they used to be. He also admitted to feelings of guilt that the argument which had taken place between his wife and his mother had inadvertently been the cause of Molly's accident on the

stairs and subsequent miscarriage. Altogether, the whole incident had been disastrous and best forgotten, he said. He wanted
life to return to normal, or as normal as it could be with his wife
and his mother still not speaking to each other.

Eve sighed as she recalled their conversation. There was no
way Mario – or many men for that matter – would be able to
understand the devastating loss of a baby you'd carried inside
you, no matter how early on.

CHAPTER FORTY-THREE

Vanessa

Vanessa loved her new home in Teddington. It had four bedrooms, a leafy garden and a spacious garage for her latest car.

The nanny, whose name was Clare and hailed from Liverpool, had her own room and shower. Fortunately, little Jon had taken to her straight away, which was a relief as well. The only problem was that Vanessa could hardly understand a word she said.

'I thought people only spoke like that in films,' she complained to her mother. 'I believe it's referred to as "Scouse"?'

Hermione, in the meantime, was preparing for her trip to Kenya, minus Desmond, who'd decided it wasn't for him. But Hermione was dead set on going and had contacted some old friends in Nairobi, who professed to be delighted at her impending arrival. Since Vanessa had managed to get her a free ticket, she was having the time of her life buying a completely new wardrobe for this much-anticipated holiday.

And then there was Johnny, who was about to attend a retirement course and had phoned to say that he'd need a bed for several nights. Her bed.

Four glorious nights! Vanessa knew she had to make the most of this because who knew what excuses he'd be able to come up with to enable him to continue visiting her after his retirement. His eldest daughter was now living in Spain and that, apparently, was where Bryony wished to spend their retirement. Spain! And Skyline didn't even fly to Spain!

Vanessa felt sick with worry.

Johnny arrived on Monday afternoon, after the first day of the course.

'Thing is,' he said sadly, 'I really don't want to retire. Flying is my life. And I love you, and my new little son!'

'Is Bryony still set on this Spanish idea?'

'I'm afraid so. I can't honestly blame her for wanting to be near Susie and the grandchildren, or for wanting to get away from our erratic climate. But the other two are in this country, and now there's Jon, and, not least, there's you.'

Vanessa rested her head on his shoulder.

'I've given this a lot of thought,' Johnny continued, 'and I'm beginning to wonder if now is the time for Bryony and I to live separately.'

Vanessa sat bolt upright. '*What*?'

'She could live in Spain, and I could live here, and I daresay we could get together from time to time. And it would mean that you and I could be together for most of the time. What do you think?'

'Oh, Johnny!' Vanessa could feel her eyes brimming with tears. 'That would be perfect! What does Bryony think of the idea?'

'Well, I haven't actually mentioned it to her yet. But I will.

She may be suspicious because I have a feeling she already suspects something. After all these years, I can hardly believe that she *doesn't* suspect something. Fortunately, she doesn't check the bank statements often and, anyway, I've arranged for my monthly payments for Jonathon to be shown as an assurance policy. Ness Assurance I call it; appropriate, don't you think?'

Vanessa was already dreaming of a future with Johnny: to appear with him in public, to introduce him to all of her friends, for him to be a 'proper daddy' to Jon. What bliss!

'It would be heaven,' she confirmed happily. 'Incidentally, I'm going back flying next week, just part-time. I did the jumbo conversion course last week, and I'm off to Los Angeles next Monday.'

'I'd like to be able to look after you so you don't need to work again,' he said, 'but let's see how it goes. The Spanish move for Bryony is just an idea at the moment.'

'It's a brilliant idea,' Vanessa confirmed with enthusiasm. 'And don't forget that your grown-up children don't really need you anymore, but little Jonathon certainly does. He needs a daddy; a daddy to take him to football, swimming and things like that. Little boys need their daddies.'

The week passed in a flash and was one of the happiest times in Vanessa's life. Johnny attended the course daily until 3 p.m., which gave them four evenings together before he had to return to Dorset on Friday. He was marvellous with the baby, with feeding, burping and nappy changing. Clare looked confused at times with Vanessa's domestic arrangements, so Vanessa gave her an extra day off to compensate for the change to routine.

They went out to eat, they went to the theatre and they even walked along the riverside with Jonathon in his buggy. One elderly couple stopped to admire the baby in his pram. 'You must be very proud grandparents,' the woman said.

Vanessa spent a great deal of time scrutinising her face in the mirror after that.

'It was me they were looking at,' Johnny consoled.

Vanessa hoped that two trips a month wouldn't be too strenuous. She didn't want to be away from Jon for more than a few days at a time, and although she trusted Clare implicitly, she was going to find it very hard to leave her little son behind. She could hardly believe how her attitudes had changed since she'd given birth to Jon. Her priorities had completely altered and, for the first time in months, she thought more and more about Eve, and how devastated she must have been handing her baby over.

Jonathon's christening had been arranged for November, and she prayed that Johnny, who'd be retired by then, would be able to be there. She couldn't believe he was at retiring age; weren't they all getting so *old*! And her being mistaken for a *grandmother*!

Perhaps she'd be able to leave Skyline completely if Johnny was with her most of the time. Apart from a base in Spain, which she hoped he'd buy for Bryony, he'd need somewhere to live in England. A pied-à-terre perhaps, somewhere near Teddington?

In the meantime, she'd heard that Eve had got married. To a *steward*, would you believe! According to Molly, they'd got married in a registry office and grabbed two people off the street as witnesses. Typical Eve of course. She was quite a business-woman these days, and a senior training stewardess as well, so she must be raking in the money. Chief stewards weren't earning peanuts either, so those two must be very comfortably off. She only wished Eve would get in touch as she'd like both Eve and Molly to be Jon's godmothers.

· · ·

Johnny called in briefly, to say goodbye, when his course finished on Friday afternoon.

'We've had such a lovely week,' he murmured into her hair as he held her close. 'I never wanted it to end. But I'm more determined than ever now to sort everything out with Bryony when I get home, and I'll let you know how it goes.'

She nodded mutely.

'I see that I get back from Kuwait the day after you get back from LA, so I'll call you then. Now, let me have a last look at that gorgeous little son of mine before I leave.'

Vanessa brought Jon down from the nursery, where he'd just woken up from his afternoon nap, and presented him to his father.

'You are both very precious to me,' he said, holding the baby close to his chest. 'Whatever happens, Nessa, I shall always look after you both.'

When he left, Vanessa stood gazing out of the window, with the baby in her arms, long after Johnny's car had disappeared at the end of the road.

CHAPTER FORTY-FOUR

Eve

Eve gasped when she studied her crew list. She was to report on one brand-new steward, one stewardess due for promotion and one stewardess returning from maternity leave: Vanessa Carter-Flint.

She looked round the office. 'Is Vanessa here yet?' she asked.

'Haven't seen her, but she was always known to appear at the last minute.'

Eve swallowed. This was going to be difficult. She'd been wondering for months how best to make contact with Vanessa again, and now the decision had been made for her.

She introduced herself to the nervous new steward who, according to the clerk at the desk, had been hanging around for an hour, looking terrified. 'You'll be fine,' she said in what she hoped was her most reassuring tone. 'Don't let me scare you! I'm here to help, you know, and sort out any worries you may have – not add to them!'

He nodded mutely.

She then turned her attention to the stewardess who was

due to be promoted and who seemed confident enough. Now, *where* was Vanessa?

Fourteen cabin crew were surrounding Bill, the chief steward on the Los Angeles flight. There was the usual chatter while some introduced themselves and some recalled past trips together.

'Right! Are we all here?' Bill shouted above the hubbub, waving a sheaf of papers. 'Where's the first-class girl?'

As if on cue, the door swung open and a flustered-looking Vanessa rushed in.

'Sorry I'm a bit late! The name's Vanessa!'

Eve noted that some of the stewards were already admiring her as she signed in.

'OK,' said the chief, 'we're all here now. Let's see the briefings: usual smattering of celebrities, four kosher meals in economy, two wheelchairs...'

Eve stood well back while he read out the briefings, wondering how long it would take Vanessa to spot her amidst the sea of blue uniforms.

'Good to have you back with us, Vanessa,' Bill went on. 'Now, three of you are being checked out on this flight by our training stewardess, Eve Muir.' He pointed towards Eve. 'I've flown with Eve a lot, and I promise you she won't bite!' Pause for some nervous laughter. 'She's on your side – don't forget that!'

Vanessa turned round and locked eyes with Eve. Eve smiled nervously as she made her way across to where Vanessa was standing, as if rooted to the spot.

'Hi, Nessa,' Eve said. 'It's really good to see you.'

'Oh, Eve!'

Eve moved forward and hugged her friend until she felt her rigid body relax slowly. 'Nessa, I'm sorry. I just didn't know how to go about resuming our friendship after such a long time. I know now that I overreacted to the baby business, and I'm truly sorry. I guess I'm my own worst enemy.'

Vanessa visibly relaxed. 'Haven't I always said that?'

Suddenly they were both giggling.

'This is just a formality, me checking on you,' Eve said. 'I know you can do this job with your hands tied behind your back, but I have to write something. God, it's good to see you! We have so much catching up to do! How's your little baby, and are you gutted at having to leave him?'

Vanessa's eyes filled with tears. 'I guess I'll have to get used to it. Fortunately, I've got a good nanny.'

Eve laughed. '*You* don't change, Nessa! Just as well we have a couple of days in LA to catch up with each other.'

'And *you've* gone and got married!' Vanessa exclaimed. 'Whatever next!'

It was a long, non-stop flight, over the Pole, and at first Vanessa said that she found the layout of the 747 very different to the smaller planes she'd been used to. But by the time they were halfway there, she'd regained her self-confidence and was enjoying herself, sailing through the first-class section and chatting to some of the well-known personalities heading for the film capital.

'She's back in her stride now,' Bill murmured to Eve in the galley. 'I gather she's just had a baby and that you're friends?'

Eve nodded.

'I'm not one for gossip of course, but everyone knows – or thinks they know – who the father is.'

Eve smiled but said nothing before heading back through the cabin before the conversation could progress any further, where she helped Vanessa collect some empty glasses.

'I hear you've taken to this monster aircraft like a duck to water,' Eve said as they headed back to the galley.

'You know what? It's great to be back, and I'm loving it!'

The Bellevue Inn faced the beach at Santa Monica, separated by a wide avenue which led to a variety of shops and restaurants, not least Ye Olde English Pub, which the crews usually frequented. Apparently, the beer there could almost pass for that at home. They even had a barman from Streatham. Eve was constantly amazed how crews always managed to find drinking establishments which resembled, as closely as possible, their local pubs at home. However, it wasn't the place to go to have a meaningful chat.

'There's a great seafood place recently opened a couple of hundred yards along the beach,' Eve said, 'so let's go there.'

'Nothing changes,' Vanessa said, looking around at the sunbathing bodies.

Los Angeles cared a lot about beauty. Everywhere and everything was dedicated to the body beautiful – exercising it, bronzing it, clothing it – and that was never more apparent than on Santa Monica beach. Old men with bronzed bodies and bulging muscles; young, fit men with film-star looks strolling arm in arm with each other; women jogging, swimming, somersaulting, vaulting. More than the average quota of weirdos, talking to themselves. An old guy with flowing hair and beard bearing a placard warning them that the end of the world was nigh.

Vanessa giggled. 'Hope we've got enough time to catch up! Where *do* all these people come from!'

They arrived at The Sea Shack, which wasn't a shack at all but a very smart single-storey wooden building with a great menu and very comfortable sofas to sit on while you waited.

Eve and Vanessa sipped large, exotic cocktails, gazing out at the sun as it set over the Pacific.

'Don't we get a green flash or something at the exact moment the sun disappears over the horizon?' Eve asked.

'Don't know. You're supposed to see it all the time in the Caribbean, but I never have. Now, tell me about this Andy!'

'Well, he's kind and he's caring, and he's funny,' Eve replied. 'Sometimes nostalgic of course. You know about his little boy? I don't know what it is about him, Nessa, but it's a winning combination! He's not particularly good-looking, quite ordinary really, average height, a bit overweight. But you know something? I'm always happiest when I'm with him.'

Vanessa looked wistful for a moment. 'I'm really looking forward to meeting him. I have to say, though, that I thought you were destined for eternal spinsterhood.'

'I didn't ever intend to marry, you know. Mainly because I didn't want to have another child, and it would hardly have been fair to any prospective husband. But Andy was different...'

'Well, it's never too late to procreate, as they say!'

'You just made that up! No, I really wouldn't want to cope with a baby at my late age, thank you very much.'

'Best be careful then. There was Molly and myself, both hitting forty and pregnant. It might be catching!' She looked serious for a moment. 'But I love my little guy, and I'm so glad I had him, Eve.'

Eve smiled. 'Times have changed, thank God. How's Johnny?'

Vanessa told her of Johnny's impending retirement and the prospective plans. If only, she told Eve, they could get Bryony off to Spain, there was some hope of a future of sorts with him.

'It's certainly stood the test of time,' Eve remarked. 'Longer than half of marriages these days.'

'Familiarity never breeds contempt when you only meet up once or twice a month, believe me. We're always overjoyed to see one another. There's none of the nitty-gritty of normal married life. He always sees me looking my best, and I never get bored with him. But, yes, I would like more of him now that we have little Jon.'

They were still chattering non-stop as they drove back in the crew bus to the airport a couple of days later.

'You two must have sore throats by now,' one of the stewards quipped.

The two of them had spent most of their time lazing by the pool, except on one occasion when they'd had a stroll along Rodeo Drive. The newer crew members, including the steward on his first trip, had done the usual routine of the Beverly Hills tour, Disneyland and Universal Studios. It was a lot to pack into a couple of days, but they'd managed it.

As they approached the air terminal, they could spot the distinctive blue tail of the Skyline jumbo as it taxied round on its arrival from London.

A little later, the incoming crew, looking exhausted, arrived in the office.

Eve ran up to the captain. 'Hi, George! How are you? How's the family?'

Her old lover beamed at her. 'I'm fine, Eve, just a bit knackered. Good to see you. Have you heard the news?'

'News? What news?'

'One of our 707s has just crash-landed. It's just come through on the radio from London.'

Eve felt shock waves ripple through her body. It was the kind of news everyone dreaded. 'When? Where? Do we know who the crew are? Were people injured? Killed?'

'Only a few hours ago, I believe. Coming into Kuwait. Johnny Martell was the skipper apparently, and he had a heart attack or something at the crucial point of landing. I gather the first officer took over in the nick of time, with Martell slumped over the controls, dead as a dodo. Only a few passengers at the back appear to have had minor injuries as far as we know.' He stopped, staring at Eve. 'Oh my God, is that who I think it is back there?'

Eve felt sick. 'Oh, George, this is horrendous. How am I going to break the news to her before someone else does?' She looked round, relieved at least to see that Vanessa hadn't started chatting to the incoming crew. 'I must take her somewhere quiet.'

Her heart thumping, Eve grabbed Vanessa's arm. 'Quick, quick, I need to tell you something important. In private.'

'What on earth are you talking about? Can't you tell me here?'

She hustled Vanessa towards the ladies' room. 'No, I can't.'

Eve prayed the toilet would be empty, which, fortunately, it was. 'Sit down on the seat, Nessa. This is serious. There's been a problem on a Skyline 707 going into Kuwait.'

Vanessa stared at her then froze and began to shake. 'What sort of problem? It wasn't Johnny, was it?'

Eve put her arm round her friend. 'I believe it was, but we haven't got all the details yet, only what George was able to tell me.'

'No, no, it *can't* be him!' Vanessa was shaking her head.

'It seems he had a heart attack during the landing. I think the rest of the crew are OK but, Nessa, brace yourself: I believe Johnny might be dead.'

'No, he can't be! Not Johnny! He's retiring soon, and we're going to have lots of time together!' Vanessa looked as if she'd been turned to stone. She was staring ahead, glassy-eyed.

Eve touched her lightly on the arm. 'I'm going to get you a glass of water, and then we'll get you some brandy on board. We need to get you home, Nessa.'

Vanessa got to her feet obediently, as if in a trance.

As they emerged back into the office, the chief was awaiting them.

'The skipper's just been on the blower to London,' he said quietly, 'and I'm afraid it's true.' He looked at Vanessa. 'I can see she's been told. Heaven only knows what I'm going to do with my first-class passengers.'

'Don't worry, Bill, I'll work the galley,' Eve said. 'I've written up most of my reports and I'm happy to replace her, if that's OK with you.'

'Thanks, Eve, that's a relief. Now, let's get her on board.'

They took an arm each and shepherded Vanessa across the tarmac, up the steps and into a spare first-class seat in the back row, where she sat like a zombie. Eve wondered if she should have got some medical attention for her friend, who was plainly traumatised.

At that point, the captain came into the cabin. 'I presume she's heard? It's common knowledge that those two were more than friends. Not that I approve of course, but this is one helluva place for the poor woman to find out.'

They all jumped at the sound of a loud wail, followed by deep heart-rending sobs.

Vanessa had begun to cry.

CHAPTER FORTY-FIVE

Molly

Molly hoped that having the plaster removed from her leg would make her feel better, but it didn't. The underlying problem was that things were still not right between herself and Mario. Outwardly, all appeared much the same as usual, but they hadn't made love since the miscarriage and the Patrick business. That, along with the row with Graziana, had constructed an invisible barrier between them.

She was still deeply hurt that he hadn't altogether believed her explanation about Patrick, which was her own fault of course, because she should have told him about the first meeting. She and Graziana were cool and polite to each other, and the boys went backward and forward between home and their grandmother's, seemingly unaware of any friction. It needed a damned good row to clear the air, but, with her luck, it would probably only make matters worse. She missed her old friends, and she missed her parents, who were now ageing. Her father had heart problems, her mother was almost crippled with arthritis, and they weren't going to live forever. She felt a strong urge to visit everyone back home.

Molly hadn't watched television that morning, but, still limping, she hobbled down to the *edicola* to buy her newspaper. She scanned the headlines of *la Repubblica* as she walked back, but Italian politics continued to be a mystery to her and, anyway, no government seemed to be in power long enough to make much difference one way or another. Then a headline lower down caught her eye: 'Skyline jet crash-lands in Kuwait'.

Molly stopped in her tracks. *Please, God*, she prayed, *don't let anyone I know be injured – or worse.*

The details were sketchy; all the facts weren't yet known. Only a few passengers appeared to have been injured, but Captain John Martell, due to retire shortly, had died at the controls. Thought to be a heart attack.

Molly felt physically sick as she entered the apartment, but she'd already made up her mind what she was going to do. She must go to London to comfort Vanessa and then Bristol to visit her parents. Mario had the following week off, supposedly to play golf, which was his new passion. There was no reason why he couldn't look after his sons as well.

Just then, the phone rang.

'*Pronto! Chi?* Patrick! Oh, how good to hear from you! How are you?'

Patrick was in transit at Fiumicino Airport, heading towards London. How was she? Had she heard about the Skyline jet? He apologised for not having any time in Rome.

'Did you say London, Patrick? You're going to London? Will you be there next week?'

Yes, he'd be there all next week as he had lots of meetings to attend. He'd be at the Hilton, in Park Lane.

'I'll contact you there,' Molly said, glad to have another friend in London. She wondered if she should tell Mario, but he'd probably get the wrong idea. So perhaps not.

. . .

Mario wasn't over-delighted at the prospect of his golf being interrupted by childminding, although he couldn't very well refuse when he heard about Vanessa's loss. And Molly knew perfectly well that it was Mina and Graziana who'd do most of the childcare anyway.

'Perhaps Vanessa will find someone single now,' was Mario's only comment, which further irritated Molly. At a time like this, the morals of the situation shouldn't be up for criticism.

Feeling nervous at her possible reaction, nevertheless Molly phoned Vanessa, only to be told by the nanny that Vanessa was due back from Los Angeles later that morning. Then she rang Eve. No reply.

In the evening, she rang Vanessa again, having spent all day trying to come up with something suitable to say. She was more than a little surprised, and not a little relieved, when Eve answered the phone and filled her in with the details.

'How is she?' Molly asked.

'She's in a hell of a state. I got her to the doctor after we landed because she'd wept most of the way back and, as you know, that's a *long* flight. He's given her a sedative, I've brought her home and now she's out for the count. I don't know whether to stay here or go home.'

'You must be exhausted!'

'I am. I just want to go home, and Andy's on his way to collect me. Clare assures me she'll keep an eagle eye on Nessa.'

'I'm coming over tomorrow, Eve.'

'Oh, that's wonderful! She's going to need us, you know. At least Nessa and I had renewed our friendship, thank goodness. What time do you land? I'll meet you at the airport.'

. . .

Molly had never seen Vanessa look so awful. At 3 p.m., she was sprawled on the settee, still in her dressing gown, ashen-faced, swollen-eyed and lank-haired. 'It was good of you to come,' she said listlessly as they embraced. 'What would I do without my friends? And what the hell am I going to do without Johnny?' She burst into tears again.

'Nessa,' Molly said, 'what you're going to do is be both mother and father to your little boy. Where is he anyway? I'm longing to see him.'

Vanessa showed no inclination to move, so Eve went into the hallway and called for Clare, who bustled in a few minutes later with an immaculate baby.

Molly cuddled him for a moment before placing him gently on Vanessa's lap.

Eve turned to the nanny. 'Have a break, Clare; we'll keep him with us here for a while.' Then she studied Vanessa for a moment. 'He's beautiful, Nessa, but then he has a beautiful mother and a handsome father, so no surprise there. And Molly's right – he has to be your first priority.'

The baby burped, which seemed to awaken Vanessa from her torpor.

'I shall never fly again,' she announced. 'Never. Who would look after him if anything happened to me?'

Molly sighed. 'Give yourself time. You know perfectly well that you're much more likely to perish on the roads than you ever are in the air.'

Vanessa appeared not to have heard. 'And what am I going to do for money? Oh God, I want to die.'

Molly spent two nights on Eve's bed-settee. She wondered, and not for the first time, why Eve and Andy hadn't pooled their resources and bought a place together, but they seemed perfectly happy to keep their own flats and sleep wherever was most convenient when they were both at home.

They spent two afternoons at Vanessa's, encouraging her to shower, wash her hair, get dressed and put on some make-up.

Vanessa remained listless and only became more animated when, on the second night, the three of them got very tipsy.

Her time in England limited, the following day, Molly headed into town to have lunch with Patrick, after which she planned to get the late-afternoon train to Bristol for a quick visit to her parents. Eve had promised to keep an eye on Vanessa.

'I'll call in again on my way back to the airport at the end of the week,' Molly said, 'and I hope to goodness she's a bit more like her old self by then.'

Eve sighed. 'I can understand that she's devastated and that they were in love and all that. But have any of us spared even a thought for his poor wife and family?'

'You've no idea how pleased I am to see you,' Molly told Patrick as they embraced in the Hilton lobby. She felt a twinge of guilt because she hadn't told Mario they were meeting.

'I can assure you the feeling is mutual,' Patrick replied. 'You're looking lovely as usual, if a little tired.'

'Hungover, I'm afraid,' Molly admitted. 'We've been drowning Vanessa's sorrows.'

'How is she?'

'Not good. She's going to have to pull herself together for the sake of the baby. She's threatening to give up flying, but goodness knows if then she'd be able to afford a nanny. Or, for that matter, whether the allowance from the baby's father will continue. It's all very messy. Anyway, enough of all that; how are things with you?'

Patrick said he was travelling a lot, not getting home as often as he'd like, and missing landmarks in his daughters' lives.

They ate a leisurely lunch in Trader Vic's and exchanged some family news.

'You're going to Bristol tonight?' Patrick asked.

'There's a train about seven o'clock.'

'Well, I think we should order some champagne to celebrate being able to meet on British soil for a change! I have a very luxurious suite, so why don't we sit in comfort until it's time for your train?'

Her hangover largely forgotten, Molly thought that champagne seemed like a very fine idea. She still hadn't told him how things were with her and Mario – and why. But she needed to explain, in case he ever phoned her at home again and, God forbid, Mario answered.

In his sitting room, Molly settled herself in one of the squashy, comfortable chairs while Patrick ordered a bottle of Bollinger. It arrived promptly, and Patrick poured.

'I'd sworn to avoid alcohol today,' Molly said as she sipped. 'Is it decadent to be drinking champagne in the afternoon?'

Patrick laughed. 'It's never decadent to drink champagne at any time of day. Now, we've talked about everyone else, but how are things with you? Am I imagining that there's something you haven't told me?'

'No, you're not imagining it.' Molly then proceeded to tell him everything that had transpired since their last meeting in Rome: the accident, the broken leg, the miscarriage, the dramatics with Mario and his mother. 'So there it is,' she said, 'and why the hell didn't I tell Mario about the first time we met up?'

Patrick sighed. 'You should have told him of course. But he should have believed you, and I cannot believe that your mother-in-law could cause so much trouble.'

Molly found it such a relief to talk. She would normally have unburdened herself to Eve about how things hadn't improved since her visit, but they'd been far too occupied with Vanessa.

'I'm going to order some more of this,' Patrick said, filling up their glasses. 'I don't have to be anywhere this evening, and you could always get a later train?' He looked at her hopefully.

She knew she shouldn't. But she was feeling so much better, having offloaded her problems, and Patrick was so understanding.

They talked, and they talked, and they got through a lot of Bolly. She hadn't felt so relaxed in years.

'Molly,' he said, 'why don't you postpone Bristol until the morning? You look exhausted. You've had so much stress one way and the other. We'll order some sandwiches later, and then you can have the bed and I'll have the settee. It's *very* comfortable.'

This sounded like a brilliant idea. She rang her parents, trying not to slur, and told them she'd been unavoidably delayed in London, but she'd get the first train next day. They mustn't worry; she was absolutely fine, but Vanessa was not. The O'Haras quite understood how much her bereaved friend needed her.

Patrick ordered a light supper, washed down with a couple of glasses of something-or-other. Was it Sauvignon? Probably, but she was becoming too fuzzy to care. She swayed a little as she stood up, and Patrick held out his hand to steady her. Dear, kind Patrick.

'Come,' he said. 'Come to bed, Molly.'

CHAPTER FORTY-SIX

Eve

'I was thinking,' said Andy, 'how nice it would be to come home to a country cottage somewhere.'

Eve laughed. 'And a pipe and slippers?'

'No, seriously. It's a bit crazy having two places, don't you think?'

'Hmm, yes, I do get a bit fed up with all the traffic sometimes.'

'Well, I was thinking I might sell my flat and put the money towards a place in Hampshire perhaps – or Oxfordshire. Not too far out. It would be handy enough for the airport. But we have to consider your business.'

'As you know, young Liz runs it most of the time and, as it's got so big now, she thinks we should move to larger premises and take on more staff.' Eve pulled a face. 'She's probably right, but I rather liked it when it was just Nadia and myself.'

The days of bringing back carvings, lamps and silks were very much in the past. She now had worldwide suppliers and import licences. Liz was right – they did need somewhere bigger, which meant more rent and more staff. But if she wasn't literally living above the shop, would she be able to keep an eye on things? There was a lot to consider.

It wasn't exactly a conventional marriage because she and Andy were frequently at opposite ends of the earth from each other. Then again, she wasn't sure she could see herself as a country housewife. It was unlikely she'd be joining the Women's Institute, the church flower rota or any other Aileen-type activities. She didn't want to be too far out in the sticks either, because she liked being close to her friends, Vanessa included. Although Eve was glad to have re-established contact with Vanessa, she often felt worn out with all Vanessa's problems, and then felt guilty because she herself was happier than she'd ever been.

Now that his body had been brought back from Kuwait, Vanessa was determined to be at Johnny's funeral – and to have Eve along for moral support.

Eve had been cautious. 'Do you think that's wise?'

'Of course it's wise! He was my lover and the father of my child. I *have* to be there!'

To make matters worse, there had been considerable television and newspaper coverage of the incident.

'We had such a happy retirement planned,' Bryony had wept to the BBC reporter. 'In Barcelona, near our daughter.'

'Happy retirement, my arse!' Vanessa had exploded. 'Little did *she* know what he was planning.'

Eve had decided it was probably best to say nothing. The man was dead and, even if he had been planning more time with Vanessa, there was nothing to be gained by informing his widow of the fact. She'd have liked to talk it over with Molly, but Molly seemed preoccupied these days. Perhaps things still weren't right with Mario. Perhaps he'd got wind of the fact that she'd met Patrick again in London? Mario certainly didn't know his wife very well if he thought she was likely to engage in any extramarital activity, because Molly was straight as a die!

Eve turned her attention back to her new husband. 'Maybe somewhere along the Thames?' she suggested. 'Henley? Marlow?'

'Expensive,' he said, 'but we can look.'

Aware that Andy wanted her to move and to ease up on the business, Eve was confident Liz would be happy to buy her out. So she had to make a decision. But to add to her confusion, Skyline offered her the position of chief stewardess, the most prestigious position, which came with a top salary. They awaited her reply. On top of all that, Vanessa wanted her advice continually, and then she had a phone call to say her mother had had a further heart attack and wanted Eve to come home.

Eve, already exhausted, flew up to Scotland.

Shortly after Eve had left for her flight to Inverness, a young man came knocking at the big red door in Chiswick. He knocked and he knocked, but there was no reply. Finally, he stood back and surveyed the interiors shop next door and wondered if there might be some connection. This time it was open, but, when he glanced in the window, he saw a young woman his own age busily stacking some cushions into a display.

Well, *that* couldn't be her.

With a sigh, he turned and walked away.

Eve hired a Mini in Inverness and went straight to visit her mother in hospital. Aileen was making a good recovery, but, nevertheless, Eve could see a marked change in her. Aileen had aged, and she'd lost weight. Propped up on pillows, she looked pale and frail. She smiled weakly at her daughter.

'Oh, Mum, so good to see you! I'm told you're recovering well!'

Aileen then recounted her trip with the Strathcannon Ladies' Guild to the Isle of Skye, and how she'd felt 'awful peculiar' on the return journey.

'Och, it would be good if you could stay up here for a wee while?'

'I might manage a week,' Eve said doubtfully, visualising Andy with his estate agents' lists, Skyline awaiting her reply, Nadia wanting to talk about the business and Vanessa desperate to attend Johnny's funeral. 'Yes, a week, Mum,' she added, patting her mother's hand.

It felt strange being in the house in Strathcannon on her own. Eve felt exhausted, yet still suffered from insomnia. At night, her brain refused to shut down, and she wondered about sleeping pills as a temporary measure so decided to visit Dr Mackintosh, who'd been the family doctor for years, and who was still practising part-time in his seventies.

'Everything seems to be happening at once,' she told him, 'and my head is buzzing all night long.' She yawned.

'Och, you young people never relax,' he sighed. 'Your mother's making good progress, and I'm going to recommend that she goes into a convalescent home for a few weeks when she gets out of hospital, otherwise she'll be chasing around again far too soon. Now, let's have a look at *you*.'

Shortly afterwards, he said, 'Well, there's not a lot wrong with you, Eve, as far as I can see. Your blood pressure and everything's fine. But I hear you got married recently, and I think it might be a good idea if you had a pregnancy test.'

Eve was suddenly wide awake. 'A *what*?'

'I think you might be having a baby, Eve.'

'You *cannot* be serious! I'm over forty and I've been having irregular periods ever since I came off the pill a year or so ago, because I was pretty sure I was having an early menopause.'

He smiled. 'Get yourself a pregnancy test at the chemist on the way back. I haven't time to give you the required examination now, but I will give you a mild sedative because you need your sleep. This will do no harm if you are pregnant.'

There had to be a mistake! Eve *knew* she wasn't pregnant; it was the menopause. Dr Mackintosh was a lovely man, but it was plainly time he retired.

But what if it was true? She'd been protecting herself from this for all these years. As she made her way home, Eve could barely see the road ahead through the blur of tears in her eyes.

CHAPTER FORTY-SEVEN

Vanessa

Vanessa checked her appearance in the mirror for the umpteenth time. The black two-piece fitted in all the right places, but it gave her a washed-out look and, God only knew, she was washed out all right after weeks of weeping and lack of sleep. If she didn't have Jonathon, she would probably have lost all hope by now; that was how dreadful she felt. Still, it wouldn't do to look too pallid, so she returned to her dressing table and applied some more rouge.

She wondered who else might be attending the funeral from Skyline: all the bigwigs and some pilots, she supposed. Some of them would know why she was there, but she'd do her best to stay in the background until everyone had moved away from the grave, and then she'd throw her little posy onto the coffin and say her private farewell. She was composing a little poem to say quietly.

As she drove westwards, Vanessa wished fervently that Eve was with her for moral support – and to share the driving. But Eve's mother's ill-timed heart attack had thrown a complete spanner in the works. She was now quite sure that she'd be crying her eyes out all the way home and would have to keep stopping to recover so she could see where she was going. Her own mother was on an extended holiday in Kenya, and goodness only knew what she might be up to. Most mothers would be on the next plane home to comfort a bereaved daughter, but not hers.

'You'll get over it,' Hermione had informed Vanessa on the phone. 'It's not as if you were even living together. But do make sure you don't lose your monthly allowance.'

And how exactly am I supposed to do that? Vanessa had wondered.

Vanessa didn't have much idea where she was going and found the road map incomprehensible. Little Poddington was somewhere near Dorchester apparently, so she headed there. She had to stop and ask directions half a dozen times in one chocolate-box village after another, which got her wondering what on earth people *did* here in the sticks.

Vanessa found Little Poddington purely by accident and drove straight through it and out the other side without spotting a church. Then there was nowhere to turn round because the road became narrower and narrower. It was a lane, and not a road at all, and she wasn't going to risk dirtying or damaging her precious Stag by trying to turn in one of those mucky farm gates. Finally, she came to a T-junction and managed a scary U-turn, by which time she was almost in tears, and there was only ten minutes before the service was due to begin.

As she drove slowly back through the tiny village, she finally spotted the sign which pointed down a lane to the church. Why on earth couldn't they build their churches on the main road? she wondered irritably. As she turned down the lane, she could see the cars, dozens of them cluttering up the place, which meant she had to reverse back up the lane again and park close to the main road.

Staggering down the lane, she questioned the wisdom of choosing to wear the killer heels she'd chosen, but she didn't really have any other kind.

Vanessa managed to get into the church minutes before the doors were closed. She, who had hoped to keep a low profile, had caused quite a stir as she'd rushed in, her blonde hair windswept, her heels click-clacking on the floor.

From the very back of the church, she was able to recognise several pilots, plus the chief executive of Skyline for good measure.

The coffin, bedecked with white hydrangeas and roses, was situated in front of the altar. Sitting in the front row, next to the coffin, Vanessa recognised Bryony in a black feathery hat. Her eyes filled up again as she recalled that flight from New York to London, being sweetly polite to the woman. There was a young man in a dark suit, obviously the son, and two very attractive young women, who had to be his daughters.

The service lasted almost an hour. Vanessa heard how Johnny Martell was a great family man, a wonderful pilot, a pillar of the community, wonderful father. On and on it went, before his son gave an emotional eulogy, and Vanessa wished she, too, could go up there and talk about her gorgeous lover. Wouldn't *that* set the cat amongst the pigeons! She was beginning to wish she hadn't bothered with the mascara as she blew her nose and dabbed her eyes every few minutes, and tried not to weep too noisily. She was aware that several people were glancing in her direction, probably wondering who she was.

Finally, it was all over, and the solemn procession exited the church. As she emerged into the sunshine, Vanessa realised she'd run out of tissues. She took a hefty sniff, and then a young man touched her arm and offered her his pristine, nicely ironed handkerchief.

'Are you a relation?' he asked chattily.

'No, just a friend,' Vanessa replied, hoping he'd go away.

She badly wanted to run her fingers along the side of the coffin, to feel the oak. She shuddered at the thought of his beautiful body in that box. 'Thanks for the hankie.' She really couldn't return it to him now. 'Are you a relation?'

'No, I'm a neighbour. We're still all in a state of shock round here. He was such a great guy and *so* devoted to his family. Poor Bryony! Did you know they were building a retirement place in Spain? Architect designed and all that. Don't know if Bryony will carry on with that because it was his idea. Said he couldn't wait to get out of here.'

You've got that wrong, Vanessa thought. *You didn't know him* that *well*.

She smiled at him and moved away, standing back some distance as the family surrounded the grave and the coffin was lowered into the ground. There was a hedge a short distance away, and Vanessa moved behind that. Some Skyline staff had nodded briefly in her direction as they'd left the church, but most had left immediately after the service.

Now that the coffin had been lowered and the vicar had finished, people began to move off. Vanessa wondered where they'd go now. Sandwiches at the local? A smart buffet chez Martell? Where did they live anyway? She could hardly ask anyone.

Finally, Bryony stood alone at the graveside, her head bowed, for several minutes, and then she, too, moved away. Slowly, Vanessa emerged from behind the hedge and, roses in hand, began to walk shakily into the churchyard, digging her heels out of the turf with each step.

Then, suddenly, Bryony turned sharply and looked around. Vanessa dashed behind a bush in an attempt to make herself invisible, stuffing the posy back in her bag, but Bryony had seen her and was heading straight back in her direction.

'You can come out,' Bryony shouted. 'I'm not blind, and I'm not stupid.'

Vanessa gulped as she emerged from behind the bush with difficulty, due to her four-inch heels anchoring her into the ground.

Bryony, her head on one side, was studying her intently. 'I've seen you before somewhere, haven't I? Was it you?'

Vanessa found her voice. 'Was it me *what?*'

'Was it you he was having an affair with? Or *one* of his affairs? I might have guessed; he never could resist tall blondes.'

'It wasn't like that at all—'

'Oh yes it was,' Bryony interrupted, 'and you weren't the only one. Couldn't you find a man of your own? How dare you come here today, to a family funeral! How *dare* you! And I've been having a good look at his outgoings since he passed away, and I see he's been paying out a generous amount of money to an anonymous someone for months. Now, *why* would he be doing that?'

Vanessa braced herself. 'I'm sorry to have to tell you this, on a day like today, but Johnny and I have been in love for years, and we have a little boy who's now seven months old. *That's* where the money was going. And he planned to spend a lot more time with us after he retired.'

Bryony rolled her eyes. 'Is *that* what he told you? Let me tell you, he couldn't get to Spain fast enough, away from this weather and probably his responsibilities. But Johnny would tell you what you wanted to hear.'

The two women continued to glare at each other.

Eventually, Bryony said, 'I'd like to see your son and have the necessary tests done to ensure that he is my husband's. If he is, I'll arrange for a sum of money to be paid to you, but there will be no more monthly payments. I'm doing this for Johnny and not for you. He was a decent man, if a bit weak where women were concerned. Find yourself someone else to finance your lifestyle.' She gave Vanessa a scathing look from the top of her head to the tips of her heels, most of which had sunk into the ground again.

Vanessa struggled to find something to say.

Bryony, however, had plenty to say. 'You'll bring your son to my solicitor's office in Dorchester next Wednesday, at 3 p.m. On the dot.' She rummaged in her bag. 'Here's his card.'

'But—'

'No buts. If you want my money, be there. Now, please get away from my husband's grave.'

With that, Bryony turned and walked quickly away, without looking back, and joined the rest of her family, who were waiting for her at the lychgate.

Vanessa, in tears, waited for some minutes to make sure that they were all gone before she approached the grave, to find two burly men had begun to fill it in and the coffin was already covered in a layer of soil. She took her posy out of her bag.

'You've left it a bit late, love,' one of them said cheerfully, resting on his spade.

'Story of my life,' said Vanessa sadly as she threw the red roses on top of the soil.

CHAPTER FORTY-EIGHT

Molly

The terracotta-coloured house nestled on a hillside with verdant views across the valley. There were large, high-ceilinged rooms, a beautiful garden and even a small olive grove. And it wasn't too far from Frascati, so the boys could continue to attend the same schools, even if Molly had to do more ferrying around.

With no less than six bedrooms, there was plenty of room for Eve and Andy, and Vanessa with her baby, and how marvellous it would be if they could all come at once!

'I think it's a good time to make a move,' Mario had said, 'and it will cheer you up because you've not been your usual lively self since you came back from England.'

That's for sure, thought Molly. Her conscience had gone into overdrive, because what Mario had once suspected had now taken place. Yes, she'd been drunk and stupid. No, it had meant nothing as far as her marriage was concerned, but it had meant the end of all contact with Patrick now that their relationship was no longer platonic. She felt very sad, because she had truly loved him as a friend. But things had gone too far. And Eve and Vanessa had been right when they'd warned her that Patrick would want more than friendship.

This house had come along at exactly the right time and, for the first time in weeks, Molly felt happier. She'd put all thoughts of Patrick behind her; for no one must ever know what had happened. She'd be relieved to have a new telephone number too, her biggest fear being that Patrick might phone.

Vanessa had given her a blow-by-blow account of Johnny's funeral and her meeting with 'bloody Bryony'. Bryony was putting a stop to the monthly allowance, meaning that Vanessa had to hire a solicitor to fight her corner, and what was she supposed to do for money?

If only Eve could have been with her! It was sad that Eve's mother was unwell of course, but the timing was less than perfect. Poor Eve.

When Mario came home that evening, he said, 'I'm going to have to go to London for a few nights, and possibly Manchester as well. If we can get the children looked after, would you like to come along?'

Molly considered this for a moment. 'No, *caro*, I don't think I will. I've only just got back, but do you know what? I'd really like it if you could pop in to see Nessa, because she needs cheering up. Maybe you could take her for a drink or something and persuade her to come out here for a few days?'

CHAPTER FORTY-NINE

Eve

Once she'd recovered from the shock, Eve decided she had three options. The first was to tell no one, not even Andy, and make a discreet visit to Harley Street. She could afford that. The second was to tell Andy and then make the visit to Harley Street. And the third wasn't really an option, not at her age and with her resolution... was it?

Having settled a protesting Aileen into a convalescent home, Eve returned to London. She decided to have the pregnancy confirmed to be sure. What she hadn't reckoned on was morning sickness, which she hadn't experienced before. First of all, she thought she might have eaten something, and then it dawned on her, and she began to wonder just how far gone she might be. It was time to take action.

The highly polished brass plaque on the wall indicated 'Dr A. Patel', followed by a long string of important sounding letters, and then 'Gynaecology'. All very discreet and very expensive.

The waiting room had sumptuous deep-pile carpeting, palms in pots and a white-clad smiling nurse gliding around noiselessly. On the glass coffee table reposed *Vogue* and *Harper's Bazaar*.

Dr Patel was tall, probably in his late forties, and disconcertingly handsome. Eve would have preferred someone less like a movie star for the task in hand – literally.

'I would estimate you are about four months gone,' he announced as he ditched the glove and rolled down his sleeve. 'If you decide to go ahead with this operation, I will only do it in the next couple of weeks, no later. Please think this through carefully and, if you want to go ahead, we will book you in.' He was looking at Eve's wedding ring but made no further comment. She was beginning to wish she'd taken it off.

'I'd like to book it for a fortnight's time then,' she said firmly.

'In that case, please make the appointment at the reception desk.'

Afterwards, Eve couldn't remember if she'd ever seen a grown man cry before. She'd planned to tell Andy when he got back from a Tokyo trip, and preferably in the evening with large gins in their hands. But the very next morning, after her visit to Dr Patel, he'd caught her throwing up.

'Oh, Evie, have you eaten something?'

She shook her head and rinsed her mouth.

'Next thing you'll be telling me it's morning sickness!' He laughed heartily at the idea.

Ashen-faced, she turned to him. 'Oh, Andy, I'm so sorry. I wasn't going to tell you until you got back from your trip.'

He stood, frozen to the spot. 'Are you *kidding*?'

'No, unfortunately I'm not,' Eve replied. 'But, don't worry, I've got everything organised.'

'Organised? What do you mean? Are you *really* pregnant? With *our* baby?'

Eve nodded. It was then that he wept.

'I'm so sorry—'

'*Sorry?*' he interrupted, wiping his eyes and blowing his nose. 'Why are you sorry? It's a *miracle*, that's what it is! After all we've been through, another *child*!'

Eve, astonished and dumbstruck, sat down on the bed.

'I've never been religious, Eve,' he went on, weeping again, 'but now I think there might be a God. For us to be given this blessing, after losing our firstborns, is truly a miracle!' He sat down beside her and took her in his arms. 'Oh, Eve, this is just wonderful!'

Eve finally found her voice. 'But, Andy, we're far too old for all this! I mean, you'll be collecting your pension while the child is still at school!'

'So what?' said Andy. 'Who cares?'

The following day, she cancelled her appointment with Dr Patel. Andy was right; it was meant to be. If Vanessa could do it on her own, then surely she could be a mother too, even at this late age, when she had the love of such a supportive man?

CHAPTER FIFTY

Vanessa

Clare, the nanny, had two days off to attend a family wedding, and Vanessa was exhausted. She'd spent the morning trawling round Sainsbury's with a fractious baby and then got stuck in a traffic jam for half an hour on the way home, while Jonathon, who had soiled his nappy, howled lustily throughout. On top of that, it was only yesterday she'd got back from the appointment with bloody Bryony and the solicitor, which had been a very unpleasant experience and now necessitated hiring a solicitor of her own in an attempt to retain the monthly payments.

She carried Jonathon and the shopping bags into the house, then had to change the horrible nappy, and discovered that she'd laddered her new, expensive tights. Thank God Clare was due back that evening.

While she was unpacking her groceries and Jonathon, was still wailing on the carpet, the phone rang. She sighed. Who now?

It was the way he said, 'Va-nessa?' The accent.

'Yes?'

'It's Mario.'

'Mario? What's happened? Is Molly OK...?'

'Yes, yes, don't worry. It's only that I am in London with a free evening and wondered if I might have the pleasure of taking you out for a drink and maybe dinner? But you are probably busy?'

'No, no, I'm not! That would be wonderful! The only problem is that my nanny isn't due back until later and I can't leave the baby. So why don't you come here and I can cook something?' Vanessa stared gloomily at her kitchen cupboards, wondering whether she'd have to brave Sainsbury's again.

'That would be nice. I shall bring some wine.'

After she'd given him directions and replaced the receiver, Vanessa began to panic. What did one cook for an Italian accustomed to exotic Mediterranean fare? Then, with relief, she remembered the Italian delicatessen at the end of the next road, which did takeaway lasagne. Problem solved.

Then she looked at herself in the mirror. She hadn't made much effort with her appearance since Johnny had died, not bothering to put on make-up or do anything with her hair. And her legs needed shaving. Not that she was about to seduce Mario – perish the thought! But the baby had finally fallen asleep, and so she decided that the precious time would be better spent on her appearance than on culinary pursuits.

Mario arrived by taxi at seven o'clock, with a large bunch of pink roses, a bottle of Prosecco and two bottles of his own wine.

He pecked her on both cheeks. 'How are you? Molly thought you might need cheering up.'

'I do,' said Vanessa as she led him into the kitchen to deposit the bottles on the counter. 'I'm so pleased to see you.'

Having inserted the roses into a vase of water, she proceeded to show him around. Mario duly admired everything, including her still sleeping baby. As they sat down with a glass of Prosecco, he imparted all the family news, showed her photos of the children and also of the house they were in the process of buying. He didn't seem to be unduly put out by the fact that he was to go to collect his own dinner from a deli five minutes' walk away. Vanessa offered to pay, but, being the gentleman he was, Mario wouldn't hear of it.

Half an hour later, with the lasagne keeping warm in the oven, they had their second glass of Prosecco, and then Jonathon woke up.

Vanessa sighed and looked at her watch. 'Clare's back soon, but I wish she'd hurry up.'

Mario stood up. 'Don't worry! I love babies, and I'll hold him until you get his bottle ready.' He picked up Jonathon, who calmed immediately and gazed up at Mario with his large blue eyes.

When Vanessa appeared with the bottle, Mario insisted on feeding him.

'Relax!' he instructed Vanessa. 'Enjoy your drink!'

How good he is with babies, Vanessa thought. Molly was incredibly lucky.

Clare had barely got in through the door before Jonathon was bundled into her arms. 'It's just that I have a friend from *Italy* here to dinner,' Vanessa explained.

Clare nodded meekly.

Mario, in the meantime, was busy making a green salad, removing the pasta from the oven and grating Parmesan over everything in sight.

'How clever you are!' Vanessa said admiringly as they sat down at the table. 'I do hope Molly realises how lucky she is.'

'Hmm,' said Mario, 'Molly might not altogether agree with that! Trouble is, I have to travel a lot, and I worry that she gets lonely.' He took a forkful of lasagne. 'Do you know a man called Patrick?' He refilled their glasses with red wine.

Vanessa thought for a moment. 'I seem to remember he was some guy Molly met on a flight. I've never met him, but I've heard her talk about him. Why do you ask?'

'Because Molly has been meeting him and not telling me. Now, why would she do that?'

'I expect she knew you'd be jealous. But Molly's straight as a die; you've no need to worry there.'

'Hmm, perhaps not. And you, Vanessa, how are you?'

Vanessa laid down her fork and sipped her wine. 'Some days I'm just about OK. Not good, but OK. Other days are hell. It's bad enough having lost Johnny, but now I'm having a legal battle with his wife to retain my monthly maintenance payments, and money's flying out of the window.' Her eyes filled.

Mario sighed. 'Surely your lover would have wished to continue supporting his son? And what about your job?'

'I'm on sick leave, due to stress. I have a very understanding doctor, but he can't sign me off indefinitely. I'll have to decide soon if I'm going to go back flying or not. I don't really want to, but I need the money. I do a little modelling from time to time as well, but it's not a regular income, and I still have some mortgage to pay off.' Vanessa gulped some more wine. 'That's not all. Johnny said that Bryony wanted to relocate to Spain, but he didn't. He was happy to be here, and we would be together more. Now she says the opposite, that it was he who wanted to go. And one of the neighbours, who I met at the funeral, said the same, and now I don't know who to believe.'

He filled her glass again. 'You'll never know, so don't torture yourself.'

'But I'm so lonely now. I know we didn't live together, but I always had his visits, or our trips, to look forward to. I really loved him, you know. The only thing that keeps me going is baby Jonathon. Without him, I would probably have…' Vanessa blew her nose.

'You must *not* think like that! Someone will come along for you before long. You are a beautiful woman, and many men will want you.'

Vanessa sighed. *Even if they do want me*, she thought, *it's unlikely I'd ever want any of them.*

They finished their meal and then transferred themselves to the sofa with the second bottle of red wine.

'That was delicious, Mario,' Vanessa said. 'It's so good to talk to a man, and you are so wonderfully understanding.' She giggled. 'And I am quite tipsy!' She moved a little closer to him on the sofa. She knew that she wasn't entirely in control of the situation and probably he wasn't either, since they'd imbibed so much wine, as well as the Prosecco. Mario was a handsome man, if somewhat shorter than her, but, as someone once said, it's all the same when you're horizontal. 'I feel so empty and unfulfilled now; what am I to do?'

He turned to face her. 'You are very lovely, Vanessa.'

'And so are you,' she murmured. Their lips touched and then he had his arms round her. 'But you should go.'

'Do you want me to?'

'No, I don't, but Molly is my friend. I should call you a taxi.'

'Indeed, you should,' he said, kissing her again.

Vanessa felt awful next day. How in God's name had *that* happened? How would she be able to face Molly ever again? Mario had called a taxi and left immediately afterwards, looking guilty and giving her a rueful smile.

In the afternoon, she took Jonathon for a long walk along the Thames towpath, to watch the boats go by and to get some fresh air. It was a cool, autumnal day, the paths thickly carpeted with leaves which crunched under the wheels of the pram. Jonathon, who was sitting up and looking around, gave her one of his beguiling toothless grins. When, she wondered, would he have some teeth? How little she knew about babies! Perhaps she should treat herself to a book on the subject and not leave everything to Clare. How long could she afford to keep Clare anyway? If the maintenance payments stopped, Clare would have to go. And then she wouldn't be able to go back flying, even if she wanted to.

CHAPTER FIFTY-ONE

Molly

Molly and Mario were about to host a housewarming party. They'd invited everyone they could think of, and Molly was particularly pleased that Eve and Andy were making the effort to come and were due to fly in that very evening. Not so Vanessa. She'd been invited, but she'd made some vague excuse about having to see her solicitor. Well, it had *sounded* like an excuse. Then again, Vanessa had been somewhat incommunicado of late, and she hoped Mario hadn't said something to upset her when he'd visited some weeks previously.

Mario, on the other hand, was much more like his old self since he'd returned from London. He was particularly kind and loving, much to her relief, and she hoped they could put the Patrick business behind them and start afresh in their beautiful new home. There were still some soft furnishings to choose, and Eve had promised to bring along some fabric samples and brochures. Now, at least all the furniture was in place and the new kitchen fitted.

Mario's brother, Alessandro, and his wife, Veronica, had

come down from Tuscany for the event, as had Donatella from Milan, with her two children but no husband because Andrea was 'tied up with work'. None of Molly's family could make it, so she was delighted that Eve was coming.

Later, as she waited at Fiumicino, she felt the usual nostalgic pang as she watched the enormous Skyline 747 touch down. It was en route to Sydney, and the only passengers getting off were Eve and Andy, although she was told there was a group of fifty getting on. And she was surprised to see a visible change in Eve as they embraced in the arrivals area.

As they headed towards Molly's car, Eve said, 'I bet you think I've put on weight.'

'No, no,' Molly said hastily.

'I have. Take a good look.'

Molly didn't quite know what to say. 'You look very *healthy*,' she managed at last.

Both Eve and Andy were laughing. 'I'm four months pregnant,' Eve said.

Molly's mouth opened, but no words came out.

'I've never known you stuck for words before, Molly,' Eve said.

'You *can't* be!' Molly exclaimed when she recovered her composure. 'You dark horse, you! A *baby*! After all you said!'

'That,' said Eve, 'was before I met Mr Right here. It certainly wasn't planned, and it's only because Andy was so delighted that I decided to go ahead with it.'

'Congratulations, both! This is wonderful! Have you told Vanessa yet?'

'Not yet. I can well imagine what she'll say though!'

Mario took Andy for a tour round his newly acquired olive grove, while Molly proudly showed Eve her kitchen.

'Wow!' said Eve. 'This is fantastic! These Italian kitchens cost a fortune in the UK.'

'They cost a fortune here too,' said Molly, 'but business is good, and Mario is pandering to my every whim at the moment. If I didn't know him better, I'd suspect he had a guilty conscience or something!'

'Well, maybe at long last he's realised just how silly he was over the Patrick business. Anywhere, where *is* Vanessa? I was sure she'd be here.'

'I thought so too, but she's got an appointment or something, which, frankly, sounded like an excuse to me. What do you think?'

Eve looked thoughtful. 'Has she been in touch much recently?'

'No, not since Mario got back. I told him to pay her a call and try to cheer her up. I wonder if he might have offended her in some way?'

CHAPTER FIFTY-TWO

Eve

The party was a roaring success. Everyone in Mario's family brought enough food and wine to feed a regiment, to add to the mountain Molly had prepared already.

'Why aren't they all fat as houses?' Eve whispered to Andy as, Prosecco in hand, they surveyed the enormous buffet.

'Italians don't let themselves get fat,' Andy said, patting his noticeable paunch. 'Feast today, famine tomorrow probably. All very stylish though.'

Later, Eve wandered out onto the terrace, nursing her glass of wine. She'd eaten enough for herself, the baby and half of Rome. Although it was now November, it was still mild, and had become very hot inside as more and more people kept arriving. It was beautiful out here, looking across the valley at the lights twinkling on the hillside opposite. She could hear the tolling of a bell in the distance and the sultry tones of an Italian love song. People inside had started to dance.

Eve was suddenly aware that she wasn't alone.

'*Buonasera*,' said Graziana. 'You are enjoying?'

'Very much. Beautiful house, beautiful view, lovely people.'

Graziana smiled. 'You married now?'

'Yes, I'm married now.'

'And having baby?'

God, thought Eve, *how does she know?* 'Does it show already?'

'Only to me. *Always* I know.' Graziana tapped her nose. 'Sometimes I know before the *mamma* does. You are pleased?'

'Yes, of course.'

'You have left it very late, like that other one. What she called?'

'Do you mean Vanessa?'

'*Sì*, Vanessa.' She sniffed. 'Time to have babies is when you young. I have my three before I twenty-five.'

'Better late than never,' Eve said politely before turning round and walking back indoors.

Eve and Andy stayed on for a few days after the party, which gave Eve and Molly the excuse to browse around the shops on Via Condotti, and then lunch in the open air at a restaurant near the Spanish Steps. In the evening, the four of them went into Frascati for *aperitivi*, and to watch *la passeggiata*, that Italian evening ritual which involves leisurely strolling, dressed to kill, admiring and being admired by all and sundry. Eve found it very amusing, particularly so because the Italians took it very seriously. She'd never seen so many fur coats on display, mainly mink, and thought that the women must be sweltering, because the weather was still unseasonably mild. She felt comparatively dowdy in her black coat, which had seemed very stylish in London, but Molly had taught her the art of draping a long scarf, in a carefully careless manner, round her neck and shoulders.

She loved this country.

CHAPTER FIFTY-THREE

Vanessa

A mahogany-tanned Hermione finally arrived home from Nairobi just three weeks before Christmas.

'Gosh, Mother, you look amazing!'

'I feel great. And I must tell you, Vanessa, that I'm only here to sell up, and then I'm off back to Kenya. I've met the most beautiful man. Gunther he's called. German – been out there for years.' She sighed theatrically. 'I've finally found my soulmate!'

'For God's sake, Mother, not *another* one!' Vanessa hesitated for a moment. 'What about Desmond?'

'What about him? He's old hat, darling, and a bit young anyway. He made a very attractive escort of course. You must meet him sometime! He's got pots of dough, you know. And he has this amazing gift for making money,' her mother went on. 'Only wish I had that gift! Never mind, my flat should be worth a fair bit. I must go up there after I've had a peep at my grandson. How is he?'

. . .

'Has your mother gone back yet?' Eve asked a couple of weeks later. They'd resumed their weekly telephone chats.

'She left last night on a one-way ticket,' Vanessa said, 'and thank God for that. All she could talk about was this bloody Gunther. Wouldn't you think, at her age, she'd be happy to take up knitting or whatever it is that old dears are supposed to do?'

Eve laughed. 'I'd hardly class your mother as an old dear, but good luck to her anyway. I'm sorry you weren't able to go to Molly's party. It was really good. Wonderful house.'

'Yes, you must tell me all about it. Let's do lunch; how about Friday? I'll book somewhere and let you know.'

'Good idea. I'll look forward to it.'

Eve

Eve was glad Vanessa had bothered to book a table, because the White Rose at Hampton was heaving, mainly with pre-Christmas works outings.

Vanessa arrived, ten minutes late, looking stunning in a cream suede coat with an enormous red fox collar.

'You look well,' she said to Eve by way of greeting.

'And you're looking sensational! You're obviously recovering?'

'Well, I am feeling a little better. I'm still missing Johnny of course.'

Eve detected something defensive in her manner. What was she up to now?

They ordered drinks and studied the menu.

'I'll just have some grilled fish,' said Eve.

'That's not like you! You were always the big steak eater. Are you slimming then? Or pregnant?' Vanessa dissolved into gales of laughter.

'Yes,' said Eve.

'Yes what?'

'I'm pregnant.'

Vanessa dropped the menu. '*What?*'

'I. Am. Pregnant.'

'*You* are pregnant! Careful, canny, sensible Eve!'

'Don't be so callous! I really thought you might be pleased for me.'

'Oh, Eve, I'm sorry!' Vanessa squeezed her friend's hand across the table. 'Of course I'm pleased! It's just such a shock, that's all. What about Skyline?'

'I'm doing a couple more trips and then I'll work on the ground for a few months. After the baby's born, who knows? I'm keeping my options open. What about you?'

'I hate flying now,' Vanessa said. 'I'm looking for a way out. Barty's got me some modelling and, provided I get Johnny's payments, I'll be able to keep Clare on for the moment.'

Eve studied her friend. 'How did you get on with Mario when he came over some weeks ago?'

Vanessa sipped her wine. 'Yes, it was good to see him. Why do you ask?'

'I just wondered. Normally you would have rung and told me about his visit, but it was Molly who told me.'

'It honestly didn't enter my mind. Now, what shall I have? The fillet perhaps?'

Andy was watching football on TV when Eve got home.

'Arsenal are rubbish today!' he said. 'Anyway, how was the grieving widow? Or merry widow? Or merry mistress?'

'Oh, she was fine and glamorous as ever. Promise me one thing though, Andy: if I'm ever indisposed for any reason, don't go anywhere near her on your own!'

CHAPTER FIFTY-FOUR

2015

'I keep remembering your lovely wedding in Rome,' Eve said.

'It felt strange at the time though,' Vanessa recalled, 'thinking of you over there in Italy.' She refilled the glasses.

'It felt strange to me too,' Molly agreed, 'particularly with my bloody awful mother-in-law! Things got better when we got our own place.'

'And you kept meeting a certain person who just *happened* to be visiting Rome,' said Eve, giving Molly a wink.

Molly rolled her eyes. 'And I have something very interesting to add to that,' she said. 'But not right *now*,' she added quickly as both sets of eyes swivelled enquiringly in her direction. '*You* gave us a few surprises, Nessa!'

'I suppose I did,' Vanessa admitted, 'and so did Eve.' She shuddered. 'That *awful* lunch...'

'Let's draw a veil over that,' Eve said quickly.

'Never mind – we're all together now,' Molly said. 'Sometimes I can't believe we're all still *here*. Alive, I mean!"

'Why wouldn't we be?' Vanessa asked.

'I must admit I sometimes worried about that too,' said Eve.

'All those time differences! Getting up in the middle of the night to fly from A to B! It couldn't have been healthy.'

'Sunbathing on the equator in a sea of olive oil!' added Molly, remembering Nairobi all those years ago.

Vanessa snorted. 'And drinking far too much everywhere we went! Still, no point in stopping now!' She lifted the champagne bottle. 'Or would you prefer wine?'

1992

CHAPTER FIFTY-FIVE

Eve

The M4 traffic kept coming to a standstill, and the drive was taking forever. Molly's plane was due to land at 9.30 a.m., which, unfortunately, coincided with the morning's commuter crawl into London.

Flo, securely belted in the back, was becoming increasingly bored. 'Why do we keep stopping, Mummy?'

Eve surveyed her eight-year-old daughter in the rear-view mirror. Flo had inherited Andy's creamy skin and blue eyes, and her own hair, which, in Flo's case, was more auburn than red.

'Lots of people going to work, darling. Auntie Molly knows what the traffic's like at this time of the morning, so she won't worry if we're a little late.'

'No boys?'

Eve smiled to herself. Flo was already quite smitten with the fourteen-year-old Carlo.

'No boys. Both Marcello and Carlo have exams, and

Stefano's working with his dad.' *And his dad*, Eve thought privately, *is working far too hard for a man of his age*.

She'd finally persuaded Molly to come over for a visit. Mario had been invited too but sent his sincere apologies because he was in the middle of negotiating a new contract with someone from Saudi Arabia, and the talks were at a crucial stage.

Eve's thoughts were elsewhere as they crawled along the motorway. Yesterday, she'd gone to visit an ex-stewardess friend who lived in Putney and had had to leave her car some distance away from Pam's house because of parking problems. On the way there, she'd walked past a big old church, where the bells were ringing and a beaming couple had emerged.

She didn't know what made her stop to watch because she wasn't a fan of formal weddings, or any weddings for that matter. Perhaps it was because they were such a good-looking pair; the pretty blonde bride in an elegant off-the-shoulder creation, and there was *something* about the groom. Déjà vu? Had she seen him before? If so, where? And when?

The guests had emerged and the photographer was dashing around trying to organise photographs, and the young newly-weds were swallowed up in the crowd.

Eve had moved on, but her thoughts kept returning to that couple.

The traffic stopped again. Eve, studying her pretty little daughter in the mirror, could scarcely believe how little Florence Aileen Mason had transformed her life. Farewell Skyline! Farewell Chiswick! Welcome to rural Berkshire, mothers' groups, bucket-and-spade holidays and the endless quest for good schools. Eve sometimes felt self-conscious amongst twenty-something-year-old mothers at the school gates, but, as Andy pointed out, she'd done so much more *living*. She'd made a success of flying and setting up a business, the latter providing a substantial income, since she still retained a major share.

Eve knew now that she had been too emotionally crippled throughout her twenties and thirties, due to the loss of her son, but Flo had helped so much to heal the wound. She often wondered about the other single mothers in that nursing home all those years ago. Had they gone home, married a nice local lad, had more babies and put the whole thing to the back of their minds? Had they too avoided emotional contact? She'd never know but, hopefully like her, they'd eventually found some solace.

'Eve, you look amazing!' Molly hugged her friend and then turned her attention to Flo. 'And you, young lady, have grown so tall! You *must* be older than eight – twelve at least!'

Flo flushed with pleasure. 'How's Carlo?'

'Carlo's fine, but he's in the middle of exams.'

'Anyway, you'll meet young Jon when we go to lunch at Auntie Vanessa's,' Eve said to her daughter by way of compensation.

Flo made a face. 'I don't fancy *him*!'

Molly roared with laughter. Flo sounded so confident but, after all, times had change greatly since their own childhoods.

'How are all the Bellinis?' Andy asked as he helped himself to a generous chunk of Gorgonzola from the cheeseboard. He carefully avoided Eve's eye, because he knew she was concerned about his increasing girth.

'All present and correct,' said Molly. 'But I worry about Mario because he's working far too hard. He's been diagnosed with a heart condition and told to take it easier, but does he listen? No, he does not! He doesn't know how to delegate, that's his trouble. Stefano's working with him now, which is good and takes some of the burden off his shoulders. Then Marcello will hopefully go to university. He'd like to study law and will probably go up to Pisa, where his Uncle Alessandro can keep an eye on him. And Carlo? Well, Carlo has more than his share of charm, but at the moment, I can only see him as a gigolo!'

'What's a gigolo?' Flo asked with interest.

'Someone who works hard at school,' Eve got in quickly, 'and who does his homework and eats his greens.'

'Oh, indeed,' agreed Molly, rolling her eyes.

'But Mario should take the doctor's advice,' Eve said, 'because he doesn't want to end up with a heart attack or something. And how about the fearsome Graziana?'

'Coming up to eighty and strong as a damned ox! She'll outlive us all!'

Molly had lost her father with cancer the previous year, around the same time Eve had lost her mother with that final heart attack. Molly's mother, crippled with arthritis, had moved in with Siobhan, while Connor had married a Spanish girl and lived in Malaga, running a hotel for British tourists and procreating profusely. At the last count, there were seven children and Molly couldn't actually remember if her sister-in-law might be pregnant again.

'Getting back to Vanessa,' Molly said, 'I believe she's having to look after her own child these days, so I bet she's finding that tough.'

Eve nodded. 'The saintly Clare got married and disappeared off the scene. I'm betting it'll only be a matter of time now before Jon is packed off to boarding school somewhere.'

'How's your mother, Nessa?' Eve asked politely as they sat quaffing champagne on Vanessa's manicured lawn.

'Yes, well.' Vanessa was studying her newly manicured nails. 'At least *she* seems to be permanently settled now, in her beloved Kenya.'

'So what about you, Nessa?' Eve asked. 'No new man on the scene?'

Vanessa shook her head. 'I don't want a new man, thank you very much. Johnny was my one and only love.'

'That was a long time ago, and you still have a life to lead,' Eve said. 'And what's wrong with some security for your old age?'

'I'm quite secure, thank you, and I'm sending Jon to boarding school shortly. I've got a new modelling contract with Barty. Did you know he's *still* with your Marty, Molly?'

'He was never really *my* Marty,' Molly said with a sigh.

CHAPTER FIFTY-SIX

Molly

Molly loved meeting up with Eve and Vanessa again, but she missed Mario, and she missed Italy. When had she become so *Italian*? She must plainly have changed in the twenty years she'd been living there, and she was aware that she wouldn't willingly live in the UK again. Perhaps it was the leaden skies and unpredictable rain; perhaps it was something else. She couldn't define it. She'd miss Italian people, Italian food, Italian music. Even Italian mothers-in-law!

From time to time, she thought how lucky she was to have met Mario and offered up a prayer of thanks that he'd never found out about that crazy night with Patrick. Occasionally, she'd wonder if Mario had ever been unfaithful to her. After all, he did travel a lot and must have had many temptations. Then she'd immediately dismiss the idea.

Molly still felt exhausted as she grabbed her bag off the carousel at Fiumicino before emerging from the terminal building, where an ashen-faced Stefano awaited his mother.

'Ah, Stefano!' She kissed her son. 'Where's your father? Why are *you* here?'

Stefano continued to hug his mother. 'Mamma, he's in hospital.'

Molly's hand flew to her heart. '*Hospital*? What's wrong? Why did you not *call* me?'

'Because this happened late last night, and you couldn't have got here any sooner.'

'What is it, Stefano? His heart?'

'Sì, Mamma, his heart. It's bad, and he's in intensive care, all wired up and barely conscious.'

Molly was in tears. 'Get me there quickly!'

I mustn't cry, Molly thought. *He must not see or hear me cry.* But as she gazed at the grey, shrunken form of her beautiful husband, amid a myriad of tubes and wires, she couldn't prevent the tears from streaming down her cheeks.

'I'm here, *caro*,' she said softly as she caressed his limp hand. 'I should have been here last night – forgive me. But now you must get well again.'

She thought he squeezed her hand, although the feeling was barely perceptible. Molly wasn't sure if he could hear her but hoped that, if she kept chattering, he might stay partly conscious. Stefano, in the meantime, was standing at the door with a tall man in a white coat who was obviously a doctor.

'It was good to see everyone,' she whispered, 'but I missed you so. They're all fine and send love.' Chatter, chatter, chatter – *could* he hear? Did she detect the shadow of a smile on his lips?

The doctor had advanced into the room. '*Signora*, it is good you are here.'

'Oh, *dottore*, what now?'

'Just come outside for a moment please.'

Unwillingly, she removed her hand from Mario's.

The doctor looked grave. 'I am sorry, *signora*, there is little we can do. He's had a massive heart attack and the heart is now so badly damaged that the rest of his body is closing down.'

'Oh, *dottore*, there must be *something*...?'

He shook his head sadly. 'We are doing everything we can to keep him free of pain and to make him comfortable. That is all we can do. It is best that you stay with him now.'

Molly nodded mutely and blew her nose.

'I'll get us some coffee, Mamma,' Stefano said.

'Thank you. What about Marcello and Carlo?'

'They're on their way. They'll be here soon.'

Although she'd only left him for five minutes, Molly felt that Mario had slipped further into the abyss. There was so much she needed to say to him.

'Mario, I love you so much. You're my rock, my life. Come back to me, *caro*, so I can take you home and never let you work again. Never!' The tears were flowing freely now. 'Who else would correct my Italian? Like the time in that restaurant when I asked for a plateful of *peni*? I didn't know it meant "penises" – I thought I was asking for pasta!'

She was sure now that she could decipher the ghost of a smile on his lips, just before everything started bleeping and everyone rushed in.

He'd gone. Molly knew he'd gone because, almost at once, she realised that the body on the bed wasn't her Mario. Her Mario was in the air, in the sky, in her heart, and not in this shell. Molly knew that hearing was the last sense to go, and hoped that he'd heard her to the end and known she was there. In the years ahead, she'd like to think that he'd waited for her to be by his side before he left her forever.

. . .

'Why God do this to me?' Graziana, shrouded in black, was leaning heavily against Molly as they finalised the funeral arrangements. 'He take my Luigi when he only thirty-five years old, and now he take my Mario! My *younger* son! Nobody should outlive their child.'

Molly hugged her. 'I know, I know. There are no answers, Graziana. But we shall get through it somehow.'

Both Alessandro and Donatella, with their respective families, were staying with Graziana. Molly had a full house too. Apart from the three boys, her mother had insisted on coming, even though she was partially crippled with arthritis. Connor had flown from Spain to collect her and bring her to Rome. And, later, Eve and Vanessa were arriving from London. Stefano was already on his way to the airport to pick them up.

It was late and everyone, exhausted with grief and travelling, had retired, apart from the three friends. They were still sitting out on the terrace after midnight when Vanessa filled up Molly's glass for the umpteenth time. 'Don't argue,' she said. 'You need it.'

'I don't know how I'm going to get through tomorrow,' Molly said.

Eve leaned forward and took Molly's hand. 'You're strong, and you're going to be OK.'

'And I know *just* what you're going through,' said Vanessa.

Eve raised her eyebrows. 'Not *quite* the same, Nessa.'

'Exactly the same!' snapped Vanessa. 'When you've been with a man for more than twenty years—'

'Except you *weren't*!' Eve interrupted. 'You only saw him occasionally, so it's not the same at all!'

'And how would *you* know?' Vanessa countered. 'You've never been with a man for that long!'

Molly spread out her hands. '*Please* don't start squabbling, you two – not now.'

But there was no stopping Vanessa. 'And, like Molly, I had his child, so I know what it's like to lose the father of your child.'

Molly put her fingers in her ears. '*Please!*'

Eve was contrite. 'I'm sorry, Molly. Of *course* we shouldn't be squabbling.' She looked daggers across at Vanessa.

Vanessa was filling the glasses again. 'I'm sorry too. I think we're all a bit over-emotional at the moment. The thing is, Molly, we're here for you.'

'And we'll always be here for you,' added Eve.

'Thanks, girls.' Molly gave a weak smile. 'It only seems like yesterday that we were young and carefree at Bellingham Road, and now we're at that age where awful things begin to happen.' She let out a sob. 'And yet I'm so lucky. I have my three boys, who are being bloody wonderful. I have Connor, and my ma, and my two best friends – everyone who really matters to me. I even feel love for Graziana, who's aged twenty years in the past few days. She may not be the world's best mother-in-law, but she doesn't deserve this. Just as well she has the constitution of an ox.'

Vanessa drained her glass. 'Have you decided what you're going to do, Molly?'

'Do? I shall stay here in our home. Alessandro will run the business with Stefano. And you two must come over often to keep me company.'

Eve

Eve, still feeling emotional, was relieved to get home. She'd worried a little about leaving Flo, although she knew that Andy was more than capable of looking after his daughter. There had been no opportunity to do any shopping, but she'd bought Flo a little leather purse at Fiumicino Airport, and some limoncello for Andy.

'Anything exciting happen in my absence?' she asked them both.

'Nothing, except Arsenal won, at last,' said Andy.

'No phone calls?'

'There was a double-glazing phone call, Mummy,' Flo said, 'but I told him we already had it. And there was a man came to the door, yesterday I think it was.'

'A man?' Eve asked as she carried her case into the bedroom.

'Yeah, nothing important. I was on the phone to Holly, 'cos there's this boy in our class she really fancies and—'

'So what did the man want?' Eve interrupted.

'Oh, he was looking for Evelyn Somebody-or-Other,' Flo replied. 'I didn't catch the second name, but I told him we were the Mason family.'

Eve sat down heavily on the bed. 'He asked for someone called *Evelyn*?'

'Yeah, I'm pretty sure that's what he said, but—'

'Did you get his name, Flo?'

'No, he was very nice though.'

'Flo,' Eve said, 'Evelyn *is* my name. Nobody's ever called me that, but it's on my birth certificate and...' She paused. 'What did he look like?'

'Mum, he was just a *man*. He was quite tall, I think. I didn't pay much attention because—'

'Was he dark, fair, *anything* you can remember, Flo?'

Flo shook her head. 'I didn't *study* him, Mum. He was dark, I think, and quite good-looking. Does it *matter*?'

'I really don't know,' Eve said wearily.

2015

CHAPTER FIFTY-SEVEN

Vanessa

'The guest bedrooms have been made up, just as you asked. Will there be anything else, m'lady?'

Lady Vanessa Delamore looked up from the list she was compiling in preparation for her visitors. One had to write everything down these days, because one was becoming extremely forgetful. 'No, Zara, that's fine. And I trust you put some nice toiletries in their bathrooms?'

'Yes, m'lady. And I put some cream roses in the English lady's room, and pink ones in the Italian lady's room.'

Lady Delamore nodded. 'Good.' No point in telling her that one lady wasn't really English, and the other wasn't really Italian. 'Thank you, Zara.'

'Zara' indeed! Had the poor girl's mother envisaged her becoming an accomplished horsewoman perhaps? Or marrying royalty? Instead, here she was, cleaning and polishing, along with an army of estate workers who kept Stourton Hall up to the standard her dear late husband, Dicky, would have wished.

Lord 'Dicky' Delamore had been fifteen years her senior

when they'd first met at Ascot. She herself had been fifty-nine and gone there with a friend who had successfully contrived to get them both into the Royal Enclosure. 'We need to meet classier types of chaps,' she'd informed Vanessa. And, sure enough, along had come his lordship.

'You're the most beautiful woman I've seen in years,' he'd told Vanessa, removing two glasses of champagne from the proffered tray and handing one to her.

'Why, thank you, Lord Delamore!' she'd murmured, attempting to appear demure.

'Call me Dicky, m'dear; everyone does.'

So she did. And, at that first meeting, established that he was widowed, childless and incredibly rich. Naturally, she'd accepted his invitation to meet again, when further investigation revealed Stourton Hall in Somerset was the ancestral country 'seat', and then there was the pied-à-terre in Mayfair, not to mention the holiday home of great character in Provence, nestling in the hills and overlooking the Mediterranean. Just a stone's throw from Cannes and Nice.

Vanessa had decided she could become very fond of Dicky; after all, she had been feeling a little lonely.

Dicky had been lonely too, having been widowed for years and sorely in need of female companionship, but he'd admitted that his sex drive had got up and gone. This didn't bother Vanessa in the least. Although she was very fond of him, she was looking for security, not sex, and she didn't fancy him that much anyway.

Vanessa had willingly acquiesced, and became the second Lady Delamore on her sixtieth birthday, a day on which she gave no thought whatsoever to pensions or bus passes as they set off on a three-month Pacific cruise.

.   .   .

On this occasion, she'd decided to pull out all the stops to give Eve and Molly a few days to remember. Eve had had a tough time battling cancer and was in dire need of some pampering. Molly, on the other hand, was in a permanent state of anxiety about her irrepressible and irresponsible youngest son, Carlo, who fancied himself as a film actor. Without any great success, it had to be said; none of which was any good for Molly's dodgy heart. Why did one's offspring so rarely achieve what one had hoped for them? she wondered, thinking of Jon. All that money sending him to the best schools, and where did it get him? Certainly not a pilot like his late, lovely father! No, he was a reporter on a *tabloid* – a downmarket tabloid at that! Johnny must be spinning in his grave!

'I just want to *write*, Mother,' he'd informed her, 'and I've got to start somewhere. Just give me time and I'll be pumping out bestsellers!'

Oh, indeed, Vanessa had thought. Then he'd capped it all by getting married – to *Eve and Andy's daughter*! Flo was a nice enough girl of course, but still... She had rather hoped he might have chosen someone just a little more *aristocratic* perhaps?

Vanessa had taken to downing a few gin and tonics before dinner. That's if you could call it dinner because, here at Stourton Hall, she generally had just one course, delivered on a tray by Zara, while she watched the news on television. Of course the routine gins, and the routine wine that accompanied the tray were way beyond those ridiculous units, or limits, or whatever they were called, that you were supposed to stick to on a weekly basis. *Try telling that one to cabin crew back in the sixties*, she thought, *and I'm seventy-three and feeling just fine, thank you very much. Who wants to live forever with one measly little drink each evening?* she wondered. *At least I'll die with a smile on my face!*

She could hear the phone ringing and Zara answering it,

followed by the knock on the door as Zara entered and handed the phone to Vanessa.

'It's your son, m'lady.'

'Thank you, Zara. Hello, Jon.'

'Hi, Mother. How are things out there in rural Somerset?'

'They're just fine, thank you. I've got Eve and Molly coming tomorrow.'

'Good, good.' He paused. 'Before Eve tells you, I thought I'd let you know that Flo's in the pudding club again.'

'*Again*? But Joshua's only fourteen months!'

'Yes, but we did want our kids close together, so we're really pleased.'

Vanessa sighed, visualising their tiny two-bedroomed terraced cottage in Clapham. She waited.

'Thing is, of course, we're going to need an extra bedroom before long.'

'Now, why am I not surprised you just said that? Am I expected to dig out my cheque book again?'

'Oh, *Mother*! Nobody uses cheques these days! You just transfer money across on the internet!'

'I've no doubt *you* do, but *I* don't. Give Flo my love and hope she keeps well.' She paused, remembering her own mother. 'I suppose I could arrange a bank transfer though.'

CHAPTER FIFTY-EIGHT

Eve

Drip. Drip. Drip. Eve sighed as she looked up at the latest chemical cocktail being fed into her veins. *Another hour and I should be out of here*, she thought. She was so relieved that, this time, she'd kept her hair, because she didn't relish the idea of arriving hairless at Stourton Hall. Vanessa had treated her to a mega-expensive wig the last time, but she hadn't really enjoyed wearing it, and now that her hair had come through again, short, white and curly, she decided she rather liked the look.

And as she looked round the chemotherapy unit, she knew she was one of the lucky ones. All around were people undergoing long, long sessions, including blood transfusions. Worst of all was a beautiful young girl who couldn't have been more than sixteen or seventeen undergoing treatment accompanied by her anxious mother. Eve couldn't bear to think of Flo in that state.

'Ah, Mrs Mason, time's up!' The cheerful nurse removed the canula and placed a sticking plaster on Eve's arm. 'This is your final session, isn't it?'

'I hope so!' Eve said. 'I'm keeping everything crossed.'

'Well, good luck, and don't take this the wrong way when I say I never want to see you in here again! Oh, by the way, we have a new oncologist who's asked to have a word with all the patients, so I'll just check if he's in his office.'

Eve sighed. She felt exhausted and wanted to get out of the place as quickly as possible. She sincerely hoped the man wasn't in his office, and she could make her escape.

The nurse reappeared. 'Mr Warner will see you now.'

Mr Warner: the man was obviously a surgeon. Should she be worried? She'd really thought her treatment was completely finished.

Sighing, she made her way through the door.

She'd seen him before. But where? When? He held out his hand. 'Mrs Mason? Do sit down. I see you've finished your treatment, which I'm sure is a huge relief.'

Eve sat down and studied him. Tall, dark, good features, brown eyes. Nice.

He was checking her details on the computer. 'Your name is Evelyn?' he asked.

'Yes, that's what I was christened, but no one *ever* calls me that,' she replied. 'I'm Eve.'

'Please forgive my asking,' he said, 'but what was your maiden name?'

'Oh, Muir,' she replied, wondering what that had to do with anything. She saw him staring at her.

There was a long pause while they studied each other.

Then, suddenly, she *knew*. And so did he.

He appeared speechless for a moment. Finally, he said, 'And you're seventy-three now?'

'Yes.' She was trying very hard not to cry. It *couldn't* be!

'Did you...' He still seemed to be at a loss for words.

'Have a baby? Out of wedlock?' she provided for him.

He nodded. 'I have to know. I'm fifty-two.'

'And your name is Robert?'

He nodded. 'I've been trying to find you. It *is* you, isn't it?'

'Yes.'

He crossed to the door and called for the nurse. 'Can you cancel any further appointments this afternoon please? Something urgent has cropped up.' He sat down again. 'I think we need some tea, or something stronger perhaps?'

'I think you're right,' Eve said, tears streaming down her cheeks.

Because they were both driving, they went to the hospital café, which, fortunately, was almost deserted, and had a large pot of tea.

He'd been a medical student in London, and he'd tried to contact her a couple of times without success and had decided she must have moved.

He'd got married in London.

'I *saw* you,' Eve said.

'I've been practising up in Manchester for the past few years, but when this opportunity came up, I decided to grab it. My wife, Cindy, is a Londoner and she wanted to get back to the south-east. We have four daughters.'

'Four daughters,' Eve repeated, trying to get her head round the fact that she was a grandmother to four girls.

'I tried to find you again after my adoptive parents died,' he said. 'I think I might even have come to your door—'

Eve thought hard for a minute. 'Did my young daughter answer the door?'

He nodded. 'We have *so* much catching up to do! But we have time.'

Afterwards, Eve wondered how she'd ever managed to drive home, shaken to her core, in the Range Rover which had caused Vanessa so much amusement. 'Don't tell me you've got a

Chelsea tractor!' she'd exclaimed. 'Next thing, you'll be appearing in a Barbour and green wellies!'

For the past ten years, Eve had lived in a large rambling cottage, up a private, muddy lane, bordered by fields, where Andy, since his retirement, kept two horses and six ewes, and where Eve had a large vegetable garden. They had happily taken to country life, although Vanessa, naturally, had had plenty to say at the time they'd bought it.

'It's we *aristocrats* who are supposed to live like that,' Lady Delamore had said, crossing one elegant leg over the other and gazing with appreciation at her new Jimmy Choo stilettos. She did, of course, at that time, own acres of Somerset, where, as far as Eve could gather, she rarely set foot, stilettoed or otherwise. The estate manager kept everything under control, while Vanessa occasionally roared up in her Porsche or the large Mercedes to 'check on everything'. Eve would have given a lot to know what the army of estate workers really thought about the lady of the manor.

'How did it go?' Andy asked as soon as she stepped through the door.

'You'll never believe it,' Eve said. 'Any phone calls?'

'Only Flo, confirming the pregnancy. She's got the dates now. I said you'd call her back. Have you been crying? What's wrong?'

Eve sat down and told him.

He took her in his arms. 'Oh, Eve, how bloody *wonderful*!'

Eve knew it would take time to assimilate this encounter, this reunion – after *fifty-two* years! So many times their paths had almost crossed, and she was trying hard not to resent that. She'd spent all her adult life thinking about him, wondering about him. He'd certainly done well. Even if she'd been able to keep him, he wouldn't have had the life, or the education, that his adoptive parents had provided. It had been best for him, and probably for her as well. In retrospect, she was beginning to see things much more clearly.

And it wasn't too late. She was now, hopefully, clear of cancer and had the time to get to know him and his family. He'd hugged her and they'd made arrangements to meet again the following week.

Eve knew full well that Vanessa thought Jon should have made a better marriage. Eve and Andy had also been less than delighted with the match. What was he after all? Only a reporter on some second-rate rag! Flo had followed her mother into interior design after she'd graduated from art school and had taken over the business. She was so successful that she'd been consulted by any number of celebrities and even minor royalty, and she was definitely going places. And then she'd met Jon again.

They'd met up occasionally during childhood, but Jon went to boarding school and then their paths had rarely crossed. She'd got over her crush on Carlo, who'd found himself a rich wife, eighteen years older than he was, who was prepared to support him in his continuing quest for acting roles.

Flo had met Jon again at Eve's sixty-fifth birthday bash. He was tall and good-looking with piercing blue eyes and slightly-too-long blonde hair. Flo thought he looked like Robert Redford and was immediately besotted. Eve considered him rather feck-less, although, like his mother, he wasn't lacking in confidence. She couldn't forget that his father had been a serial two-timer and only hoped Jon wasn't tarred with the same brush. She vowed to throttle him if he ever two-timed her lovely daughter.

Still, Flo seemed happy enough. She lugged young Josh around to and from work, but how would it work out with *two* of them? And in that tiny house? No doubt Jon would go, cap in hand, to his mother for financial assistance. And she, doubtless, would give him a stern lecture *and* the money. One day, of course, he would inherit considerable wealth from his mother.

'Should I go blonde, do you think?' Eve was surveying her short white hair in the dressing-table mirror.

'Whatever for? I like you just the way you are!' said Andy.

The trouble was that Andy always liked everything about her, even when she'd been bald as a coot.

'It's just this get-together we're having at Vanessa's stately pile. M'lady will be groomed to the nines, and expensively clad as usual, Molly will be very Italian, and very chic, and I just don't want to look like the proverbial country bumpkin!'

Andy kissed the back of her neck. 'Country bumpkin, *you*? Never! Just dig the earth out from under your fingernails, leave your wellies at home and you'll be the belle of the ball! Anyway, when you tell them your earth-shattering news, they won't give a damn what you look like! A grandmother of *five*!

'Five and a *half*,' she corrected.

CHAPTER FIFTY-NINE

Molly

London was cloudy. Molly arrived early evening and booked into a hotel near Victoria. On a previous occasion, she'd tried to book into the hotel where she'd first met up with Mario in London, only to find the entire building had been replaced by a glass-fronted office block.

Normally, she went straight to Eve's or Vanessa's, but, on this occasion, she fancied a clear day to browse around in London to do some shopping, before Eve came to pick her up for the drive to Vanessa's country pile. Afterwards, she planned to spend a few days with her sister Siobhan in Bristol. Since her mother's death, Molly found that she got on much better with her sister, so perhaps old age had mellowed them both.

In the meantime, London was calling, and she enjoyed being back. She ate early in a small bistro close to the hotel, then took a walk along the embankment to admire all the landmarks. Tomorrow, she decided, she would take a boat trip down the Thames to Greenwich, to look at all those luxurious waterside developments that had sprung up over the years.

. . .

It was chilly, with a stiff breeze, as Molly boarded the boat at Westminster the following day, but at least it was sunny.

The boat moved slowly downriver. Molly, from her seat halfway back, found herself studying the other passengers with interest as they sailed under Tower Bridge. Something about an elderly man who'd just walked forward caught her attention. She hoped he'd turn round and walk back so she could get a better look. When he did, she sat rooted to the spot for a moment. But he hadn't seen her.

She found herself scrambling out of her seat and navigating her way to the back of the boat. Perhaps she was mistaken, but she had to know.

Molly caught up with him and touched his arm. 'Patrick?'

He turned. Those same blue eyes, now wide with astonishment.

'Molly? Molly, is it really you?' He took both her hands in his.

'Yes, Patrick, it's really me.' She was astonished to see tears in his eyes.

He blinked them away quickly. 'This is incredible! I've thought about you so much over the years – every damned day in fact! But I couldn't contact you in Rome anymore.'

'We moved, Patrick.'

'I realised that, and I knew it was for the better really, but, oh, how I envied your Mario!'

'Mario died twenty-three years ago.'

'Oh, I'm so sorry. Really. And so you're living back in England now?'

'No, no,' Molly said, 'I'm still in Rome. Just here to visit some old friends and having a day to myself first. What about you?'

He was still staring at her. 'I just can't get over meeting you again!' He paused for a moment. 'Well, my wife died three years ago and the girls are now married with families. I see them all regularly. I retired years ago, but I really missed my trips to Europe, so thought I'd have a final fling before I get too ancient. London, Paris and Rome are on my schedule, but I didn't think I stood a cat in hell's chance of ever finding *you* again!'

Molly swallowed back tears. 'I've thought of you often too, Patrick. But I had a great marriage and I didn't want to rock the boat, particularly after London.'

'Are you staying in London tonight?'

'Yes, but I'm heading off to Somerset tomorrow.'

He beamed. 'Good! Then I'm taking you out to dinner. We've *so* much catching up to do! And tell me, is there any chance you'll be back in Rome when I get there a week from now?'

Molly grinned. 'Yes, Patrick, I'll be back in Rome.'

'Molly, I've never seen you look so good,' Eve said as she manoeuvred her way through the heavy Friday-afternoon traffic on the M4. 'You're positively glowing!'

'Thanks, Eve, I feel good. And you're not looking bad your-self! Your hair really suits you.'

'It's a bit different from the old coppery locks, isn't it? I did wonder about going blonde.'

'Absolutely not! It looks great, and you're lovely and slim too.'

'The gardening keeps me in shape these days. I expect Nessa is her usual elegant self, but I haven't been down to Stourton Hall since Flo and Jon's wedding. Normally we meet up in town, but she doesn't come up so often these days.'

'That was *some* wedding!'

'Wasn't it just! Fortunately, Vanessa footed the lion's share of the bill. By the way, Flo's pregnant again.'

'Are you pleased?'

Eve shrugged. 'Yes, of course. It's just that they never seem to have any money.'

'I don't think this generation *ever* have any money, no matter how much they earn,' Molly said with feeling. 'I guess we were damned lucky to have low house prices and high salaries. Any other news?' Molly asked.

Eve smiled. 'Lots to tell you both later!'

CHAPTER SIXTY

Vanessa

Vanessa, wearing designer jeans and a pink cashmere sweater, awaited her guests, who'd just been shown to their respective quarters. She was in the smallest of the four reception rooms, her expensively highlighted and lowlighted hair expertly coiffured. It was a cool September evening and she'd had the heating put on and the fire lit so the room was almost cosy, no mean feat in this sprawling mansion. The coffee table was laden with trays of canapés and bottles of champagne in ice buckets.

Eve appeared first. 'Wow, Nessa! This is all so grand! I love the four-poster in my bedroom, and all the goodies in the bathroom!'

'Good. Now, I've several fizzies here: Moët, Bolly, or Dom Pérignon?'

'Blimey, that's some choice!'

'You know me!'

'Oh, OK then, I'll have the Bolly.'

'Good. *Love* the hair, by the way! Ah, here's Molly.'

The drinks were poured, and the three raised their glasses and clinked them together.

Eve looked round. 'Well, we don't damn well look as if we're in our seventies, do we?'

Vanessa snorted. 'That'll be down to the pure, innocent lives we've led!'

'And because we've stayed young inside,' said Molly, taking a large gulp.

'I must say *you're* looking very perky, Molly!' Vanessa was studying her over the rim of her glass. 'What did you get up to in London last night?'

'You'll find this hard to believe,' said Molly and proceeded to give them a short account of her meeting with Patrick.

'So will you be seeing him again?' Vanessa asked, refilling the glasses.

'Yes. He goes from here to Paris, and then on to Rome.'

'Next thing we hear, you'll be moving out to the States,' Eve said.

'No way. I'm staying in Italy, but it would be nice to see him occasionally. Anyway, that's enough about me. How's the treatment going, Eve? We didn't get round to talking about that much on the way here.'

Eve updated them. 'I'm feeling good, they seem happy with all the scans and things, and, thank God, the chemo's finished.' She grinned. 'I met a *very* nice oncologist.'

'You're not planning on two-timing Andy I hope?' said Vanessa.

'No, I don't believe in incestuous relationships,' Eve replied.

'*What*!' Molly and Vanessa chorused.

Eve told them.

'Un-believe-able!' Vanessa exclaimed.

'Oh, *Eve*!' Molly had tears in her eyes.

'He's fifty-two! I can hardly believe it myself!' Eve wiped her eyes.

'Do you still feel sad about all the years you missed out on with him?' Vanessa asked.

Eve nodded. 'Sometimes, especially when I think that, if it had happened now, I'd be given a nice flat and no end of benefits. But these lovely people gave him a great education, which I certainly couldn't have afforded to do. I did what was best for him, and so I can have no regrets.'

An hour and several glasses of champagne later, Vanessa cleared her throat. 'Before I forget, I'm planning to get rid of the Porsche because I have an Aston Martin on order, and I'd like to give you first refusal, Eve.'

Eve gasped. 'I really couldn't afford it, Nessa!'

'Yes, you can,' Vanessa said, quoting a silly price.

'But that's ridiculous!' Eve said, almost choking on her champagne. 'That's *giving* it away!'

'Take it or leave it. I don't need the money. It's yours from tomorrow if you want it. Here, let me top up those glasses again...'

Eve

Zara served the five-course dinner at the round table in the Reading Room. 'The dining room is so large and formal,' Vanessa said, 'so I thought this would be cosier.'

As Eve sipped her after-dinner liqueur, she wondered how this place could ever be made cosy with its huge rooms and ornate high ceilings.

'You know, Andy and I had a week in New York last month,' she said. 'Would you believe that Korvettes no longer exists?'

'We so loved shopping there,' Vanessa said. 'All those bargains!'

Eve noticed Vanessa's dreamlike trance and remembered New York was 'her' place with Johnny Martell. 'And the Pan Am building is no longer Pan Am of course, but something really boring, like insurance.'

'Well, Pan Am no longer exists, and neither does TWA – names you never thought would disappear,' Molly said sadly.

'And Old Joyless has gone to tart up the angels in heaven!' Eve added.

'Rumour has it that Dipstick Dave's got dementia and having the time of his life chasing the nurses around in some care home in Bognor Regis. Apparently, he spends most of the day displaying his willy to anyone who passes by.'

'No change there then,' Vanessa said drily.

'So what's happening with you, Nessa?' Molly asked.

'I've sold the house in Provence.'

'Why?' Eve asked.

'Well, I didn't get out there all that much,' Vanessa replied. 'And, although I try to avoid them, sometimes I have to use these awful *budget airlines*! They hardly allow you to have any luggage! And don't get me started on the cabin service – or lack of it. It's becoming a nightmare. I've driven down the last few times, but I'm getting too old for that now.'

'Well, *everybody* flies now; it's not like it used to be,' Molly said.

Vanessa snorted. 'It is such an ordeal! All the queueing with all those people – some of them even have *tattoos!*' She paused to let the horror sink in. 'And then they have the nerve to charge me for daring to have any check-in baggage!'

'It is like a cattle market,' Eve agreed.

Vanessa wasn't finished yet. 'All that security palaver, a twenty-mile hike to the gate and then some disinterested flight attendant – *flight attendant*, if you please! – chucks a cellophane-wrapped tacky sandwich at you to have with your cardboard cup of so-called coffee!'

'Thank God we flew when we did,' Eve said.

'And then,' continued Vanessa, 'they come round with a *black bin bag* to collect all the rubbish!'

Eve was remembering the genteel queues of passengers back in the sixties, when the ladies wore smart suits, dresses, gloves and even hats. And all the men wore suits, collars and ties. No screens, no multi-channels, no headsets, no entertainment of any kind. Just friendly stewardesses ready to chat, provide endless drinks on silver trays and keep smiling.

'Anyway,' Vanessa continued, 'you know that Dicky's younger brother and his family will inherit Stourton? And the title? Well, the house in Provence was in Dicky's name only, and that seemed to be a good reason to sell it and buy something in my own name, which I did. I've bought some holiday cottages in Cornwall, so not too far to go, and it gives Jon some extra inheritance.'

'But you'll keep the flat in London?' Molly asked.

'Of course. This place really isn't my scene even if it *had* been left to me. But there's so much more space here and, if we'd had this reunion in London, you two would have had to share a bedroom.'

'Just like Bellingham Road!' said Eve.

'Good old Bellingham Road! And good old Skyline! Didn't we have a great life back then?'

'We did,' Eve agreed. She nudged Molly. 'Even the New Year's party!'

Molly laughed. 'How could I ever forget it?'

'Marty and Barty had a civil wedding recently, and I can't tell you how glam they both looked,' said Vanessa. 'They've retired now, moved to the country and become fanatical gardeners. Happiest couple I know!'

Eve found herself becoming increasingly tiddly. 'How's your mother, Nessa?'

'The old bat's outlived all of her men-friends, and she's still out there in the sticks in Kenya with a houseful of staff. She's ninety-six, you know, and last I heard, she'd got matey with some ancient Maasai warrior. She's probably shagging him as we speak!'

Molly nearly choked. '*Nessa!*'

Vanessa shrugged. 'Probably true though. Let's change the subject: God, I *hate* being old!'

'You still look fabulous,' Eve said, wondering if Vanessa had had some work done on her face, which was suspiciously unlined. 'And, even more important, you've kept your health.'

'I've been lucky,' Vanessa agreed. 'But I get so stiff, and I fall asleep everywhere except in bed at night. And I am so forgetful! Trouble is, I'm not *ready* to be old! There's a young me inside, hammering to get out!'

Molly peered at her empty glass. 'Talking about being forgetful, see how you've forgotten to top up my brandy?'

'Bloody hell!' Vanessa slid the bottle across the table. 'Fill it up yourself!'

'I guess we all drink too much,' Eve said, giggling. 'Heaven only knows how our livers survived the years with Skyline, never mind now!'

Vanessa took a large swig of her brandy. 'I got a long lecture from my doctor about all the nasty things that can happen to old biddies who drink too much. I told him I'm ready to go anytime, preferably with a gin in my hand. I mean, who wants to end up as some ancient, dribbling old crone in a nursing home?'

Eve hiccupped. 'Very *profound*, Nessa.'

'Yesh indeed,' Molly agreed.

CHAPTER SIXTY-ONE

Vanessa

Vanessa woke up with a crashing headache and a raging thirst. She staggered into her bathroom to find a glass of water and to try to locate the Alka-Seltzer. *Never again*, she thought, then wondered how many times she'd said that over the years. They'd overdone it last night, but it had been so good to see those two again and to reminisce. She'd been bowled over by Eve's news, after *fifty-two* years! They hadn't got to bed until nearly two o'clock.

She glanced at her Rolex: only seven o'clock. The other two would likely sleep for hours yet. Well, of course, they needed their sleep more than she did, Eve with her cancer and Molly with her dodgy heart. She couldn't bear to contemplate life without either of them. Somehow, as the years had passed, their friendship had become more and more precious to her. *I must remember to tell them that before they leave*, she thought.

Vanessa opened the curtains and looked out at the early-morning autumnal sunshine dappling the fields and trees which stretched far into the distance. *Soon*, she thought, *the frost will come again, and the fields will be dull and brown. You really notice the seasons when you live in the country, and I shall miss that.*

Fresh air was called for. A nice walk to clear her head.

Vanessa donned her jeans and a warm sweater, and pulled her hair up into a ponytail. She padded downstairs, grabbed a body warmer and slipped her feet into some walking shoes before leaving by the back door. No one seemed to be around yet, so she'd follow the footpath across the field to the single-lane road, which, at this hour of the morning, was always quiet, and then continue down to the little river at the foot of the valley.

It was a beautiful cloudless morning, the air sharp and bracing. She staggered slightly, aware that she was still a little drunk, and took deep breaths of air.

When she reached the road, she found herself thinking of Johnny. Dear, dear Johnny. She thought of him most days, but, this morning, he seemed to pervade her thoughts as never before. How she had loved that man! Nobody could understand why she'd given him the best years of her life, but she didn't regret it for a single minute. She suddenly remembered the Top of the Sixes in New York, Johnny holding her hand across the table as she sipped her Cloud 66 cocktail. She'd worn the emerald-green silk minidress. 'You're the most stunning woman in here!' he'd said. The Top of the Sixes! Did it still exist?

Vanessa could almost see and hear him as she crossed the road and didn't notice the pothole which sent her sprawling, or the noise of an approaching engine. She'd done something to her ankle and wondered if it was broken. Try as she might, she couldn't get to her feet, and now the engine noise was becoming louder and louder.

The last thing she saw, as the souped-up car came roaring

round the corner, was the look of horror in the eyes of the boy racer behind the wheel, and the last thing she heard, drowning out Johnny's voice, was the squeal of brakes.

EPILOGUE

Eve

The red Porsche hurtled along the country lane leading from the cemetery towards Stourton Hall, which was just visible at the top of the hill.

Molly, in the passenger seat, blew her nose again and said, 'I still can't believe she's gone! We're going to miss her so much, after all these years!'

Eve nodded, concentrating on driving as she wasn't yet entirely familiar with the instrument panel. 'She was certainly a one-off!' she agreed eventually.

'Well, at least now she'll be with *him*! After all, he was the great love of her life.'

It had begun to rain. 'It could get a bit crowded up there, don't you think?' Eve asked as she located the windscreen wipers. 'The wife died some years ago, and three's a crowd, you know.'

'I wonder how *that* works out?'

'Do you really believe in heaven? I wish I did. But I got some wonderful news this morning.'

'Which is?'

'All the scans are clear, and I seem to be in remission, and they don't want to see me again except for an annual check-up.'

'Oh, that's terrific! I'm *so* pleased! I couldn't bear it if I were to lose you as well. Let's have a holiday somewhere together, shall we?'

They'd entered the driveway leading up to Stourton Hall and the wake.

'Brilliant idea! How about Vienna? I've never been there.'

'Me neither.'

'Great!' said Eve. 'Right now, I could murder a drink!'

'You and me both,' agreed Molly.

A LETTER FROM DEE

Dear reader,

I sincerely hope you've enjoyed *The Sunshine Club* and, if you'd like to catch up with my other women's fiction books, or the Kate Palmer cosy crimes, just sign up with the link below. Your address will never be shared, and you can unsubscribe at any time.

www.bookouture.com/dee-macdonald

People have asked if any one of these three ladies might be me – and the answer is no, but there are some characteristics and experiences that we share – and I'm not about to tell you what they are!

It's social history now, so please do not be offended by the lifestyle, or any language or events that took place then, because that is how it was sixty years ago and I wanted to report everything as accurately as possible.

If you did enjoy the book, I'd be grateful if you could leave a review. I love to know what my readers think, and it also helps new readers to discover my books for the first time. You can get in touch with me at any time via Facebook or Twitter.

With many thanks,

Dee

KEEP IN TOUCH WITH DEE

facebook.com/AuthorDeeMacDonald
twitter.com/DMacDonaldAuth

ACKNOWLEDGEMENTS

A huge thank you to my wonderful publisher, Natasha Harding, and everyone concerned at Bookouture, for publishing this book, which was the first one I wrote – and so particularly important to me. The team at Bookouture are second to none, and my grateful thanks must go to all the people concerned with the publication, including Lizzie Brien, Kim Nash, Melanie Price, Lauren Morrissette, Mandy Kullar, Hannah Snetsinger, Ruth Tross, and the rest of the publicity, marketing and editorial teams!

I will always be grateful to my agent, Amanda Preston at LBA, for introducing me to Bookouture, and a special thanks to my good friend and mentor, Rosemary Brown, without whose expertise this book might never have taken shape. Thanks to my husband, Stan Noakes, for patiently enduring my long writing sessions, and to my son, Daniel, who keeps a close eye on my sales and sorts out my technology problems.

A huge thank you to my friends from my own flying days back in the sixties and seventies, particularly: Sylvia (Pryke) Morrell, Margaret (Walton) Perkins, Maggie (Kenny) Boucher, Jan (Stanley) Hunt, Silvia (Caligari) Gridley and the late lovely Sue (Mattingley) Thomas. These enduring friendships form the very heart of this story.

Finally, thanks to my late mother, Anne (Sutherland) MacDonald, who encouraged me to write 'wee stories' to help pass the long, dark Scottish winter evenings (no TV, just a crackling radio!) back in the forties and fifties.

She really was the instigator of all this.

Made in United States
Cleveland, OH
08 February 2025

14167659R00204